GUY QUIGLEY
THE REBEL SON

THUNDERSMOKE

This book is for my wife Wendy
A true child of Africa

PROLOGUE

It was March, 1978, and despite shining over a Nassau beach, the mid-day sun was not unbearably hot. Bill Fallon relished the low humidity that hung in the air as he watched the pale-blue net curtains on the veranda wave gently in the sea breeze. He kept an ivory-handled cane by his side, which he stroked gently between thumb and forefinger as he listened to the conversation between the handsome couple sitting across from him in wicker chairs with plush cushions.

This was the winter home of this handsome couple, Bill's mother and father, Patrick and Mary Fallon. The wealthy Philadelphians had long ago abandoned the unpredictable north-eastern winters of the United States in favor of the Bahamian sun. They would typically depart this paradise near the end of April – always on time for Memorial Day, in any regard – where they would turn to spending their summers on the family's forty-acre farm in the safe, rural Bucks County township of Solebury.

But until that day, all family counseling would have to take place here; here in this gleaming white, six-thousand-square-foot villa. The home bore a Moorish style, one more in keeping with Southern Spain or Mexico rather than the festive colors of the

Caribbean. But that was the way Bill's father had wanted it, and how could his mother refuse the man's persuasive manner? After all, Patrick had been a contractor all his life and knew the true essentials of building in hot coastal locations.

A silence fell over the group, and Bill used it to assess his father. Patrick Fallon, gazing over the calm ocean as if it belonged only to him, was a muscular man in his mid-sixties. Perhaps due to his years in construction, if not his half-yearly retirement in the sun, he was tanned to the point of almost bronze. Save the lines of toil on his face, he carried a pleasant look.

"Another hot day in paradise," he rumbled.

Bill's mother chuckled politely. Mary Fallon was a sophisticated woman from the right side of the tracks in Philadelphia society. Bill knew that she had never really worked a day in her life, unless one counted the chores of the socialite as work. Even before marrying Bill's father, the lifestyle she lived had been in keeping with the wealth of her own Main Line family.

"To think they've just had nine inches of snow up north," Mary said with a wry smile. "It's all snow shovels and backaches."

Bill nodded and turned to assess the sea. Its dark blue waters glinted in the high, white sun.

"Thank God I don't have to do that anymore," Patrick said, chortling.

"Oh, hell, Patrick," Mary said, "you've *never* had to do that."

Bill watched his father break into a slow, knowing smile.

"Let's hope Belston's plowed the road up to the house," Bill said, rolling his eyes for emphasis. "Jake'll charge up in that stupid Porsche Carrera or whatever he's driving these days."

"Suppose he'll bury it a couple of hundred yards from the house," Patrick offered.

"As usual."

"As usual."

Bill gritted his teeth as he looked down at his fingers, still working over the head of his cane, which was itself the result of a snowmobile accident. The look of its dull white crest still brought to his mind painful memories – memories of distressing times for his entire family. Every day, he would see this cane, and every day, he would remember how he and his fiancée Amanda were to be married at the cathedral on Philadelphia's Logan Square. And then he would inevitably recall the funeral.

Bill sighed to break himself from his train of thought more than anything. "I know Jake makes a decent income," he said, referring to the Philadelphia real estate company his brother shared with his best friend, Brian, "but they'd both be better off if they sold to a franchise and moved on."

"Listen to the investment banker," Mary said rather sarcastically. She offered a caustic smirk as she tipped back her mimosa.

Bill frowned at the casual barb. She might have been joking, his mother, but that didn't mean her comment wasn't correct. Bill, after all, was an extraordinarily successful investment banker in Manhattan – so successful that he owned a twin-engine aircraft that allowed him to fly from work in New York to play in Nassau on a whim – while his brother, successful though he may have been, still seemed to have an unreasonable amount of growing up to do.

His mother apparently noticed Bill's brooding. "Oh come on, Bill. You know your brother. And Brian, Jesus. Since those two came back from the war, they've just gotten used to living off the extra fat of the land."

"Yeah," Bill said. "But in this case, it's *your* fat and *your* land."

Mary leaned over and patted her son on his good knee. "Don't be so hard on the boy. He's your baby brother, after all."

Bill chuffed. "Boy? Some *boy*. Mother, he's twenty-eight years old. And as his older brother, I'd like to know what he's going to do with the rest of his life."

"Maybe you should lay off him a little," Patrick said.

Bill felt taken aback. It was not like his father to defend Jake's wayward spirit. The surprise in his eyes was apparently enough for his father to notice.

"Listen," Patrick said, holding out a defensive hand, "your brother did a three-year stint in the Army. He survived Vietnam."

Bill scoffed, turning his eyes back to the ocean.

"Besides all that," Patrick added, "when did you become his keeper?"

Piqued, the young man furrowed his brow. "I'm not his keeper. Only his older brother. And as for Vietnam, he was *drafted*, remember? And you seem to be forgetting the fact that he smoked pot through the whole affair." He paused for a moment, running his soft hand over his stubbly chin. "And correct me if I'm wrong, Dad, but didn't you once threaten to cut off the cash flow if he didn't straighten himself out?"

Patrick sighed and massaged the bridge of his nose. "Bill," he said through a long breath. "He was only twenty-two when I told him that. He's been to *war* since then."

For Bill, there was no ignoring the degree of pride in his father's voice.

"We should all count ourselves lucky he didn't come back seriously disturbed like a lot of those other boys," Mary added.

Patrick offered a curt nod.

"Or with some gook wife."

Patrick's eyebrows blew back as they always did when his wife's comments drifted off the track of polite. But as usual, he said nothing. Bill waded through the tension that hung in the air as everyone tried to put the remark out of memory. The waves kicked up a soft mist, crashing melodically against the white, sloping sand.

"If you don't trust real estate," Patrick said, breaking the silence, "why don't you take Jake and Brian into your business?"

Bill groaned, as he always did at this question. "C'mon, Dad," he said. "We've been over this. I've *tried* to take them in. *Several* times. All he ever wanted to do was mess around with the girls in the office."

Mary chuckled so suddenly that she appeared to have to suppress a belch.

"I love him dearly," Bill added. "But boy, oh boy, does he ever need to grow up."

"Bill, please," Patrick said haughtily. "Some of the stuff your brother does can be aggravating, but remember the things he's accomplished. Back in '76, for example. After the war. That diamond mining in East Africa."

"That was a stroke of luck as far as I'm concerned," Bill said with a snort.

"What do you mean luck?" Mary asked, looking suddenly skeptical about the giant rock on her finger.

"Forget it, Mary," Patrick said, terminating the conversation with his eyes.

Bill felt compelled to enlighten his mother, but the hand his father held in the air cooled his blood and warded him off.

"Let's not bring up old news," Patrick added. "Kid made a killing on the diamonds, and that's it. I just don't know why you don't give him a break, Bill."

The young man scowled at the sea.

"Hell, he and Brian have that company running on auto-pilot with those other four agents they hired. And the boy owns a shit load of hot stocks. He's got the golden touch, I'd say. Why would you want him to give all that up? What kind of job would you have him pursue?"

Bill pressed his chin to his neck. "Anything that'll hit him between the eyes with some fiscal discipline."

Mary stood, casting her arms to either side. "Enough of this," she said sadly. "We're family. A good, white, God-fearing family."

Bill noticed his father's wince.

"So let's not drum up any negativity," Mary added. "Especially since Jacob isn't here to defend himself." The older woman turned toward the villa, pausing for a moment to look back at her son. "I know you are flying back to New York this afternoon, so I'm going to get Harry to make some lunch."

Bill nodded and watched his mother depart, a kind of drunken confidence in her stride. He did what he could to keep his eyes off his father for a while, but after a time, it couldn't be avoided. What he found when he relented was a rather disappointed-looking old man.

"Why'd you have to bring up that luck shit about Africa?" Patrick asked his tone almost jovial despite his solemn expression.

"What do you mean?"

Patrick fired one paranoid glance back toward the house. "You and I both know those diamonds were probably stolen. Hell, that one on your mother's finger probably spent more than a day up some African's ass."

Bill offered a knowing nod.

"But, damnit, Bill, some things you just have to keep to yourself."

The young man sighed, shifting in his chair. Again, he gazed back down at his cane; his knee seemed to throb whenever he did so.

"I don't mind quibbling about Jake, son," Patrick said softly. "I know he's got plenty of growing up to do. I'm not blind."

Bill pursed his lips.

"But let's not forget that he *never* has anything negative to say about *you*."

The young man drew a shuddering breath. "You're right, Dad. I'm sorry."

Patrick folded his hands – worn from many years of championing a contracting company with a hands-on approach – over his lap.

"I guess it's just my self-pity," Bill added. "Jake always had it so good. Plus, he did all kinds of stuff to you guys that I would *never* do."

If this line annoyed Patrick Fallon, he did his best to hide it. "Like what?"

Bill shrugged. "Like sky diving. Rock climbing. Fast cars, fast girls. Smoking pot. Drinking in high school. Drinking *heavily* in college. You know etc. etc. etc . . . the immortal line from *The King and I*."

Patrick grunted. "You were no angel, either."

"Yeah," Bill said, fidgeting with his cane. "The *fallen* Angel."

"Now I get it," Patrick said, his cynicism evident. "The bad knee and the cane. You're supposed to have fallen from grace the day Amanda died on that slope."

Even if he'd wanted to, Bill couldn't look his father in the eye. Instead, he stared at his cane and addressed all the painful memories it represented. The Poconos. Only a year hence. Bill and his lovely fiancée were out on the snowmobile on the third day of what should have been a romantic two weeks. Amanda begged Bill to let her drive.

The young man, getting on now at thirty-one, could still remember the flames. They kicked up in flickering wings on either side of the wide pine tree. He could still remember the stark contrast of his fiancée's dark blood against the pure white of the snow all around.

Amanda had died silently there in that snow, her future husband wailing for her not to close her eyes.

After the funeral, Bill would be left to live his life with a mere smashed knee. A minor injury by comparison, but one that would lead to several knee replacement surgeries, the need for the cane, and would in the end serve as an eternal reminder.

"Your life isn't over, boy," Patrick barked. "For God's sake, move on. Nobody blames you. And that includes her parents."

Bill recalled his fiancée's parents. The pain in their eyes when they'd arrived on the scene. The hollowness at the funeral.

Mary shouted from the kitchen that the salads were on the table. Both men rose, Bill utilizing his cane for support. Feeling rather hollow himself, he followed his father toward the house.

"Don't worry, son," Patrick said, offering a pair of soft and sympathetic eyes. "Everything will be well in the end. For you *and* for your brother."

CHAPTER 1

J ake Fallon watched the sneering mechanical arm of the tractor raise its snow shovel into the air. The beast turned slowly in its odd salute, weaving along the plowed portion of the gravel farm road. Jake then sat back in the bucket seat of his Porsche Carrera, his head returning from its recent position craned out the window. He clucked his tongue at the sight of the bowels of the tractor immediately before him. In front, it plowed through the virgin snow. Behind, it dragged the Porsche at a slight upward angle, its giant tires kicking up chunks of snow on the low-engine profile.

Jake, a man of twenty-eight, boasted rugged good looks and clear blue eyes. His was a solid build. His mousy colored hair framed a chiseled face that nonetheless bore a calm demeanor. The only visible imperfection was the war scar he carried under his chin.

He turned up this chin and fired an impish grin at his best friend and business partner, Brian Wilson, who chuffed from the passenger seat.

Brian shook his head as he always did at his bullish friend: with a hint of silent but highly reluctant approval. Brian, despite what his rock-legend moniker might suggest, was also twenty-eight and a Philadelphia Main Liner. He sat, and by consequence stood, two inches taller than Jake, but was more slender and gaunt. Beyond his winning smile, the thick mass of blonde hair that flared atop his head seemed to draw whatever young woman his best friend chose to send his way.

Both young men wore bomber jackets, gloves, and knitted hats pulled down over their ears. They smoked rampantly, the windows on either side of the vehicle standing open.

Jake stewed. Not because he felt guilty about getting his friend into this predicament again, but because he had professed such certainty that the modifications he'd ordered for his Carrera would ensure successful passage through the snow. This time. But no, here they were sitting with sober heads and crossed arms, a rain of gravelly snow against the windshield the only entertainment.

"No problem, man," Jake said, blowing smoke out the window. "Belston'll get us there. Man knows his way around a backhoe."

Brian snorted.

Jake flicked the butt of his cigarette into the passing snow outside. Then he leaned forward and crossed his arms over the top of the steering wheel, resting his head on the meat of his forearms. This trip from respective bachelor apartments in center city Philadelphia to Jake's parents' country home was to serve two purposes. The first was to fulfill Jake's standing promise to his parents that he would check the vacant property every couple of weeks to ensure that Belston, the ever-faithful caretaker, was on the job. The second, as it was the right time of the year, was to fulfill Jake's and Brian's desire to fly over forty acres of fresh powder on the family's stable of snowmobiles.

"Thank God Belston was here with that thing," Brian said with just a hint of frustration. "Otherwise, we'd've been out here all night."

Jake picked up his head, incredulous. "Are you nuts?" he wheezed. "We'd've roared through that snow, man. I only needed another couple minutes to rock."

Brian laughed, but it did not sound like a laugh of mirth. "Man, you had us *buried*. You woulda smoked this car out first. The ass end woulda ripped right out."

"Fuck you, Brian," Jake snarled.

The passenger shrugged and offered a slow, disapproving smile. "Not my fucking car, man."

Almost half an hour passed before the tractor finally rumbled to a stop beside the towering Fallon farmhouse. Jerry Belston, a rotund little man in his late sixties, climbed down from the cab and began the chilly prospect of unshackling the Porsche. He began by bundling the tow-rope in a ball and throwing it on the back of the tractor. Then, without a word, he climbed back aboard and drove in the direction of the stables, disappearing around the side of the house.

Secure on the ground, Jake and Brian hopped out of the car, retrieved a case of Yuengling from the trunk, then slipped and slid their way into the mud room. Inside, they removed their Italian shoes and shuffled into the family room. Brian plopped the case of beer down on the sofa. The two young men stood with hands on hips for a while, silently assessing the empty and half-dark room.

It was a large family room with cathedral ceiling. The entire affair was painted in earth tones. Pale-green velvet curtains fell majestically onto the solid mahogany floor. On one side of the room stood a full-size and solid-wood bar, matching stools with leather seats and brass studs. Two large Persian rugs offered quiet elegance to the well polished wooden floor. Strewn on end tables and coffee tables about the room were a series of travel mementos and an abundance of framed photographs of the two Fallon boys spanning from grade school to graduation. Several valuable original paintings and low-numbered prints adorned the walls.

From the lacquered lid of the grand piano in the extreme corner of the room to the shelves behind the bar was a wealth of strange and obviously treasured gifts bestowed by Bill and Jake on their parents. Mary Fallon would rotate these gifted items from time to time and strategically place them in other areas, apparently to ensure that each of her boys would never feel that one was less important than the other. A warm and inviting log fire flickered in the Inglenook fireplace.

"They were expecting us, I guess," Brian said, pointing at the fire.

"Must've been Alice," Jake said with a shrug.

Alice Belston, the Fallons' cook and housekeeper, was the dutiful wife of Jerry Belston. Her rotund stature matched that of her groundskeeper husband perfectly.

Jake turned to look at his friend, who seemed locked in a reverent smile at the fireplace.

"Shall we?" the host asked.

Brian nodded, and the two barreled like schoolboys up the back stairway to the bedrooms. Splitting off to their usual rooms, Brian and Jake each changed into lighter and dryer indoor clothing before returning to the family room and settling before the fire.

"You want a beer?" Brian asked, motioning over his shoulder at the case still waiting on the couch.

"Nah, fuck that," Jake said.

Brian arched a blonde eyebrow.

Jake smirked as he stood and made his way to the bar. "I don't even know why we brought that shit." After a moment of fiddling around behind the bar, he returned to his seat carrying a pair of brandy balloons filled nearly to the brim with Patrick Fallon's best cognac.

Brian took his glass eagerly, then clearly enjoyed his first healthy nip. He leaned back in his chair, sighing and stretching out his legs.

Jake nodded approval. Then his eyes caught something expected and yet unexpected. His lips parted into a smile as he assessed the large framed print that sat backwards on the floor beside the Inglenook. Its brown paper backing called to him to be replaced to the wall. And so he stood, shaking his head, and turned it around to its rightful place. A Dalí print.

"What's that all about?" Brian asked as Jake returned to his seat.

"Look at it," Jake said, firing a finger at the painting. "It looks like the devil eating a mermaid. Mom despises it. And it scares Alice witless."

Brian shrugged through apparent confusion.

"Deal is," Jake said, "when Dad's not home, one of them always takes it off the wall."

Brian chuckled. Then he held up his glass, toasting the print. After a time, he settled the glass back in his lap, cupping it with both hands. "She going to have dinner for us, then?" he asked. "Alice, I mean."

The host directed his nose to the air. "Can't you smell it?"

The guest drew breath through his nostrils and smiled. "Now I do."

"That's right, my friend. Smells like her famous roast beef to me." Jake set his cognac on the table between him and his friend, then leaned forward and rested his elbows on his knees. "So," he said, "you as excited about this trip as I am?"

Brian affirmed with his eyes before taking a long sip of cognac.

This didn't satisfy Jake. He slapped his friend's arm with the back of his hand. "Jesus, man," he said. "You don't take hunting trips to Africa every fucking day."

Brian wiped the cognac that had spilled over his lips with his forefinger, then nodded. "Sorry," he said. "I'm excited. *Really* excited."

"Hell yeah," Jake agreed.

"I hope to shoot a lion."

Jake chuckled. "Yeah. Unlike the gooks, they can't shoot back."

Brian smiled, then buried his nose in his glass.

Jake stood and made his way for the bar again, where he retrieved a dark black humidor and produced two giant Cuban cigars. He returned to his guest and offered one up. "You concerned at all?" Jake asked. "You know. About Africa?"

Brian took the cigar as if it were a precious jewel, then examined it with delight. "I'm not too concerned," he said, still assessing the cigar. "Tourists go there. It's a far cry from Nam."

Jake fished through the drawer of the table between him and his friend, then sat back with a box of long matches. He rotated his cigar through the light, then offered the box to Brian.

He took a long pull as he watched his friend light his own cigar. "After Nam," he said through a slow exhale, "I'm dying to get a little excitement back in my life."

"Me, too," Brian agreed. He paused and examined the cigar. "Great smoke."

"The best."

"Your old man will be pissed."

Jake shrugged. "Fuck it. He's not supposed to have Habanas, anyway."

The pair chuckled and then got down to the business of razzing one another about the women in their lives. For Jake, "women" was the more proper term. For Brian, the "women" referred to one woman, Bertha Strauss, a young lady with a wealthy lineage and an uncommon beauty that didn't match her unfortunate name. Jake would tease Brian endlessly about the relationship, given that the latter didn't seem to care much for the romance, or lack thereof. Brian would remain standoffish, blushing at various cracks before dealing back a few of his own.

"Tell you what," Jake said the moment he tired of the game. "I've got an idea."

Brian's eyes perked some. He lifted his chin from its defensive position.

"Tomorrow afternoon, after beating our asses to death on the snowmobiles, let's hit the road for Manhattan."

"But our flight doesn't leave until Friday."

"Fuck it, man. We go in a day early. You know. Celebrate."

Brian pursed his lips. "What would we be celebrating?"

Jake thrust his hands to either side. "What the hell you think? We'd be celebrating Africa."

Brian shook his head incredulously. "You're talking about celebrating a *vacation*. A *vacation*."

Jake cackled and tossed back the last of his cognac. "There's nothing in life not worth celebrating, my friend." He stood up to refill his drink, motioning to Brian to ask if he needed one, as well.

Brian nodded and Jake returned with a fresh snifter.

"Who knows," the host said jovially. "Maybe we can pick up a couple of chicks. Make you forget all about Bertha."

The guest snorted dismissively.

"If not chicks, there's always roosters in the Village."

Brian finally snapped out of it. He punched his friend in the arm. "That's not funny, man," he said, donning a macho tone. "Fuck that gay shit."

Jake shrugged, his smile broad. "If worse comes to worst, we can always grab a couple of hookers."

Brian shook his head, beaming. "I guess you can take the soldier out of Saigon but you can't take Saigon out of the soldier."

Jake chortled, but Brian got suddenly serious.

"Listen," he said, placing a hand on Jake's forearm. "Whatever we do, none of that 'My friend here is the real Brian Wilson from the Beach Boys' shit, okay?"

Jake laughed as if he'd never heard anything so funny in all his life.

At that moment, Alice waddled into the room to advise the men that dinner was ready. The first thing that Jake noticed when he turned to smile at her was that her eyes immediately settled on the Dalí print beside the fireplace. She pressed her hands over her eyes and did an about-face, shaking her head from side to side as she fled.

Jake and Brian grinned at one another as they stood and followed the round little woman into the dining room.

CHAPTER 2

Bill Fallon stood before the broad north window of his Manhattan apartment, the one that overlooked Central Park. The apartment admittedly lacked a woman's touch, with its distinct and very definite leaning toward the bachelor's lifestyle, but the place still seemed to possess a kind of quiet opulence. In sum, it was outfitted with mostly leather furniture, thick carpeting, and bric-a-brac from all over the world. An open counter shared by the living room and the kitchen crowned a trio of walnut barstools and served as a comfortable breakfast or cocktail area. As he'd learned from his parents, Bill refused to adorn his walls with anything but original or low-numbered prints, his tastes ranging from Norman Rockwell to Picasso. Several photographs of Bill and Jake lined the walls – one as little boys playing on the beach in Long Beach Island, others featuring the pair of them outside the Bahamian villa with their smiling parents. The only truly macabre photograph captured Amanda's smiling face, enclosed in a solid black frame.

Bill played furiously with one of the tassels flanking his floor-length gray velvet curtains as he listened to the conversation playing out over the phone. He gazed out over the park as he waited for his turn to speak, feeling more and more like he wanted to destroy something. When that turn came, he spoke sincerely into the mouthpiece. "You must be insane," he grumbled.

"Less insane than going to Nam," came the furtive reply.

Bill's father, surprisingly acting as the voice of reason to this point, butted in. "That's different, Jake," Patrick said. "You *had* to go to Vietnam. You were drafted."

"Please, Jake," Mary pleaded. "I'm concerned." Bill could imagine her sitting in her favorite sunny chair in the corner of the villa's grand sunroom, fanning herself with a magazine, as she often did.

To Bill's dismay, his brother began laughing, low and long. "No need for concern, Mother," he said once he'd finished. "Where I'm going, they still have tourists. Victoria Falls. You've heard of it."

"I've heard of it," Patrick and Mary said, their voices lacing awkwardly over one another.

"It's one of the seven fucking wonders of the natural world," Jake quipped. "And a serious tourist trap, to boot."

A short, tense silence followed – one that Bill felt obligated to break.

"This is no laughing matter, Jake," he said. "I'd wager you know nothing about the place."

"Oh yeah?" Jake said with a scoff. "And I bet you know every goddamn thing there is to know."

Mary cleared her throat. "No need to take the Lord's name in vain, son."

The line fell dead for a moment.

"Tell us about the place, Bill," Patrick offered.

Bill paced back and forth in front of the window, massaging the bridge of his nose as he called to mind everything he could remember. "Rhodesia," he whispered, as if speaking its name might help him conjure up facts he'd forgotten. "Thirteen years ago, give or take, Ian Douglas Smith declared UDI, which means a Unilateral Declaration of Independence, effectively breaking Rhodesia away from the UK. This came about because the RFP, or Rhodesian Front Party, opposed black majority rule in the then-British colony. Strangely, even though the Party declared independence from the UK, it maintained allegiance to the Queen of England. Black Africans have been waging a terrorist war ever since."

Silence fell anew.

"Sounds like not the kind of place to be a tourist," Patrick offered after a time.

Bill could sense his brother's childish insolence coming before it even hit the telephone wire.

"Dad," Jake whined, "we're going on a hunting safari with a reputable big-game hunting organization. They've assured us that we'll be far removed from any aggravation." He took a deep, audible breath. "For God's sake, they've got little kids going to school every day."

"Using the Lord's name again," Mary blurted, clearly annoyed by more than just the blasphemy.

"Well, shit, Jake," Patrick said, though his tone sounded more angry than resolved. "You're well over twenty-one, so what the hell? I guess a couple of Vietnam vets should be able to keep their heads down and their powder dry."

"Then you don't *mind*?" There was no hiding the surprise in Mary's voice.

"How can I?" Patrick offered. "Jake's a big boy."

From half an ocean away, Bill fumed.

"And besides, Bill," Patrick added, "if you're so concerned, then why don't you go along?"

A strong swatting sound could be heard over the phone. Judging by Patrick's grunt, Bill guessed that his father had just been whacked. Suspicions were confirmed when his mother next spoke.

"You go from concerned to encouraging *both* the boys to go out to some remote part of the world," Mary hissed. "Bill's not going, and that's that."

Bill rolled his eyes. "Well, Mother," he said with more than a hint of sarcasm, "thanks for allowing me to respond for myself."

"You'd go then?" The desperation in her voice was clear.

"Oh definitely not."

Mary sighed long and hard.

"I'm too busy to go gallivanting around Africa."

"Too scared, buddy?" Jake asked, laughter beneath his words.

"Boys!" Mary barked.

"That's enough," Patrick interjected. "Jake, you can't expect your brother to go limping through the African bush with his cane."

Tension lay so thick it could practically be heard through the phone lines. Bill sat down in his favorite plantation chair beside the window. He worked his free hand up and over the rounded wooden armrest, an anxious fidget.

"I'm sorry, Bill," Jake finally said – and with what sounded like an honest sigh. "You know I'm only kidding."

Bill considered accepting the apology, but instead kept silent.

"Look," Jake continued, "I'll keep in touch. Wherever there's a phone, I'll call home. And, Mom, I'll bring you home a lion skin."

Mary scoffed. "I'll have no smelly animal parts of any nature in any of our homes. Give it to your brother."

"No thanks," Bill said sardonically.

"Fine," Jake said. "I gotta run. Brian's expecting a call from me. We'll talk again before I leave."

The click came over the line so suddenly that it startled Bill. Here he was, left to make awkward goodbyes with his equally miffed parents. As he hung up the phone and returned to examining the park below his building, he imagined his brother, the rebel son, winging away to Africa with a highball in hand.

CHAPTER 3

Having slapped the phone down on his family, Jake strode for the kitchen in search of Alice. He found the rotund little woman where she always seemed to be: in the pantry, gathering up spices for the evening's meal. The young man requested that Alice put down what she was doing and make him a sandwich. And in three minutes flat, he was returning to the family room, peanut butter and jelly in one hand and a bottle of Yuengling in the other. He placed the beer on the nearest coffee table, then picked up the phone and dialed Brian's number.

"Hey, man," he said when his friend answered.

"Jake," came the solemn reply.

"You sound like hell. Your folks give you a barrel of shit, too?"

Brian groaned. "Big time. It's like I'm ten years old."

"Yeah, well—"

"I mean, seriously," Brian interrupted. "I'm a grown man who can't vacation in Africa without catching holy hell. But when Uncle Sam sends me to dangerous, hot, humid, shitty Vietnam, everything's copacetic."

"I hear you, man." Jake smiled at his friend's rare show of cynicism. He took a swig of his beer and a bite of his sandwich.

"Hell," he said, his mouth still full, "we're getting on in years. It's time our parents let go and realize we're big boys."

"No kidding."

"But on the other hand, fuck it. We can't piss them off completely. We've got inheritances to think about."

Brian chuckled. "Let's just go hunting, all right?"

"So you got the green light?"

"Yeah."

Jake took another swig of his beer, burped, and then laughed aloud. "All right, man. But you're forgetting something."

"What's that?"

"New York, asshole. We've got celebrating to do."

"Right. Forgot about your need to celebrate a vacation."

"We'll shack at Bill's."

"He gonna be all right with that?"

"Fuck him. We'll get him a nice piece of ass. Make his mundane life worth living."

Brian chuckled, sounding nervous about the whole situation.

~ ~ ~

Disappointment struck the two excited young men when their Safari could not be confirmed as a go until mid July. This would eventually unfold as a bad omen – leaving Jake and Brian to deal with their collective parents, who continually drilled them negatively about their upcoming hunting trip. Thus, the long awaited celebration in New York had to be postponed for what seemed an endless period of time.

Jake woke with a blonde to his right, an empty bottle of Gentleman Jack to his left, and a raging goddamned hangover. Such was his throbbing headache that it took him several minutes to even remember where he was. Then it occurred to him. The larger of Bill's two guest rooms. As the blonde stirred, bits and pieces of the previous night returned to him. A nightclub in Manhattan. Brian with a long-stemmed brunette. Bill striking out with a beautiful Asian that Mommy never would've approved of, anyway. Drink after drink. A limo ride home, arranged by Bill. And then a drunken haze.

Jake had gotten quite adept at sliding out of bed without waking his nameless companions, but on this occasion, his arm was pinned in the space between the blonde's slight shoulders and her lovely head. He would have to get her to roll over first, which he did with a gentle nudge and a cooing whisper. As she rolled, he took in the sights. A supple young body, soft and cream-white skin, the subtle smell of lilacs. A familiar and yet unfamiliar conquest. A considerably rewarding one.

When he stood, the room swirled for a moment, sending him off his balance. But he caught himself quickly with a deft step forward. In the corner of the white-walled room, he found his clothes lying on the marble floor, his boxers knotted up in his tangled slacks. With a conqueror's chuckle, he unfurled the mess and slipped on his pants. He'd wake Brian with a rumbling knock on the door to his room. Then a loud banging around of pots and pans would wake his brother. All in the name of rising on time for breakfast and a long flight to Africa – if not simply in the name of good old-fashioned hangover fun.

He shuffled into the kitchen and fiddled with the coffee machine. He'd never had to make his own coffee, so he didn't bother attempting. He simply examined the empty pot, then slammed it back down in its cradle. A quick glass of water and a handful of painkillers would precede the trip to Brian's door. There, he hammered on the wood like a man yelling "Fire!"

Despite the display, it would be a good long while before Brian could be heard to stir in the guest room. It would take him even longer to reach the door and answer it with a look of searing anguish.

"What?" he wailed.

Jake craned his neck to look over his taller friend's shoulder. In the bed, he saw no one. "Where's the brunette?"

"Left last night, I guess," Brian said.

"Ouch," Jake said. "Couldn't even keep her to breakfast, eh?"

Brian turned, running his hand through his hair as he returned to the bed to sit down. He looked sick. "Shut the fuck up, man. It wasn't like that."

Jake chuckled.

Brian winced.

"You ready for a long, long flight, or what?"

Brian groaned.

Jake bent down and scooped up Brian's designer jeans from the pile of clothes on the floor. "C'mon, buddy. You can get some sleep on the plane." He fired the jeans at his friend's head.

Brian unfurled his pants and started pulling them on, a reluctant smile forming on his lips. "Africa," he breathed.

"Africa."

~ ~ ~

A long, slow jaunt through New York traffic preceded an early evening of ushering through check-in and waiting in the airport bar nearest the gate. Bill had chosen to park and head into the gate to wait with his brother and his brother's friend for their plane to depart. At the bar, the older Fallon had ordered a Bloody Mary, then made a face of disgust with every passing sip. Jake had positively punished two thick pints of beer – so quickly that Brian had to remind him that getting a drunk on too early in a flight always spelled disaster.

Jake hadn't listened. And now he walked beside his best friend and down the jetway, his face alcohol-warm and his spirits high and jovial. They walked like penguins in a scrum behind the dozen or so other first class passengers.

He grunted. "Let's get a move on," he said loudly.

Brian elbowed him in the ribs and he laughed.

"Just trying to get to my seat, man," he explained, still rather yelling.

When they reached the door to the plane, Jake winked at the young stewardess, who grinned politely in reply. Then he smacked the pilot on the shoulder, stirring the older man out of his apparent trance.

"Let's try to keep her in the air, buddy," Jake said with a chuckle.

The pilot tipped his cap, but his expression appeared less than friendly. Jake cared little. He simply found his seat near the bulkhead, fired his carry-on into the bin, and then ordered a round of champagne for him and his friend.

"We're not even off the ground yet," Brian said, protesting rather feebly.

Jake scoffed at his companion, then winked at the stewardess again. "I'm gonna see if she's staying in London during the layover."

Brian leaned over his friend. "Who?" he asked, pointing at the stewardess. "Her?"

"Yeah."

"Wouldn't have thought her your type."

Jake sized up the stewardess. She was a redhead with glasses, sure, but her features were soft and her curves ample.

"Why not?"

"She's just . . . I don't know . . . a little bigger than your usual, I guess."

Jake blinked as if clearing a cloud away from before his eyes. When his vision crystallized, he still saw an attractive stewardess ducking through oncoming foot traffic to fetch his champagne.

"I don't know what you're talking about, man," he said. "I like 'em all shapes and sizes."

Brian laughed, then reached into his travel bag to fish around for a while, then pulled out a black eye-mask and slipped it over his head.

"Goodnight then, Cinderella," Jake said.

Brian sighed. "Goodnight, Jake."

The stewardess returned with a pair of champagne flutes. Jake snapped them both up, communicating with his eyes that he'd be drinking for his friend. The stewardess giggled before turning back to her duties. Jake watched her, licking his lips before downing a flute of champagne in one long swig.

~~~

Jake drank himself into a stupor on the flight to London. It would be a blurry layover in that bustling city – a rejection by the curvy stewardess followed by a few more pints in the pub nearest their connection gate. Once aboard the London-Johannesburg leg of the journey, Jake finally managed to drink himself into a deep sleep. There, they changed planes once again, and given that he'd had so much to drink, Jake felt extremely well-rested as the Vickers Viscount aircraft touched down at Victoria Falls Airport.

He'd argued with Brian throughout the rickety car ride from the airport to the Victoria Falls hotel about whether it would be best to get a good night's sleep prior to the hunt or spend considerable time and money gambling at the Victoria Falls Casino Hotel, less than half a mile away. Jake had taken the gambling end of the argument, and had won his friend over, as always.

So after a quick welcome-to-Africa toast from the mini-bar, Jake and Brian showered and changed and stalked the short walk down to the casino. In no time, Jake found a seat at a mid-stakes blackjack table, a highball of scotch in his hand. Brian, mean-
~~~

while, passed the time by shoveling coins into no fewer than three slot machines at once.

An hour and several dozen up and down hands later, Jake found himself bored with blackjack. His concentration drifted. As the dealer flicked cards here and there, tending to the other players, he took in the hustle and bustle of the grand casino. The ringing of slot machines. The smiling of tourists. Attractive, tanned Rhodesian colonial girls. The head-rubbing of old men on long bouts with bad luck or hard booze. Nubile young women, dark-skinned and beautiful, all of them, sauntered this way and that, some serving drinks, others simply milling around wealthy-looking white men.

Jake's eyes followed down the carpeted aisle between the blackjack tables and the slot machines, to where they settled on the glass door leading out of the casino. There, he caught a brown-skinned vision in a long red dress. Her hair, auburn mixed with jet black and done up in a little bun behind her head, appeared far straighter and more pliable than that of most Rhodesian African women. Her features were not so classically broad, but with eyes as big and as lovely and as brown as Jake had ever seen. Her lashes were so long and pouty that they could be seen to flutter even from this distance. She was gorgeous. So gorgeous as to stop the young man's heart. So gorgeous as to render him incapable of looking anywhere else but in her direction.

"You playing or not?" came the gruff voice to his left.

He pulled his eyes away from the woman only for a moment, just long enough to answer the voice. He glanced at the overweight, middle-aged, obvious American sitting beside him at the table. "Hold on there, buddy," he said.

"C'mon, kid," the man barked. "You're playing like an asshole."

"Jesus, mister," Jake said, disgusted. "That's the kind of talk that makes us Americans so popular around the world."

"Screw off," the man said through his teeth.

Jake groaned, then picked up his chips, neatly arranged into two short stacks. Taking a cursory look at the door, he threw a chip to the croupier. He then leaned over to the man. "I fold," he whispered. "And it's a good thing for you that I've got better things to do." He locked a threatening eye onto him. "Otherwise, I might fold your cock right into your ass."

The man made a gesture to stand up, but Jake held out a hand.

"I wouldn't do that, buddy. I'm younger, stronger, and faster." He curled his lip back. "And I've killed or maimed more gooks than you've had hot dinners."

The older man opened his mouth to speak, but seemed unable to think of anything clever to come back with.

"No, fat-ass," Jake said, turning away, "you sit and enjoy your losses."

Ignoring the man, he gazed back at the door. The woman he'd spied no longer stood there. The huddle of children that had been trailing her was missing, as well. He strode quickly to the entryway, where he pushed through the glass and scanned the opulent gardens outside the casino hotel. A handful of tourists stood bartering with locals – porters and drivers, mostly – but no gorgeous young women could be found. He stood there gawking for a moment, his mouth hanging open.

"May I help you, sir?" came a voice, its command of English unreasonably proper.

"No," Jake said, shaking his head. He glanced down to see the short, squat valet beaming up at him with improbably white teeth. "Just getting some air."

The valet bowed and retreated to his stand beside the entry. Jake took one last long look over the grounds, greenery and palm trees breaking to the vast wilderness of Rhodesia beyond. He sighed.

Retreating back to the casino, Jake crossed to where he'd left Brian. His friend had remained in the same seat all this time, still pumping money into his various machines.

"Did you see the girl at the door?" Jake asked.

Brian shook his head distantly. "Nope," he mumbled. "Too busy losing money."

"She was gorgeous."

Brian snapped out of it and smirked up at his friend. "They're all gorgeous."

"Yeah," Jake said, looking back over his shoulder. *Not like this one,* he thought. Her form would remain with him for the rest of the evening, lingering with him as a deep and frustrated longing, a yearning to find a woman he'd felt oddly connected to, a woman he'd likely never see again.

"Fuck it," Brian said suddenly. He slapped his hand against the machine directly in front of him. "We should get some sleep anyway."

Jake nodded, still staring toward the door.

"We've got things to kill tomorrow."

CHAPTER 4

ankie National Park, Rhodesia's largest game reserve at over 5,600 square miles of Kalahari sand terrain, stretched before them. Saltpans and grassy plains with one of the largest concentrations of wildlife in Africa had set forth an abundance of game. The hunting party had already borne witness to great herds of elephant and buffalo, pockets of giraffes, zebras, wildebeest, and cheetah. They'd been flanked for a time by wild dogs, kudu, and hyena. They'd spotted impala, roan, waterbuck, jackals, foxes, and even the elusive sable antelope.

This had struck Jake and Brian as remarkably fortuitous, but as their guide – a white Rhodesian with three-day stubble and bad teeth – explained, seeing an abundance of game was not unusual. He pointed to the protectionism that had followed two decades of unmitigated slaughter of the animals. According to him, an early African chief named Hwenge was ousted by the invading Ndebele people, who in turn overtook large tracts of Hwenge's land, setting things up for hunting. For a time, the advanced weaponry of the white settlers of Rhodesia thinned out the animal populations considerably, pushing the herds of animals further into the unwelcoming western reaches of the country. It was here that Wankie

National Park was established, as a protectionist measure for the rare beasts of Africa.

"It's no surprise," the guide explained, his breath rank even in the open air. "You really came at the best time. July to October is excellent for viewing and hunting game."

"Why now?" Brian asked, his voice carrying in a yell to accommodate the roar of the wind blowing back over the Land Rover.

"It's this time of year that the game concentrates near permanent water," the guide said, circling his hand around in a show of abundance.

"You say this is a national park," Brian said. "How can we hunt here?"

"Ah," the guide said, pointing to the stream to his right. "*That's* a national park. Everything beyond that stream. What we're driving through here is private property. Long as you gun them down on this side of the water, we're fine."

Jake chuckled at the politics.

The hunters sat perched on the back of a Land Rover that jostled through semi-open areas and wound along a track weaving in and out of Mopani trees. They passed momentarily into shade, and the moment his eyes adjusted to the light, Jake spotted what he'd been keeping his eyes peeled for since departing the hotel. The experienced, weather-beaten guide had spotted the lion long before Jake, and was already pointing at it with his finger. He banged on the roof of the vehicle, and the African driver slammed his foot on the Land Rover's brake pedal.

"There," Jake whispered. He pointed alongside the guide in a direction that lay through a thicket near the bend in the path.

"Where?" Brian whispered as he brought his rifle to his shoulder, resting its business end on the roof of the Rover.

"Just there," Jake said into his friend's ear. "Through the trees."

Brian nodded. "I see him." His turn for a shot, he took steady aim. A great cracking shot erupted over the plain. The

.318 bullet grazed the lion's neck, then kicked up a cloud of dust behind it. The lion jumped up and, blood trickling from its neck, instinctively charged toward the Rover.

Brian dropped back in his seat to reload his rifle just as the lion picked up speed in its charge. His fingers quivered. The white guide cocked his own rifle, taking aim to protect his paying customers. But before he could tense his finger on the trigger, Jake reached out and touched him on the arm. When he had the guide's attention, he pointed to himself.

The guide nodded, but kept a steady bead on the charging carnivore.

Jake fired off a single round. The shot exploded between the animal's front legs. The lion hit the ground head first, tumbling over itself and coming to rest twenty yards ahead.

All men in the truck let out a warrior's yell.

Calm settled. A rustling in the trees followed. Out of the bush, two lion cubs the size of Great Danes raced toward the Rover in full flight to protect their mother. The guide banged the roof of the vehicle and the African driver took off, tires spinning in the dust. Jake turned as they fled. Behind and losing ground, the cubs pursued the vehicle. Shortly, they gave up the chase. Just before passing out of view around the bend, Jake saw them return to their dead mother, where they stood over her for a time before lying down beside her.

"I thought he was going to jump onto the fucking Land Rover," Brian said, his eyes glassy and wide. "And then you dropped him."

"Her," Jake said.

Brian raised an eyebrow. "Her?"

"Her," the guide echoed.

"He was a she," Jake explained. "We killed a lioness." He looked to the horizon, where the sun seemed haloed in savanna haze. "Unfortunately."

"Oh my God," Brian said, putting his head in his hands.

Jake clapped his friend on the back. "Cheer up, buddy," he said. "A fucking lion is a fucking lion in my eyes."

The guide laughed. "I'll leave a couple of boys behind," he said. "When the cubs leave, we'll pick up your trophy."

~ ~ ~

Sitting now in the cabin of the Land Rover, Jake took in the sights as the hunting party entered the town of Victoria Falls. The falls, he knew, separated the countries of Zambia and Rhodesia, and as it was the last week in August, the Zambezi was no longer in flood. Jake regretted this fact since he'd read that, during the rainy season, the volume of water was so immense as to create a natural phenomenon unseen anywhere else in the world. When the Zambezi was in flood, a mist rose into the sky that could be seen twenty miles away. The mist was known as Mosi-o-Tunya or "*the smoke that thunders.*" But here in August, there was no flood, no mist, and the falls were dotted with a selection of rivers in varying sizes flowing over the precipice and crashing into the first of a series of gorges below.

On the Zambian side of the river was the town of Livingstone, named after Scottish explorer Dr. David Livingstone, while the Rhodesian town was named after the actual Falls. The falls were generally considered to be the most gigantic in the world. Not the highest, but at approximately one mile wide with a height of three hundred and sixty feet, certainly among the broadest. The unusual natural configuration of Victoria Falls permitted almost the whole width to be viewed from a central position at the top of a ravine and directly opposite. At that point, the Zambezi River dropped into deep, narrow chasms. Many rare animals and bird life could be viewed in the area of the falls, and here the Zambezi was also abundant with tiger fish and the succulent bream.

As Jake took in the magnificent sight of this natural wonder, the Land Rover pulled up in front of the Victoria Falls Hotel. Almost immediately, the doors were opened by African staff wearing red uniforms, white gloves, and fezzes. Jake and Brian stepped out. In turn, both shook the white guide's hand and then headed for the front doors to the hotel.

"Don't forget the fishing," the guide shouted after them.

They turned slightly and nodded before following several of the staff into the hotel.

Even as they passed through the doors, Jake could hear the faint sound of the falls rumbling into the gorge at a distance behind. The pair passed through reception and into the atrium, where they found a vast space of well manicured and lush green lawns surrounding an ample swimming pool. Handfuls of tourists lounged in and around the pool, many of them being served drinks by the same red-clad staff that had greeted Jake and Brian at the door.

"Let's sit and have a drink," Jake suggested.

Brian nodded, and in a moment, the two had split off from their fez entourage and taken to a set of broad wooden deck chairs. It wasn't long before each was reclined with a cocktail in his hand. From here, Jake did the talking while Brian eyed a young, bikini-clad woman stretched out on a sun-bed.

"Can you believe we've only got ten days to go?" Jake said, holding his free hand over his eyes to get a better look at the girl.

Brian seemed incapable of tearing his gaze from her. "My God, she's gorgeous," he said.

"They're all gorgeous," Jake echoed.

This seemed to snap Brian out of it. He smiled distantly. "Yeah. It's amazing how quickly three weeks can fly by."

"Three weeks," Jake breathed. "I can't believe we've been here that long."

Brian sighed.

"Three weeks, and we haven't even gotten laid," Jake quipped.

"Yeah," Brian said with a soft smile. "No broads. But that hunt was a blast."

"I guess you can kiss the deer hunting in Pennsylvania good-bye," Jake quipped. "Won't be the same after the kind of rush we just had."

Brian tossed his feet to the floor and set his drink down in the holder flanking his chair. "Remember that fucking lion," he said, his hands animated. "I just clipped the side of his neck. Scared the living shit out of me."

"Lioness," Jake corrected.

"Whatever."

Jake stood and stretched, looking up at the sky. "The sun will be down soon," he said. "Free sundowners at the tables of the Falls casino."

Brian groaned. "I've dumped more money into that fucking casino—"

"You can just sit and watch me play, then," Jake interrupted. "You'll still get the free drinks."

Brian offered a cockeyed grin before getting up and joining his friend. He took one last look at the young woman, who at that moment stood up and got busy stepping into the legs of a tracksuit.

"So where the hell are we going tomorrow?" he asked.

"Lake Kariba," Jake said, leading the walk toward the casino.

"Oh yeah," Brian said. "Our guide was all about that fishing. I wonder what makes him so sure it'll be so good. Every time I fish, I don't catch shit."

"Operation Noah," Jake said. "The government flooded the area to build the largest man-made lake in the world."

Brian laughed. "Listen to you, Encyclopedia Britannica."

"I know," Jake said with a smirk. "How my brother would be proud."

CHAPTER 5

In the morning, after coffee and a long drive into the valley, the guide would do his part to add to Jake's growing knowledge of the area.

"Legends suggest that the Zambezi River was known outside of Africa for thousands of years," he yelled over the roar of the Land Rover's engine. "The kingdoms of Hiram, Solomon, and Sheba supposedly were enriched by its gold and ivory. Evidence of early occupation by man has been discovered along most of the river, but much of its history remains a mystery."

Jake turned to Brian, who rolled his eyes regarding the lecture.

"The Zambezi meets with the Sanyati, Ume, and Sengwa Rivers in the Gwembe Valley, which is where we're headed."

"It's not exactly sterile there, is it?" Jake asked, recalling his guide books.

"No," the guide admitted. "In truth, it's a painfully hot and disease-ridden region. Mostly indigenous people. Mainly Tonga tribesmen."

Brian leaned forward. "I thought we were going to Lake Kariba."

The guide nodded. "We are. Kariba's a manmade lake in the valley."

Jake opened his mouth to say something to Brian, but was cut off by the guide's diligent history lesson.

"In 1955, the Zambezi Valley became a hive of activity with the construction of the wall for the Kariba Dam," he said mechanically. "The wall was completed by the end of 1958, despite an enormous flood that threatened to halt efforts."

Jake wondered how many times this guide had given this speech.

"In the early Sixties, media attention focused on the new township at Kariba, where Operation Noah undertook the world's largest animal rescue attempt. World media covered the effort to save wildlife from the rising waters of the new lake. Lake Kariba became a mesmerizing confusion of ecological change and parts of the area teemed with an abundance of flora and fauna."

"Mesmerizing confusion?" Jake mouthed to Brian.

Brian chuckled under his breath.

The Rover crested a hill that bent down into the valley in question. There, Lake Kariba stood in all of its shimmering glory.

"Jesus," Jake said.

"It looks more like an inland sea," Brian added.

The guide nodded with a proud smile. Then he banged on the window frame of his passenger side door, signaling that the African driver should pull over near the shore.

"Here we cast our rods," the guide said with a wink. "See if you have what it takes to catch the tough and elusive tiger fish."

Jake elbowed Brian, who offered a wry smile. The group spilled out of the truck and took to a nearby boat, a tall and powerful sport craft already outfitted with everything the big game fishermen would need to catch a thirty-pound tiger fish. After a quick briefing on what to expect, the party alighted on the lake.

In short order, the African boat driver proved himself to be an expert in all things bait. The wiry old man seemed to know all the best spoons and spinners to entice the tiger fish. They found that the shoreline of the many islands in the lake – owed mostly to the original capturing flood waters – offered a wealth of game fish. It was all Jake and Brian could do to keep up as they cast and trolled from their boat.

On shore, game life appeared equally plentiful, with enormous herds of buffalo grazing the green grass on the bluff just beneath the horizon. Hippo and bull elephants fought here and there in the crystalline water.

After several hours of fighting the tiger fish, the boat pulled into the marina and tied up. Jake and Brian disembarked, Jake thoroughly tanned from the hot days on the savanna and lake, Brian thoroughly burned.

In the marina, the pair had their pictures taken with the lone tiger fish they landed, each of them having done half the work in reeling it in. They shook hands with the African boat driver. In turn, both Jake and Brian handed the man a $50 note, which the African took with a look of extreme disbelief. When that passed, he simply grinned from ear to ear. With a pat on the shoulder and a departing wave, they parted ways with the kindly African, then turned and followed their middle-aged white guide back to the Land Rover.

The Rhodesian guide looked at them scornfully as they climbed into the cab. "You gave the Munt too much money, man," he said, shaking his head. "It bleddy spoils them for the rest of us."

Jake shrugged. "But it was worth it to us." He then craned his neck to look into the back seat. "Wouldn't you say, Brian?"

"It's only fifty bucks," Brian said.

"Only!" the white guide said, flashing yellowed teeth. "That bugger won't want to work for a month now. He'll find a beer-hall and piss it all away."

~ ~ ~

Kariba Town rested close to the Kariba Dam at the north-western end of Lake Kariba and in close proximity to the Zambian border. It endured the unpleasant geographical location of the Zambezi Valley, which made the place hot year round. Still, the town was the center of the tourist industry for the Lake Kariba region.

Jake and Brian never did have the opportunity to see the dam's wall, nor the town itself, as they had to rush to catch their flight, lest they wanted to miss their connection in Johannesburg. By the time they arrived at the airport, the plane had already boarded, and they were forced to run across the hot tarmac to the steps of the waiting Air Rhodesia Vickers Viscount. They had no sooner climbed the steps when the stairway truck backed away and the door of the Viscount was closed.

Sweating from the run and still a little disoriented, Jake led the way down the aisle of the aircraft, scanning his boarding pass. When Jake found his seat, he turned back to look at Brian, who stood some twelve rows down the aisle, looking for an empty seat next to him. There were none. The two, it seemed, would not be sitting together, Brian near the front and Jake closer to the rear.

Jake's look of disappointment at not finding a seat next to his friend quickly faded when he realized who he would be sitting next to: the beautiful African he had seen outside the door of the casino only a few days earlier.

As he took his seat, he did what he could to avoid staring, but that proved difficult. This young woman was a true child of Africa, not black and not white, but the clear product of mixed parents. She appeared to be in her mid-twenties, but regardless, she was a stunning beauty, a petite build and likely on the rather short side, with hair not totally black, but rather streaked with shades of a wavy auburn color. She wore a dowdy white dress that looked straight out of the fifties, buttons running all the way up to her neck. Still, despite this cloak, she radiated a quiet beauty. Jake couldn't believe his good fortune in having been given a seat next to her.

He smiled warmly the minute she realized he was looking at her. She returned the smile.

"Hi," Jake said simply.

"Hello." Her voice was proud, confident.

Jake arced a hand to her, bending it awkwardly at the wrist so he could shake hers despite their seated position. "I'm Jacob Fallon."

She took his hand. "I'm Sarah Malumbo," she said warmly.

"I saw you at the Victoria Falls Casino Hotel."

She shook her head. "I don't gamble."

Jake laughed. "I didn't say you were gambling. I saw you outside the door with a bunch of little kids."

Her look of consternation bled to a heart-stopping smile. "Oh, I see," she said. "They are from an orphanage in Bulawayo. The Sisters drove them in the convent bus to see the falls."

"Nice of the Sisters."

Sarah offered one long, slow nod. "How can a child be so close to one of God's wonders and never see it?"

"You're right about that," Jake said. For a moment, he found himself uncharacteristically short of words. He discovered that every time his eyes met hers, breath rather failed him. "You, uh," he stammered. "It's uh . . . it's a shame that they're orphans."

The moment the words escaped his lips, he chided himself inwardly. *Smooth, Jake*, he thought. *Real fucking smooth.*

"Oh, there is no shame in that," Sarah said, pressing her soft hand to what, even beneath her frumpy dress, appeared to be an ample breast. "I am also an orphan."

"No kidding."

"I am not kidding," Sarah said with a sad little frown. "I was brought up by the Sisters in the Convent school."

Jake was snapped suddenly from his beauty-induced trance and realized that the conversation was not going as he'd anticipated. Quickly, he tried to gain safe ground. "I'm sorry," he said. "I didn't mean to suggest that . . . But then I guess that's why you speak English so well."

Sarah's face melted into a look of subtle confirmation.

"In fact," Jake said, "some of your inflections make you sound Irish."

To his great relief, his company smiled.

"There are two nuns that are Irish at the orphanage," she said. "And one in Sinazongwe. So I suppose it must sound strange some of the time."

Jake grinned, his eyes lingering on hers perhaps a little too long. He opened his mouth to speak, to say something romantic, whatever came to mind, but just as he did, the plane began to move and Sarah broke her end of the gaze. Jake looked then to the head of the aircraft, where the air hostesses were busy presenting the usual survival ritual. Then, to his right, Jake could see the massive Lake Kariba, partially visible in the distance through the window as the Viscount gathered speed down the runway and lifted off the ground.

He watched the scenery pass rapidly by, each passing moment feeling more awkward than the last. "Where's Sinazongwe?" he asked finally.

"It's a little town halfway up Lake Kariba on the Zambian side," she explained. "I came from there originally."

"What do you do?" Jake asked, feeling a little lame that he couldn't come up with something more original in his line of questioning.

"There's a small mission there. I have a job working as the Sisters' cook."

"That sounds ni—"

"I am also studying journalism through an American correspondence course," Sarah interrupted, as if she felt the need to justify her future ambitions.

Just as she finished speaking, the *no smoking* sign switched off on the overhead panel. Jake dived into his pocket for his cigarettes, extending one to Sarah, a soft glint in his eye. "A cook who can write," he said. "And with the face of an angel."

Sarah seemed to brighten up for a moment, but then she noticed the cigarette. She looked down at it with obvious disgust as she shook her head emphatically from side to side. "No thanks," she said. "The Sisters would never approve."

She reclined her seatback and stared up in the direction of the air vent.

Jake puffed for a time, then crushed his cigarette in the ashtray. He smiled at his companion and reclined his own seat. Then he turned in Sarah's direction, looking with eyes half-closed into her lovely face. In time, it became clear that she was doing the same, facing him with the same half-closed eyes.

CHAPTER 6

The four turbo props whined vigorously on ascent as the Viscount made a steady climb out of Kariba Airport. In the distance less than ten miles from takeoff, a pocket of African freedom fighters under the supervision of a superior officer waited in a clearing in the bush. These were members of the Zimbabwe People's Revolutionary Army (ZIPRA), the armed wing of the Zimbabwe African People's Union (ZAPU), a militant Communist organization headquartered in Zambia.

ZIPRA, under the leadership of Joshua Nkomo, were regarded by the natives as freedom fighters or guerillas, while to the white Rhodesian minority, they were considered terrorists. The men crouched in the brush, dressed in a mixed bag of battle fatigues, some Russian, some Chinese. The man in the center – a huge, oafish brute with jet-black skin and a chiseled jaw – focused a Russian SAM-7 ground-to-air missile on the ascending aircraft. When the officer kneeling behind him gave the signal to fire, the guerilla fighter released the missile.

A white stream of vapor trailed through the clear afternoon as the missile sought its target. The Viscount, with its broad underside, made for an easy direct hit when the missile found its mark. Such was the impact that the aircraft seemed to stop midair before banking and spiraling from the sky, a bright red fireball following the descent.

The twenty men on the ground leapt with glee at the sight.

~ ~ ~

The Viscount hit the ground, breaking up in large pieces as it crashed through the dry matima bush. Parts of the fuselage cracked off, firing and toppling in different directions. Two of the sections rolled over like giant barrels smashing through the dry trees, crushing and breaking everything in their path until they came to a stop against thicker brush. Other sections stood in flames.

Cries and screams from survivors trapped or dying erupted into the air, echoing through the otherwise silent bush.

When Jake came to, he realized that he remained strapped to his seat; Sarah's head rested on his shoulder. A warm sensation came over his thigh, and when he looked down, what he found there made him feel weak. A sharp piece of plastic had torn away from his armrest and jabbed deep into the front of his thigh.

He turned to Sarah, who opened her eyes as if waking from a dream. With the exception of a swollen cheek, she was unmarked.

"Jacob," she mumbled.

"Yes, I'm here," Jake said through gritted teeth.

Smoke began to billow from behind. A fire raged near the back of the shredded cabin.

Sarah wrapped her arms around Jake's neck, sobbing softly. "Is this really happening?" she asked. But before he could answer, she grew tense, rigid. "Your leg!"

"Never mind that," Jake said, collecting his bearings. "We have to get out of here." It occurred to him that they were sideways. The window once to Jake's right was now directly above them; the windows from the opposite side of the aircraft now served as the floor. In their suspended position, along with the pain in his thigh, Jake could feel the extreme pressure from the tightly stretched seat belt that locked their waists to the seats, leaving their upper torsos to bend over like toy puppets.

"Okay," Jake said. "I'm gonna unhook myself and lower down. Then I want you to do the same."

Sarah looked at him with fearful eyes.

"I'll catch you."

She nodded.

Feverishly, Jake did as he'd suggested, howling as he cracked the splinter of plastic and freed himself from the shackles of his broken seat. He wailed anew as he toppled down to the other end of the cabin, all his weight coming down on his wounded leg, the plastic still protruding from the front. He stumbled over the lifeless bodies of the two people who had been seated opposite, trying to get a foothold so he could secure Sarah.

He glanced down only for a moment to confirm that the people were dead. The man's back was clearly broken. He lay sideways atop his dead female companion, both still strapped into their seats and also looking like limp puppets.

Jake straddled the unfortunate pair as he unbuckled Sarah. Despite his throbbing leg, he found his strength redoubled, spurred on perhaps by a rush of sudden adrenaline. Carefully, he secured her over his arms, then staggered toward the nearest patch of daylight. Neither spoke as they took in the horror all around them.

Over the next seat, they came to another pair of trapped passengers, these two only slightly older than Jake, but still breathing and lucid. Jake let Sarah down to her feet, and the two of them helped the other survivors escape.

As Jake watched the freed couple climb to the opening, he looked ahead, realizing that the midsection of the aircraft was gone and that there was no sign of any of the passengers who'd occupied that area. It was as if that section of the aircraft never existed.

He turned back to Sarah, offering his hand. "C'mon. Not far now."

She replied with that same stiff nod, then took his hand. They passed beneath and above several other passengers, all of them slumped, still strapped to their seats, either dead or injured beyond help.

Jake called for Brian and began pulling apart some of the wreckage, finding nothing but plastic and smoke. Desperately, he realized that there was little hope of finding his friend. There was no telling whether Brian's section of the plane remained attached to Jake's, or if it wasn't, where it had landed.

One last tug through the wreckage and Jake felt sunlight against his brow. He felt Sarah's breath hot on his neck as he threw her arms over his shoulders and literally dragged her into the clearing. There, about ten other survivors had assembled, some of them children. Jake found himself mumbling to them, but could scarcely know what he was saying. He toppled to the ground, the pain of his leg overcoming him. Sarah stooped beside him, her eyes brimmed with tears, but he nodded, mouthing that he was okay.

In time, voices could be heard in the bush. Eight more survivors emerged, some with serious injuries. A man likely in his early forties shouted to the ten, but Jake couldn't hear what he was saying. One woman crawled along the ground, clutching an injured child to her chest.

"We have to find cover!" Jake shouted, forcing himself onto his elbows and trying to make himself heard. "I think we've been shot down!"

A few cries of terror sprang up, but the man in his forties brought calm to the chaos. Apparently uninjured, he shepherded many of the women and children into a nearby cover of trees, urging with his hand for Jake and Sarah to follow.

Just as Sarah helped Jake to his feet, further shouting could be heard in the distance – this shouting distinctively not English.

"Wait here," Sarah said, helping Jake gingerly to the ground.

As the young man watched, his companion climbed a sturdy nearby tree and panned her eyes over the bush. Even as she did so, the shouting approached – close enough now to be identified as Ndebele.

"Sarah!" Jake called. "We have to go!"

The lithe young woman leapt from the tree and grabbed up Jake's arm once more, trying to pull him away from the carnage.

Just as they passed into the cover, the forty-year-old survivor began shouting at the woman with the injured child. "We've got to get out of here," he demanded.

The woman looked up at him helplessly. "But help is on the way," she said. "They'll have seen the crash from the airport."

The man rushed over and shook her. "Those men are shouting in Ndebele," he said. "They're probably terrorists. This was no accident."

"He's right," Sarah said as they hobbled past. "Rhodesian forces would not be shouting in Ndebele."

Jake looked directly at the woman. "You've got to go with him," he said. "Think of your child."

Sarah grabbed Jake's arm and yanked him away. The blood from his leg left a steady stream as she dragged him into the thick bush.

"Our plane was shot out of the sky," Jake said frantically. "I've seen this shit in Nam. No way did the plane just blow itself up."

"That's almost as impossible to believe as the crash," Sarah said.

Then Jake's numbed mind seemed to clear and again focused on his missing friend. "Gotta find Brian!" he cried, pulling away from her and limping away toward the nearest cluster of flames, another piece of wreckage on the north side of the cover.

"I'm coming with you!" Sarah called, following behind for only a moment before gaining ground and looping Jake's arm around her shoulders.

Behind them, gunfire could be heard, thunderous on the breeze. As they reached the section of the wreckage, the clearing came suddenly alive with guerrillas, all of them shooting indiscriminately in every direction. Sarah halted and, without a word, pulled Jake away from the gunfire and toward the lake, moving as quickly as Jake's leg would allow.

Just behind, a group of survivors led by the forty-year-old tore through the brush. Only eight had managed to elude the guerillas. Just as Jake looked back, they broke away from his and Sarah's path, heading back in the direction of the airport and the town of Kariba.

Just near the clearing beside the lake, Sarah's strength failed her and the pair toppled to the ground. They lay facedown in the bush as silently as possible. The pain in Jake's leg traveled in searing arcs from the plastic spike to his extremities and back again.

Sarah put her hand on the protrusion, giving it a small tug before Jake stopped her short.

"Not here," he whispered through his teeth. "We won't be able to stop the bleeding."

Sounds of gunfire and slashing poured through the trees. Screams from the remaining survivors rang out, the guerillas apparently sparing no one, not even the children. Jake lifted himself to his elbows. From here, he could just make out the killing spree. A handful of terrorists hacked at men, women, and children in their dying throes, looted the bodies from the remains of the wreckage, and made their way through the dense bush, apparently unaware of Jake and Sarah.

Sarah buried her face in the small of Jake's back and wept. The two remained like this for some time, Sarah weeping and Jake watching like a statue as the guerillas collected everything they could carry. They stole from scattered suitcases that had toppled from the luggage compartment. They pilfered women's purses, wallets, and watches from wrists of the dead. One among their lot cut off a woman's ears just to retrieve her diamond studs. Sarah shook so hard it affected even Jake. But she remained silent, to her credit.

The guerillas moved slowly through the wreckage, but when they had finished, they peeled off in a direction upwind from Jake and Sarah, much to the former's relief. But just as peace came to him, it was ripped away. Behind the first band of terrorists, a small group of maybe four surviving passengers were led at gunpoint. Among them was Brian. As the prisoners disappeared into the bush, Jake pawed at the dirt before him, a muffled cry escaping his lips as the pain shot up his leg.

"We've got to pull this out," Sarah admonished under her breath, looking at the plastic that still jutted from Jake's leg.

"I told you," Jake said between clenched teeth. "If we pull it out here, we won't be able to stop the—"

As he spoke, Sarah unbuttoned her dress to the waist, removing the blouse she wore. Jake found himself losing command of his voice, his eyes fixed on the firm breasts making themselves known beneath Sarah's brassiere.

Sarah apparently noticed, as she rather scoffed and pulled the top of her dress back over herself, buttoning it quickly. The blouse she shredded into several pieces, leaving two pieces in clumps. Then she wheeled her head around, her eyes darting here and there in the thicket.

"What are you doing?" Jake asked.

"Looking for a . . . a tree," she said distantly.

"A tree?"

"A special tree. There!" She crawled through the brush to a nearby sapling. From its trunk, she pulled a handful of leaves and bark.

Jake watched intently as she began chewing the leaves and spitting the green residue onto the bark. She then crawled back to his side, and without a word of warning, placed her hand on the protruding plastic.

Jake winced, then set his hand on hers. "We can't afford sound here," he whispered, pointing at Sarah's free hand. "Give me a piece of that branch."

Sarah broke off a piece of the branch and handed it to him.

He put it between his teeth and offered her a smirk. "Now," he said.

Sarah threw a leg over Jake's chest, sitting astride. With one swift pull, she slid the sharp plastic from his thigh. It was no less than six inches long. Jake's back arched at the quick action, so powerfully that it nearly threw her to the dry, golden grass. A burst of blood followed.

Collecting her balance, Sarah got feverishly to work, putting pressure on the wound with one of the rolled pieces of her blouse. The fabric quickly became saturated. She grabbed up the second piece of cloth and removed it quickly, sopping up the blood before placing the bark with the green concoction over the wound. She pressed hard on the bark before tying it off with a fresh strip of cloth. Her fingers fast and sure, she bound the rest of the splint with the remaining strips of her blouse.

When she finished, Jake sighed and began to shiver. For a time, she held his head close to her breast. When he became still, she turned her face down to look at him.

"You need help, and as soon as possible," she whispered. "We have to make it to Kariba. Can you walk?"

He smiled through chattering teeth. "I'm gonna have to," he said. "Unless you wanna carry me."

She offered a half-smile.

"Thank you for all you've done," he said.

"You're welcome," she answered flatly. "Shall we go?"

"No," Jake said, crossing his arms to warm himself. "We should lay low for a while. Wait for them to clear out."

"You're right," she said, sounding frustrated. "We've no idea how many or where the freedom fighters might be."

Or where they've taken Brian and the others, Jake thought, clenching his teeth against both the pain and frustration.

The two lay silently in the bush until the sun began to drop in the sky. When dusk had settled, Sarah helped Jake to his feet.

"Put your arm around my shoulder," she said.

With his much shorter and slighter support, Jake struggled through the bush, his leg oozing blood with every step. In short order, they heard voices in the distance once again. Ahead, they saw a bright campfire lighting the coming night. This stood between them and the town, and so they knew without speaking that they would have to make their way around it or die in the wilderness.

Jake and Sarah fell to the ground and crept forward on all fours. Jake clenched his teeth against the agony shooting up his leg. The voices near the fire laughed and shouted in Ndebele. After they'd inched further along, the light in the clearing brought everything into focus. Brian Wilson hung naked from a tree, upside-down, his legs lashed to a broad, low-lying branch. He bled from both sides of his head. A closer look from Jake suggested that his best friend's ears had been cut off. Beneath Brian, a naked female passenger was held to the ground by a group of the guerillas. She screamed as the apparent officer in charge finished raping her. The ugly brute stood and beckoned to the others to take over for him. Without hesitating, one of his men jumped onto the terrified woman for his turn.

Jake's heart began to pound as he watched the officer zip his pants and stare in their direction. In the firelight, he got a clear look at the face of the officer. Two large scars stretched from cheekbone to jaw on either side of his face. He seemed to sneer in satisfaction as he listened to the grunting sounds of the man who was now raping the woman.

Jake pushed up on his hands, readying to spring on the officer, but Sarah grasped him by his makeshift bandage and ripped it off. Jake glared down at her in disbelief as she grabbed him by the hair and pulled his head to her chest. Without a word, she gouged the open wound with her finger.

Jake howled into her flesh, a howl that went unheard by the men making merry by the fire. Sarah clutched a hand over Jake's mouth, still gouging his wound with the other. In a moment, Jake's eyes rolled back in his head and he lost all sense of the world.

~ ~ ~

With her life saved twice in less than twelve hours and her savior lying unconscious in the weeds, Sarah tried feverishly to stop the bleeding once again, ripping pieces from the hem of her dress and binding Jake's wound tightly. She propped herself against a tree and looked in the opposite direction, continuing to hold Jake in her arms. She wept silently and tried to cover her ears to keep out the screaming uproar behind them. Tears streamed down her face for the raped woman, who the men beat and bruised mercilessly.

Another male voice entered the fray, this one in English. Sarah stuck her head up to see what was going on. She saw that the naked man hanging by his legs had regained consciousness.

"How much more can she take, you fucking savages?" he shouted in vain. "You're killing her."

The ZIPRA men ignored him.

"Please, dear God," the hanging man shouted to the heavens, "put an end to this!"

The scarred officer, his black eyes flickering in the firelight, turned away from the screaming woman and grabbed the hanging man's blood-soaked blonde hair. He lifted the tortured man's head up to face him.

"You want an end?" he spat in heavily accented English. "You want God and you want Jesu? I will give you all these things." He turned, releasing his grip on the blonde man's hair. "In return, we want our freedom." Then he wheeled around and put the muzzle of his automatic pistol to the hanging man's temple, sneering as he pulled the trigger.

The blonde man's back arched, his head flopped forward, and his dying body involuntarily urinated.

The officer looked at his remains in obvious disgust. "See," he said. "You piss yourself like a frightened baby. Now God has put an end to this." He turned to face his men, who continued to shout and rape the poor woman in the now bloody muck. "*I* am God here. *This* is the land God gave me."

Sarah slumped back under cover, quaking from head to toe.

"That's enough," the officer yelled to his men. "Hang her up to dry."

Sarah listened as the men laughed.

"Let's leave a souvenir for Mr. Ian Smith so he can see what he has done."

One last look at the guerilla camp saw the men stringing the woman up by her legs, letting her dangle next to the now almost-headless man. Sarah shivered as the ZIPRA officer picked up Brian's ears from the earth and stuffed them into the woman's vagina. The woman, who clearly had no will left within her, simply hung like a rag doll from the limb of the tree.

Sarah squinted her eyes closed as the officer walked over to the raped woman, putting the gun to her head. She heard him fire, then his shouting to the other men in the camp. The sound of guns and packs being scooped up from the ground followed.

Sarah rocked back and forth with the unconscious Jake resting in her petite arms. Slowly, he came to, and she held her hand over his mouth to quiet him. Jake tried to stop her rocking, but she resisted, finding herself rather in shock, as if locked in a trance.

Only when Jake grabbed her firmly and shook her did she wake from distant horror.

"What happened?" Jake whispered. "I blacked out."

Silently, Sarah pointed over her shoulder, where the carnage would await her companion.

~~~

Jake sat gingerly, taking a slow look from behind the tree against which Sarah rested. "They butchered my friend," he said to her in a crying whisper. "I could have *saved* him. Why did you stop me?"

Sarah stopped shaking and looked him straight in the eye. "Because if I'd let you go, they would have killed you, too. And raped *me*."

Jake turned away, furious.

"Don't you see?" she said, placing her hand on his shoulder. "I am the perfect target for their hatred. Half white, half black."

Jake scowled. "I could have done something."

Sarah scowled right back. "You're a fool," she said venomously. "A stupid fool."

Through the trees, Jake examined again the scene of his friend's death. Two men remained there by the fire. One of them appeared to be a white man.

"See that?" he whispered to Sarah. "One of those pricks is white. What the hell's he doing here?"

Sarah got up onto her knees, crouching beside Jake. "He's not white," she said softly. "He's an albino. Probably next in command behind . . . " She paused for a long while, a look of disgust crossing her troubled but lovely face. "Behind their leader."

"How can you be so certain?"
~~~

"Africans are suspicious of albinos. The sight of an albino helps to keep the others in line with ZIPRA's way of terror."

Jake kept his gaze trained upon her. "These people are dead," he said. "Why would they leave the albino behind?"

"He and his friend are waiting to protect the bodies from wild animals," she said. "Hyenas, jackals, maybe a leopard, or even an old lion could be looking for a free meal. These men stayed behind to make sure Rhodesian forces find the bodies exactly as they want them to."

Jake rolled over, pulling at his hair. "I could have taken those two pigs," he said, his mind roiling with sudden fury.

"Sure you could have," Sarah said with more than a hint of sarcasm. "You could have limped in there with a leg oozing blood and surprised them."

Jake grunted.

"And what if they were planning an ambush for the Rhodesians? You would have stumbled into ZIPRA guerrillas lying in wait." She took his face in her hands. "No, Jacob. We've got to get out of here. By morning, they will have blended into the locals or gone back to their safe haven in Zambia."

The sound of dry sticks breaking underfoot rippled from just behind. Jake peered around the tree. A guerilla was ambling straight toward them, tracing his rifle back and forth across the brush. Jake staggered to his feet, keeping himself out of sight behind the large tree before them. He heard the unmistakable sound of a soldier loading his weapon just as the guerilla passed beyond their location.

Jake sprung forward and grabbed the fighter from behind. The man proved stronger than he looked. He struggled mightily, twisting and flailing to free himself from Jake's grip. Jake slid his hand over the terrorist's mouth and thrust both hands to either side, twisting the man's head completely around, breaking his neck. The sound of bone snapping echoed through the otherwise silent bush.

When he turned back to Sarah, she was staring up at him in horror, her hand over her mouth. Trying to ignore how wretched this made him feel, he gathered the dead man's water bottle, took up his AK-47, and pocketed his military-issued knife.

He sighed scornfully. "They'll be looking for this piece of shit," he said. "So now we *do* have to get out of here."

Sarah nodded, tears forming as she stood and braced herself gingerly against Jake. They began moving through the still night. In the distance, the mating roar of a lion rang out above the din.

Jake and Sarah hadn't gone far before the voices of men came to them from the bush behind. To Jake, it sounded like angry gibberish.

"They've found the man you killed!" Sarah said through her teeth. "We must go!"

They moved as quickly and as silently as they could, given Jake's wounded leg. In time, they came within sight of water. Jake's heart skipped as he recognized something for the first time: the marina they approached was the place where he and Brian had gone fishing.

"C'mon," he said to Sarah. "I know this place."

The pair stumbled up to a square, whitewashed building with a tin roof. Jake banged on the door frantically. In time, it eased open to the inside, revealing a bleary-eyed African – the boat driver from the fishing trip.

"Sir, we need your help," Sarah said in English. "ZIPRA shot down our plane. They're hunting everyone."

The African seemed to center his attention on Jake. "I know this Mlungu (*white man*)," he said, his poor English meshing with Fanagalo. "He was fishing here this morning. Gave me makulu (*big*) mali (*money*) for danke (*thanks*)."

"Mhlaumba wena helpa tina (*Can you help us*)?" Sarah said.

"Hamba fihla lapa lo skepe," the African said. He paused for a long while before adding, "Linda."

"What the hell's he saying?" Jake asked.

"He said, 'Go hide there in the boat,'" Sarah explained, nodding toward the largest boat in the marina. "Then he said, 'Wait.'"

The African examined Jake's bleeding leg for a moment before ducking back inside his house. When he returned, he carried a set of boat keys, a bottle of peroxide, a blanket, gauze, and three bandages.

"Mina bas (*my boss*) bamba lo (*keeps this*) for the white fishermen," he said. "Go to that skepe (*boat*). If ZIPRA come, I not help you. You must go now. Baleka (*run*)." He had apparently run out of English, because he continued solely in Fanagalo. "Mina Msebenzi kona lapa basopa lo mfazi na lo bantwana gamina. Mina tshela mina bas, wena tshontsha lo skepe."

"What the hell did he say at the end?"

"He told us to run. His job now is to protect his wife and children. And he'll tell his boss you stole the boat."

"I could give a shit," Jake said. "How do you say thank you?"

"I'm sure he understands thank you," Sarah said.

Jake grabbed the man's hand and shook it violently. "Thank you so much. I will not forget this. But I need a broom." He nodded, willing the man to understand.

In the bright moonlight, the African put his hand behind his front door and grabbed a broom. He offered a wide, almost toothless smile as he handed the broom to Jake.

Jake hobbled back on their tracks and into the bush as if heading in a new direction toward the tarred road. He then returned, walking backwards, brushing away the old tracks as well as the new, along with any dripped blood that may have fallen on the dusty road down to the marina.

The African, apparently noticing the pain Jake was in, darted forward and took the broom out of the American's hands.

He gestured them to go, and as they departed, he swept away any trail that led from the bush.

Jake and Sarah reached the docks before turning back to wave to the old man. He waved, finished sweeping, and then returned to his little whitewashed house, easing the door shut behind him. The interior light went out. Then, as they boarded the boat, Jake watched the old man place wooden shutters on the two small windows of his abode, sealing his family within.

Inside the boat, Sarah pulled the cushions off the seats and placed them in a position of viewing advantage. Jake hobbled as he untied the lines and wrapped the rope around a mooring. He limped back into the cabin with the rope in his hand and tied it to the steering wheel.

Yelling could be heard in the distance. Time grew short.

Sarah opened the bandages and the bottle of peroxide. She removed Jake's makeshift wrappings and gazed at the ugly wound in his leg. Both Jake and Sarah paused there for a moment, staring down at his leg. Then their eyes met.

She put her mouth over his and kissed him firmly. Jake, surprised, let his hands drift to the small of her back, where they lingered until he began to feel searing pain in his leg. He pulled away from her lips, looking down to see that she had poured at least a quarter of the peroxide into his open lesion. Jake flinched and drew breath to scream, but Sarah lunged forward, locking him into another kiss. In time, the pain subsided and all that remained was the kiss. He relaxed, taking her lithe body onto his.

After a long, blissful moment, Sarah withdrew in silence. Working feverishly, she gauzed and bandaged the bubbling peroxide gash with the clean materials given her by the African. Jake watched her curiously from his huddled position in the small cabin. The only continuous sounds that could be heard were the incessantly noisy crickets and the water lapping gently against the boat.

Jake flopped his head back on one of the cushions. He bit his lip, avoiding the slightest whimper. He held his leg in both hands to ease the pain.

When she'd finished dressing him, Sarah started to shiver, crying silently. Jake put his arm around her, brought her close, and covered both of them with the blanket.

"When they realize that we didn't cross the tar road, they'll be back," she said fearfully. "Jacob Fallon, this could be the time that we die."

"Not today," Jake whispered. "Not after all we've been through."

She looked at him quizzically.

"Total strangers meeting like this," he explained. "There has to be a reason."

She furrowed her brow.

"How could God put something so beautiful like you in my life and then take it away with no meaning?" he asked.

"God can be unkind if he wants to," Sarah said with obvious certainty. "He's God."

Jake nodded thoughtfully and made to stand, the boat keys in his hand. Sarah grabbed him by the arm, pulling him down to her once more and kissing him on the lips. This time her kiss was tender. Jake sighed, pressing himself to her. His left hand found the small of her back once more. His right traced through her hair.

Death or no, he never wanted this moment to end.

Voices carried from the end of the docks. His heart racing, Jake broke from the kiss.

Jake and Sarah crawled gingerly to the nearest window, peering out to see three ZIPRA terrorists banging on the door of the African's little home. When no response came, the terrorists battered down the door and rushed in. The African, his wife, and his three little children were marched out into the clear moonlight.

Jake turned to Sarah. "Can you drive a boat?" he asked. "There's no way I'm going to let this family get butchered."

"I told you we were going to die today," Sarah said with authority.

"Nevermind that," Jake hissed. "Can you drive a—"

"I can," she interrupted. "In Sinazongwe, I have to know about boats."

Jake watched as she took her position at the wheel. He eased off the rope he had tied there, untethering the boat from the dock. Then he tried to start the engine, which sputtered and died. Again he tried. Again, it struggled and failed. The sound traveled.

Jake watched as the three ZIPPRA guerrillas wheeled around to the dock. Screaming, they burst into a run toward the boat. Jake readied himself at the chain, putting all his strength into cranking the engine to life. With a triumphant howl, the Mercury fired into action. Jake's eyes immediately darted to his African friend, who used the moment of opportunity to gather his family together, then scatter into the bush.

Jake picked up the AK-47, readying it to fire. "Come on, you motherfuckers," he mumbled to himself. "Come on. This one's for Brian and that poor abused woman and all the people you bastards blew up."

The weapon danced in his hands as he moved from side to side along the boat. He fired volley after volley into the approaching terrorists. One of the men fell headlong into the dust. The other two clamored on.

Just as Sarah jerked the boat away from the dock and slowly opened up the throttle, one of the attackers took cover behind a barrel.

Jake fired mercilessly at the third man. The terrorist broke into a spring, leaping just as the boat separated from the dock. The jump ended mid-air, Jake's last burst bringing him down. He crashed onto the back of the boat, lifeless, his torso riddled with bullets, his legs dangling in the water.

Jake relished the moment. But it would be short-lived. The remaining attacker stood from his position behind the barrel, sweeping the entire dock with his AK-47. Jake leveled his fire on the barrels, hoping they were full of fuel, but the bullets died in the empty steel drums.

Then warmth came to him. It trickled from the side of his head down to his neck. He fell to one knee, taking cover, lowering his weapon, and setting his fingers to the warmth. When he pulled them away, they were covered in red. All faded to black.

~ ~ ~

Sarah's hands worked one over the other on the wheel, churning the boat away from the dock. When she got them around to facing the center of the lake, she opened up the throttle, bringing the boat soaring to life. At that moment, she heard a thud on the deck. She turned to see Jake lying prone atop his weapon. Blood trickled from the side of his head.

"No!" she yelled.

Gunfire continued to tear through the air all around her. Mechanically, she steered the craft out of the sheltered marina and into open water, then on full throttle, the boat sped out into the lake. For a time, she refused to look back, her eyes focused on the horizon, scanning for the lights of Siavonga on the Zambian side of the lake. As the boat gained speed, she spotted unwelcome bright lights off to starboard, then gunfire. A Rhodesian gunboat charged straight toward them. The gunboat unleashed its full volley.

"The momparas (*fools*) are firing at us," Sarah said to herself. "They must think we are ZIPRA." Her hand pressed to the throttle, she took one last look at Jake. "We've got to get to the Zambian side of the lake."

Sarah had read of such encounters before. She knew the Rhodesian boat would sink them first, then look for survivors.

The Rhodesians came alongside them, kicking up wake. Sarah steered into the wake, causing the boat to rock. At the motion, the dead terrorist finally bounced into the water, the carcass erupting in a terrible splash.

The lights of the gunboat wheeled onto the body hitting the water. The Rhodesians slowed and came to a stop; the spotlight flickered here and there over the water, Sarah's boat gaining ground on freedom all the while.

Dawn approached as Sarah turned to watch her pursuers. Several of the Rhodesians reached into the water and hauled the dead terrorist aboard. Then, without hesitation, the boat once again gave chase. But just as quickly as it had started, it stopped, roaring around in a complete turn, coming to a stop in the unstill waters.

"Zambia," she said under her breath. They had reached Zambian jurisdiction, and the Rhodesians would not pursue.

She eased the boat to a standstill and then strode back to check on Jake. The wounded man appeared semiconscious.

"Jacob!" she said, shaking him vigorously. "Jacob Fallon! Are you all right?"

"Where . . . " Jake breathed. "Where am I?"

A smile came to her lips. "Close to Zambia," she said. "The dawn is breaking, and it looks as if we're *not* going to die today."

Jake nodded, his head scraping the deck. Then a look of wracked worry came to him. "Who am I?"

Sarah's heart sank. "Jacob Fallon," she urged.

His eyes were hazy. Distant. "How did I get here?"

Sarah sat down in the boat and cradled his head to her chest. She put her hand to her mouth. "Oh my God," she whispered.

CHAPTER 7

J ake watched as the strange but beautiful woman docked the boat along the bank of the lake. When she had finished, she returned to him, helped him to his feet, and limped with him to what appeared to be a small mission hospital. They were greeted by a man with kind eyes and graying hair, a man who was dressed as a minister.

"You'll need medical attention," he said, almost as if it were a question.

Jake felt too weak to speak, but Sarah nodded.

"I'm Dr. Raymond Young," the man said.

The man appeared to be in his mid sixties. His face was cracked, but well-tanned, likely from daily beatings by the hot Zambezi Valley sun. Jake looked at him skeptically, his eyes centering on the white collar around the so-called doctor's neck.

Dr. Young chuckled. "Don't worry," he said. "I'm a doctor as well as a Baptist minister." He then turned and motioned for Sarah to lead Jake down the short path to a small, whitewashed building with a corrugated iron roof. As they walked, he continued filling in his history. "My wife and I have been here at the mission for twenty-five years."

When they made their way into the building, Jake could see that it was a primitive surgery, like something out of the 19th century. His suspicions were confirmed when the doctor set him up on a table and immediately tended to the deep gash in his leg. Jake winced as the old man's fingers pressed all around the wound.

"Right," Dr. Young said. He then turned and rifled through a pair of cabinets.

Jake fired a pleading glance at Sarah, who looked upon him with deep concern.

The doctor returned with a giant syringe, plunging it into Jake's leg without warning. "For tetanus," he said. When he had finished, he placed the long needle on the table beside Jake and got to work stitching the young man's leg.

Jake writhed and groaned at the pain. The doctor attempted to hold him in conversation – perhaps as a distraction – asking him a host of questions that Jake didn't bother answering. Dr. Young then examined the graze on the side of his patient's head. Apparently satisfied that it wasn't deep enough to stitch, he began to apply the antiseptic via a little ball of cotton.

"He won't speak," he said to Sarah, his drawl unmistakably from a southern U.S. state.

"He's in pain," Sarah said, her eyes still lingering on Jake.

"I need information on this man," Dr. Young said to Sarah, his focus still clearly on Jake.

"His name is Jacob Fal—"

"Let him answer for himself," Dr. Young interrupted. He thrust out his chin. "Is that true, son? Is your name Jacob?"

Jake shrugged.

"What's this?" Dr. Young said, practically glaring at Sarah.

"He regained consciousness like this," Sarah explained.

The doctor's eyes widened. "You mean to tell me he doesn't *know* who he is?"

Sarah nodded.

"Does his elevator go all the way to the top?"

The young woman cocked a brow. "Elevator to the top?"

"I mean is he a nut-case?" The doctor circled a finger around his ear. "You know . . . like the Africans say: 'Whya-whya? *(crazy).*'"

"Of course not," Sarah answered defensively. "He's not crazy."

"Are you his only friend?"

Sarah explained that Jake couldn't seem to remember anything after being shot in the side of the head.

Jake felt utterly bewildered as he listened to this odd pair converse. He tried lifting himself from the examination table, but found that the doctor held him fast.

"Hold on there, buddy," the older man said. "I'm not finished. I think that cut on your head needs a few stitches, after all."

"I'm all right," Jake grumbled, speaking for the first time since the boat.

"You obviously have some form of amnesia," Dr. Young said. "But as a starting point, you're clearly an American."

Jake looked deeply into his eyes. "I *am*?"

The doctor nodded long and hard. "Oh, very much so," he said. "An East Coast, mid-Atlantic accent, I would say."

Jake sighed, wracking his brain and finding nothing.

"Does he have ID?" the doctor asked of Sarah.

Sarah shrugged.

"Then he's in Zambia illegally," Dr. Young said with authority. "If that's the case, then you've got a problem."

"It's bigger than a problem," Sarah said. "You know if he's found, he'll be arrested."

"Oh, I understand fully," the doctor urged. "Further, if arrested, he'll be held at the President's pleasure and probably accused of being a Rhodesian spy."

"I've heard that story before."

"So have I." The doctor sighed. "Many times. But what can I do?"

Sarah grabbed the old man's sleeve. "We were never here," she pleaded.

"I can't lie to the gov—"

"We came across the lake from Kariba," Sarah interrupted, her voice frantic and urging. "ZIPRA shot down an Air Rhodesian airplane. We survived, as did some others. And ZIPRA could be hunting us."

The doctor's eyes grew wide. "Shot down an aircraft? There's nothing on the BBC."

"It happened yesterday afternoon. It took us all night to escape with our lives."

The doctor shook his head, still apparently unconvinced.

"By noon, it will be all over the country."

Dr. Young turned away, but Sarah grabbed him by the sleeve once more.

"You know as well as I that there are protected ZIPRA camps in the Zambezi Valley." She pointed back at Jake, who sat confused and bleeding on the table. "This man . . . Jacob Fallon . . . he saved my life. And during the escape, he killed at least three freedom fighters."

"I did?" Jake piped in, utterly amazed.

"Oh, you sure did," Sarah answered with compunction.

Dr. Young's breathing grew shallow and his hands became busy. "They'll be on a *rampage*!"

Sarah tried to plead with the doctor, but he turned away.

"You must leave the Valley," he said. "They'll be looking for anyone who aided this young man, and I can't put my clinic at risk."

"But the Zambian army—"

"Don't be foolish, girl," the doctor interrupted. "You know as well as I that the army can't control the forces of the rebels. There are more guerillas in this country than standing army."

Jake watched as the beautiful young woman who was apparently his friend paced away from the doctor. His heart reached out to her as she pressed a delicate finger to her full lips, apparently pondering something deeply.

"We could take the boat back up the lake to Sinazongwe," she said eagerly. "Play the game of being tourists out on a fishing exped—"

Dr. Young waved his hand in the air, interrupting her. "It's over a hundred miles of water between here and Sinazongwe. And nowhere to refuel."

Sarah's shoulders slumped. Jake gulped, wanting desperately to help her but not entirely sure why. He glanced over at the doctor, whose face had taken on a sudden look of intensity.

"Where did you get the boat, anyway?" the old man asked.

"We stole it to get away," Sarah said. "It's owned by a white man."

The doctor chuffed. "This gets better by the second." He then shook a finger at the young woman. "Tell you what; I'll do a trade with you. I buy the boat from this mysterious Mr. Fallon in return for an old Land Rover I bought on a government auction. It runs, and you can keep it or leave it at the mission clinic in Sinazongwe. How's that?"

Sarah seemed to mull the offer for a long while, sending skeptical glances now and then at the shrewd doctor.

"We'll take it," Jake piped in.

Sarah fired a confused look at him.

Jake shrugged. "Whatever's going on here," he explained, "I'm up shit creek." He banged his hand against the healthy side of his head as if trying to remember. "Whatever the hell . . . It seems it's time for us to get out of Dodge."

The doctor smiled. "You're right there, partner." He made frantic with his hands again, turning to his cabinets and pawing around for something. "I'll draw up a bill of sale."

"Doctor?" Jake said impatiently.

Dr. Young turned to look at his patient, obviously confused.

Jake pointed at his still-bleeding head. "Could you take care of this first?"

The doctor offered an impish smile, then moved in to tend to Jake's head.

~ ~ ~

Sarah looked quizzically at Dr. Young as the old man happily exchanged papers with Jake and flipped him the keys to his Land Rover.

"Do you know Dr. Caldwell?" she asked.

"Why do you ask that?" Dr. Young inquired, arching a brow.

"You said to leave the car in Sinazongwe, where his mission is located."

"Ah," Dr. Young said, his eyes darting from one side to the other. "Yes . . . yes of course I do. We're part of the same mission."

"He delivered me," Sarah said casually.

The doctor looked away. To Jake's eye, it appeared that this news was no news to him.

"I see," Dr. Young said. "And what is your last name, young lady?"

"Malumbo," Sarah said. "My name is Sarah Malumbo."

The quickness with which Dr. Young looked up at Sarah could not be hidden. Nor could his obvious surprise. "I see," he said, his eyes returning to their darting dance. "That makes a difference."

"What do you mean?" Sarah asked, her lips parting into a curious smile. "You know me?"

Dr. Young began to fidget. "Uh, no," he said. "No, my dear. I'd just heard that Willie delivered you."

Jake's face still carried its bewildered expression as he watched the conversation unfold, but his cunning remained. There was something this doctor was hiding – and though Jake still didn't quite comprehend how he knew this lovely Sarah Malumbo, he felt strongly that he wanted to get to the bottom of it.

The doctor offered a nod that urged Jake to sign the paper he had just been handed. When Jake patted at his front pockets, he was immediately handed a pen. He did not read the bill of sale. He simply signed on the dotted line, questioning how he could remember his own signature, but not his history.

Sarah handed the boat keys to the doctor.

"I guess you'll have it repainted," Jake said.

Dr. Young smiled. "The boat?"

Jake nodded, a nod that was mirrored by the doctor. The old man then beckoned the patient and his companion to follow him out to the back of the clinic. There they found a dirty and beaten army-issue Land Rover. Without hesitation, Dr. Young climbed into the old green vehicle and turned the starter. He smiled as the engine fired immediately on the first attempt. With the engine idling, he plodded over to a nearby shed and retrieved a pair of five-gallon tanks of gasoline, which he carried over and chunked down in the back of the Rover. He then repeated the process, carrying two more from the shed to the vehicle. By the time he had finished, he was sweating, and smelled of it, as well.

"Do you know the way?" he asked Sarah.

"Yes," she replied.

The doctor fired out a bevy of information as to what to expect en route. There would be a roadblock by the Zambian army at Kafue bridge, but as they were not going to Lusaka, they would be turning off prior to the bridge and out of sight of the army. He warned them to be careful going through the town of Mazabuka, a location where the police loved to hassle drivers. Since Jake had no ID, he suggested that they rest up and go through the town at night.

As for Jake and his wounds, the doctor advised that they were not to be disregarded. The wound on his leg was deep and he had lost a great deal of blood and possibly had serious nerve damage. He was given a large supply of aspirin and told not to allow the wound to reopen and to keep it clean at all times.

"You will be out of action for several months," the doctor warned Jake. "If you allow your leg to get re-infected and gangrene sets in, you could lose it."

"I'll be fine," Jake said dismissively.

"Don't do that, boy," Dr. Young said, furrowing his brow. "Never forget that you are in Africa. Things aren't the same here."

Jake thanked the old man for all he had done.

"Thank Sarah," Dr. Young said. "She's your true guardian angel, I'd say."

Jake glanced over at Sarah, who appeared quite demure. He then stared earnestly into the doctor's eyes. "You're not setting us up, are you?"

"No, son," Dr. Young said indignantly. "Your movements are safe with me."

Jake and Sarah shook hands with Dr. Young and climbed into the Land Rover. The woman took the driver's seat while the wounded man stretched out on the passenger side. The doctor waved them off, a wave that the pair in the vehicle returned. As Sarah pulled into the gravel road, Jake's eyes lingered on the doctor. He watched him turn and shake his head, then scampered a little too quickly back to his clinic.

"I don't trust him," Jake said. "We best keep a sharp eye."

Sarah nodded, her foot easing down on the gas.

~ ~ ~

Siavonga was situated on the north shore of Lake Kariba and, depending on road conditions, the town stood approximately two to three hours from the capital city of Lusaka. The lake that crowned the town served as a sore point for the local Batonga

Tribe of the Zambezi Valley. They had put the blame for the massive flood directly on Nyaminyami, their River God. Myth had it that the wife of Nyaminyami, in answer to the prayers of her people, went downstream of the Kariva to a place later known as the Kariba Gorge. Upon her return, she was trapped and could not cross – the new wall of the Kariba Dam was simply too high, towering 590 feet above the Zambezi River and crossing the Kariva. The loss of his wife angered Nyaminyami, and as a result, he ordered the river to rise and destroy the white man's bridge.

Due to the construction, the dam wall and Lake Kariba had split the Tonga people ideologically. But during the early days after resettlement, the Tongas were allowed to cross the Lake without restraint and meet relatives and friends on the other side. When the Federation of Rhodesia and Nyasaland broke up in 1963, and Zambia became an independent country in 1964, free movement between the tribe ceased to exist. Border posts were established at Kariba and Chirundu. At this, the relationship with Southern Rhodesia began to deteriorate.

To add to the situation – and certainly not for the better – Southern Rhodesia declared unilateral independence from Britain, making the country an inaccessible "mutineer" republic. Dealing with Rhodesia became politically unacceptable for Zambia and delayed the progress of construction on a power station that would lie on the Zambian side of the lake. This would prove devastating to the infrastructure of the unstable region, Zambia desperately needing additional power for its ever-expanding copper mining industry.

In 1970, the struggle for independence in Zimbabwe began, and a bitter war broke out between the Southern Rhodesian settlers and the African nationalists. Due to the unfortunate geography of this war, Zambia became a host nation for freedom fighters. The numbers were hard to establish, but it was estimated that there were no fewer than forty thousand fighters huddled in the bordering areas between Zambia and Rhodesia. This large presence made it almost impossible for the Zambian army to control their guests. Their military forces were smaller than the freedom fighters, and they had never had to fight a war, gaining independence from Great Britain as almost a gift.

It was through this tumultuous region that Jake and Sarah rode.

Sarah piloted the vehicle carefully, but not without speed over the rough terrain. In her peripheral vision, she could sense Jake smiling over at her from his place in the well-worn passenger's seat. She kept her gaze locked on the road until he huffed and gave up. When she finally looked at him, he had laid his head against the window. There, he contorted his face as if searching for something in his mind, something he couldn't quite find.

"Something's weird here," he said, clearly puzzled.

"What?"

"That doctor," Jake said, furrowing his brow. "How come your name was instant recognition?"

Sarah bunched up her shoulders.

"You're a hot-looking woman," Jake said. "Don't get me wrong. It's just that it seemed like we only got easy help because your name's Sarah Malumbo."

Sarah sighed, then nodded. "It was also strange to me," she said. "But we're out of there, and that's all I want."

Jake smiled at her. "Are we lovers?"

Her heart leapt as she tried to battle between anger and excitement at the question. "We kissed in the boat," she answered.

"I remember the boat."

She turned to him and cocked her brow. Anger had won the battle. "Do you remember something about sex?"

"No," Jake said, flashing a grin. "Was it good?"

Sarah felt utterly annoyed. "You think I would give up my virtue to you when we were being shot at?" She seethed through her teeth. "Honestly, Jacob, if you think I'm some kind of—"

Jake cut her off by placing his rough hand on her wrist. "Sarah Malumbo," he breathed, "I think nothing of the sort."

"Then why would you—"

"I don't know," Jake interrupted again. "I guess I just feel like we have this . . . this *connection*. And I couldn't help but wonder if we had a history before everything went all fuzzy."

"Well, we don't," Sarah said. She was agitated, but she couldn't hold back with either her eyes or her tone that she agreed with Jake. They *did* seem to share a connection.

"*Can* we be lovers?" he asked jovially.

Sarah broke into a wide smile. "Don't you start, Jacob Fallon." She ran her fingers through her hair, attempting to make herself look more presentable.

"I love it when you say my name," Jake said wistfully. Then he tucked his chin to his chest, looking mournful. "I only wish I knew what it meant. Knew who I was."

"You will find it, Jacob."

A time passed in cacophonous silence as the Land Rover bounced down the pothole-lined road.

"Would you want to know me as I am now?" Jake asked finally.

Her heart skipped once more. "Not just now," Sarah said. "Not at this moment."

Jake offered her a smile as the vehicle bounced along the road. Sarah smiled only with her lips, content to keep her eyes fixed on the road ahead. In time, she could sense that Jake had put his head back against the window and closed his eyes.

In silence, Sarah concentrated on driving along the tarred road, encountering few cars or trucks on the journey to Mazabuka. Given the isolation, and desperate to get to a place where she knew she would encounter friendly people, she decided to ignore the doctor's warning about the town. Luckily, they managed to pass through without a hitch.

Back into the wilderness beyond Mazabuka, Sarah looked over at the sleeping Jake. Her mind began to wander.

She could see herself at eight years old. In the vision, she walked hand-in-hand down the long passageway of a convent with a nun in her mid-forties. When they reached the front door, the nun swung it open.

A man entered through the door. A white man. Sarah looked up at him, and could see the outline of his face, but he did not return her gaze. Standing in the doorway, Sarah watched as the nun and the man whispered to one another.

The vision grew blurred, but Sarah could see a white hand reach out from the light. It patted her on the head, then handed her a white baby doll. Sarah smiled and took the toy, her eyes alight with joy and innocence. As the girl examined her doll, the man handed an envelope to the nun. Then he turned and patted Sarah on the head once more. Sarah smiled at the man, but he said nothing. Without looking back, he turned and walked away.

The nun closed the door behind him. Sarah looked up at the nun with confused and blinking eyes. The nun fell into a soft expression of sympathy. She fell to her knees, then rocked back on her haunches, facing Sarah. Even now, Sarah could feel her warm embrace, could sense the loving pat on her bottom.

In the final throes of her vision, she watched the nun take her hand and lead her down the passageway. The nun smiled, like a mother would to a daughter, as Sarah let go of her hand and ran down the hall of the only establishment that she would ever call home.

~ ~ ~

At Batoka, eighteen miles north of the town of Choma, Jake awoke. He knew nothing about where they'd traveled or where they stood on their journey, but he could read the sign for the Maamba Mines, and he watched as Sarah guided the Land Rover to the left.

"Where are we headed?" Jake asked.

His question seemed to startle Sarah, who was clearly locked in a deep reverie. "We're heading back toward the Zambezi Valley and the hamlet of Sinazongwe," she said.

"Sinazongwe," Jake said melodically.

"We are on the main Great North Road between Lusaka and Livingstone. This road will take us within ten miles of Sinazongwe."

Jake couldn't help but notice that his companion still held a rather glazed look in her eyes. He touched her arm. "Sarah, are you okay?"

"My father was a white man," Sarah blurted.

Jake chuckled. "No surprise there."

Sarah's expression grew soft and troubled. "I'm sorry," she said. "I don't want to burden you with my past."

"Burden me," Jake said with a dismissive wave. "I insist."

Sarah sighed, looking mournful. "When I was a little girl, a white man came to the orphanage. He gave me a doll, but never said a word. A Sister told me he was my father and he paid to keep me there."

Jake drew an audible breath, trying to imagine.

"I only saw him once," Sarah continued. "He never came back. He must have been ashamed of me."

"What the hell do you mean 'ashamed?'" Jake asked.

"Mr. Mysterious Jacob," Sarah said with a sorrowful smile. "The man with no memory. Have you also forgotten that you are in Africa?"

"So what if I'm in Africa? What's the shame?"

Sarah furrowed her brow. "Here," she said darkly, "when a white man and a black woman . . . or vice versa—" she removed her hands from the wheel for a moment, interlocking her fingers on either hand "—enza tanda, it is scorned upon."

"'Enza tanda?'" Jake asked.

"It means to make love." She took on a look of disgust. "The whites in Africa say 'jiga-jigging,' and you foreigners say that awful 'fuck' word."

Jake suppressed a chuckle. "Not good dialogue for a convent girl," he quipped. "I prefer your enza tanda to the 'fuck word,' anyway."

Sarah broke into a mild little smile.

"And anyway, you're not all African. You're half and half."

The beautiful driver sighed. "But I am colored."

"What difference does that ma—"

"Being colored makes me more of a misfit," Sarah interrupted – and her tone was that of defeat.

Jake grabbed Sarah's arm. "Not in my eyes," he said.

For a moment the two locked eyes, lingering there. Jake longed to kiss her. Longed to reach out and make her understand that everything would be all right. But he knew he couldn't. Not here. Not now.

The Land Rover rolled over a pothole, snapping them both back to the reality of the situation.

"I must drive," Sarah said.

Jake pondered the state of things for a long moment. "I will say this, Sarah Malumbo," he said after a time. "We sure are a sorry sight, you and I."

Sarah looked over at him, obviously confused.

"I have no memory of who I am, and you have no past. Just a couple of sorry souls in the African wilderness."

She smiled.

"How many more miles to go?"

"About eleven miles," she replied. "What a mess I have made. No good is going to come from any of this."

Jake chuffed. "No bad, either. It was you who saved my life, remember? That's the good. You let me take care of the bad."

"You're in no position to take care of anything," Sarah said sarcastically. "No identity, no memory, no way to prove you are not a mercenary. Plus, you are in Zambia illegally. There are plenty of men in power here who would love to make an example of you."

"Jeez, listen to you. Little Miss Pick-me-up."

Sarah grew stern. "As I said, no good can come from any of this."

Jake turned away, watching the foreign land speed by endlessly.

"Put on the radio," Sarah said after a time.

Jake fumbled with the radio, eventually choosing a station from one of only a few that came to tune. When he landed the frequency, a song burst into the cabin of the Rover: "Fooled Around and Fell in Love," the 1976 song by Elvin Bishop.

Jake smiled over at his companion. "How appropriate is that?" he said.

"What do you mean?" Sarah asked.

Jake chuckled silently, deciding it best not to answer.

By the time the song had ended, the Land Rover had left the tarred road in favor of the last ten miles of gravel. The sound of the stones from the gravel crashed against the inside of the fenders, kicking up a great stir of noise. Sarah turned up the radio, smiling at Jake as she blared the pop song and drowned out the noise. Jake's heart skipped as he watched her turn back to the road, biting her lower lip as she took it all in.

CHAPTER 8

The town of Sinazongwe proved even smaller than Siavonga. It stood roughly halfway between the border town of Livingstone, at Victoria Falls, and Siavonga, by the dam wall of Lake Kariba. The town was situated on high ground, the center uphill and away from the lake. It boasted a small hospital, but as Sarah pointed out, the post office was over a half-mile away, at Sinazeze.

At the flooding of the lake, Sinazongwe had a busy harbor, complete with the only lighthouse on the shore. It was a convenient hub for white farmers of the Southern Province of Zambia, who established fishing camps out in the lake, all on islands and within Zambian borders. At times, there would be a half-dozen or more farmers and their families fishing on the various manmade islands left after the flood waters had settled in the basin.

Sarah pulled the Rover off the road, where Jake climbed out of the vehicle and sought cover. Through the rearview mirror, she watched him huddle into some trees as she drove toward the mission hospital and parked at the rear.

She entered via the back door and was greeted by an African nurse named Betty, a young woman who could always be counted on to wear an immaculately starched uniform.

"Sarah!" she said with surprise. "You scared me."

Sarah smiled warmly.

"And you look like you're gula maningi (*very sick*)."

Sarah brushed away the hand that Betty pressed to her forehead.

"Where have you been?" Betty asked with wide eyes. "The Sister and the Father have been asking the government for help."

Sarah hugged her old friend. "I escaped from freedom fighters at Kariba. They shot down the flaimashim (*airplane*), but I got away."

Betty gasped, placing a hand over her heart. "That was on the news," she said. "Oh, sweet Jesu, I thank him you are safe."

"Is Dr. Willie here?" Sarah asked, glancing over Betty's shoulder.

"Yes," Betty said. "He is in his office. I will tell him that you are here."

"Do not bother," Sarah said, holding up a hand in protest. "I will surprise him."

Betty grinned with pearly white teeth.

Sarah slid past, then headed down the hall, where she opened the familiar door to the doctor's office. Beaming, she watched as the surprised doctor looked up from his cluttered desk.

"Sarah!" he said.

The young woman moved in for the expected hug, which was given as tightly and warmly as that of a father.

"Hello, Dr. Caldwell," Sarah said happily, and with much relief.

William Caldwell hailed from Carolina, and Sarah knew this because he often talked proudly of his homeland. He was a rather rotund man in his sixties. The relative lack of hair on his head left his dome to take on a permanent red hue from years in the blazing sun without a hat. He offered his usual warm and friendly smile as he kissed Sarah on the cheek and held her hands in his.

"Sarah," he said. "Our beloved Sarah. We thought we'd lost you."

"I am fine, Doctor," Sarah said with a blush. "I was helped along by a young ma—"

"Yes, Dr. Young called me and told me about your experience," Caldwell interrupted. "Did that young man help you get back?"

"Yes," Sarah said with a sigh.

Caldwell cocked a bushy white eyebrow. "Tell me, child. Is he a Rhodesian soldier? Or worse . . . a *mercenary*?"

Sarah felt herself flush. "No and no!" she said defensively. "He's a countryman of yours, in fact. At least, that's what Dr. Young believes. Jacob cannot remember who he is."

"Jacob, then, is it?" Caldwell asked, running his fingers over either side of his rounded chin. "Then he's in Zambia illegally. Do you want me to look at him?"

Sarah explained that Dr. Young had already tended to Jake. "You can see him, I suppose. But not until he has had some rest." She turned away from the doctor, unsure of how to proceed. "That's why I've come here, actually. To see if Father Burke would be so kind as to put him up for the night."

"He is with you still?" Caldwell asked, his eyes going wide.

"Do not worry," Sarah said. "I've asked him to hide in the bush. He will not endanger you here."

The doctor sighed with obvious relief. "That's good, Sarah. Good thinking." He wagged a finger. "You always were the smart one, weren't you?"

"It does not take a genius to realize that bringing a man such as this into your clinic would jeopardize you here. I know he wears a target on his head."

The doctor nodded, apparently satisfied – but his nod was not without sympathy. "You're right about Father Burke," he said. "As a priest, he might feel morally bound to take the boy in."

"Listen, Dr. Caldwell," Sarah said, snapping the doctor from his apparent ruminations on the subject. "I have a Land Rover out back that I would like to leave with you."

"Leave with me?"

"Dr. Young loaned it to us. He thought that perhaps if we left it with you, you could get it registered and put it to good use."

Dr. Caldwell smiled. "Well the old codger's right about that."

"In any case," Sarah said, placing her hands on the doctor's crossed forearms, "it is no good to Jacob and me. We cannot continue riding around in such a high-profile vehicle."

Dr. Caldwell casually extended his hand. "Well, I guess I should do as the good doctor wishes."

Sarah smirked and dropped the keys into the old doctor's hand.

~ ~ ~

The door was opened by a man wearing shorts, sandals, and a t-shirt. It was Father Joseph Burke, a Catholic priest in his mid-fifties and a veteran of the Biafra War. He was tall with dark, graying hair and sported a tan to the envy of any Mediterranean sun-worshipper. His expression was nearly that of astonishment as he gazed at his charge, the lovely and grinning Sarah Malumbo.

His expression changed dramatically when he turned his attention to Jake. He looked back at Sarah, and then once again at Jake.

"My good God," he said. "It's Sarah herself." Then he stepped aside, waving the young couple inside.

Once they had passed, he fired a glance to and fro outside his house, apparently checking whether anyone had seen them enter. He then closed the door and followed his guests into his tiny living room, where he offered them a seat before shouting to his old cook, Shadrick, to make some tea.

"And bring some of the cake that Sister Margaret made!" He offered a jovial glance at Jake and Sarah. "The cake tastes like a wet sponge," he whispered. "But I promise it won't poison you."

Jake offered an approving nod. Sarah blushed and covered her smile with her hand.

"The kitchen has been in sore need of your skills, I'm afraid, young lady," Father Burke added. "We've been falling all over ourselves with disgust since you left. Shadrick's a bear with that stove."

Sarah giggled. "What about the Sisters?"

"Oh, them?" Father Burke scoffed through a lighthearted smile. "Sister Bridget is over in England on a retreat. And as for Sister Margaret, well . . . she's no gourmet chef, I'll tell you that."

Sarah giggled louder. "That is no way to talk about the Holy Sisters, Father."

Father Burke waved it all off. "I suppose you're right, as always." He winked. "In any case, it's good to have you back."

At that moment, Shadrick strode into the room. Sarah looked on him fondly. The hardened old African in his sixties, barely a shade over five feet tall, had often found himself the butt of Father Burke's jokes. He had grey hair and was missing more than a few teeth. He bent at the short table between Father Burke and his guests, dropping an overlarge tray onto its surface with little flare for the serving arts. He chanced a quick glance at Sarah, who smiled politely. The smile was not returned. Shadrick simply straightened up and walked mechanically back into the kitchen.

Sarah started to pour the tea, offering the first to Father Burke and the next to Jake.

"So, is it true?" Father Burke asked, his little finger upraised from his teacup.

"Is what true?" Sarah asked, cocking her head to one side.

The priest fired a thumb over his shoulder. "What Willie Wonka at the hospital factory over there told me over the phone?"

"Willie Wonka?" Sarah was bewildered.

The priest chuckled. "I mean Dr. Caldwell. He passed on whispers that you two were on the plane that ZIPPRA shot down."

Sarah's heart skipped a beat. "You men talk a great deal."

Father Burke became deadly serious. "We know about the plane, yes. And even if we hadn't been talking, it's on the news, by now. They say there were no survivors."

Sarah gently squeezed Jake's good leg as the priest spoke. "Jacob was also on the plane. But as I am sure Dr. Caldwell explained, he has no idea who he is."

"Yes. And that is very curious."

"But if it were not for him," Sarah continued, her dewy eyes directed at Jake, "I would be dead."

"And don't believe all that you hear on the news," Jake added. "Sarah told me earlier that we saw other survivors run into the bush."

"Did they get away?" the priest asked, acknowledging Jake for the first time.

Jake shrugged. "I don't even remember the crash. Or how we got to the mission hospital."

"May God protect them as he did you," Father Burke murmured.

Sarah became suddenly resolute. She felt somehow desperate and at peace all at the same time as she assessed her patron's mood. "Father, I beseech you; Jacob has no identity—"

"You mean he's—"

"He's in this country illegally," she interrupted. "At least we think so. He has no passport."

The priest crossed his arms over his chest, taking on a defiant look.

"Father, please," Sarah pleaded. "He simply needs time and a place to stay while he figures things out. You have to help us."

"Help *us?*'

"I mean him." She nodded in Jake's direction. "Please hide him. At least until he has a chance to remember who he is."

The priest sighed, crossing one leg over the other. "Are you a Catholic?" he asked of Jake.

"I don't know," Jake said with a smirk. "But I am today."

"You sure you're not a mercenary?"

Jake shrugged again. "I don't know. I really don't know."

~ ~ ~

Having left Sarah to seek new clothes from Sister Margaret, Father Burke directed Jake to a spare room off the belfry in the church. "The six a.m. Angelus should keep you alert," he quipped.

"I can't thank you enough for this, Father," Jake said, limping ahead of the priest.

Father Burke stopped his guest with a tug at the wrist.

Jake wheeled around to face the priest.

"I want you to hear me now, boy," Father Burke said, holding Jake's gaze with a pair of steely eyes. "If it wasn't for Sarah, someone I've known for a great portion of her lifetime and have quite a soft spot for, I'd have quickly turned you away." The priest looked down at Jake's oozing leg, his face taking on a much more pious look. "Are you in much pain?"

Jake grimaced. "My leg hurts like a son of a bitch." His eyes went wide. Then he shook his head in apology. "I'm sorry . . . it's just that you don't look like a priest."

Father Burke cracked a smile. "God knows I've heard worse than that." He chuckled. "But pray tell, what's a priest supposed to look like?"

The young man ran a hand over the front of his neck. "Well, a Roman collar for one thing."

"In this heat?"

Jake nodded. "Point taken."

The two men continued down the hall toward the belfry, now side by side.

"So, Jacob?" Father Burke asked.

"Jacob Fallon," Jake said. "According to Sarah."

"And what have you been up to with our Sarah?"

Jake offered a wry stare. "*Your* Sarah?"

"Figure of speech."

The priest attempted to turn away, but Jake stopped him with a hand on the shoulder. "No. You called her *your* Sarah." He held up a finger. "The doctor at the mission hospital suddenly wants to help when he hears Sarah's name." He held up another finger. "And lo and behold, the doctor right here in this godforsaken blip on the African map *delivered* her into this world!"

The priest looked rather beside himself.

"What the hell gives?" Jake asked, almost breathless.

The priest became visibly irritated. "To use your vernacular," he said, his cheeks burning red, "what the hell gives with you and Sarah? I saw all the touchy-feely stuff."

Jake shrugged. "I'm not sure. She says we're not lovers, though, if that's what you're getting at."

"But you'd *like* to be."

"Yes, she said we kissed on the boat."

The priest looked up to the ceiling and waved his hands as if in contact with his creator. "Well now, isn't this getting as muddy as a bog?"

Jake snapped his fingers in front of Father Burke, bringing him back to earth. "You haven't answered my question."

"What question?"

"Why's Sarah the most popular girl in the African bush?"

Father Burke looked somehow conspiratorial. "I fear that that would be too much for you to comprehend in your current state."

Jake opened his mouth to protest, but was silenced by the priest's quick hand.

"All will be revealed in good time, my son," the older man said. "And if you'll get anything here, it's time."

Jake tried to protest again, but found himself rather shoved down the hall.

"All you need now, Jacob, is a hot bath and a change of clothing. After, you and I will embark on a bowl of Shadrick's Irish stew that, save the recognizable potatoes, will be made from some mystery meat and a varied selection of other miscellaneous indigenous vegetable ingredients."

Jake turned to object, but was shoved again.

"Thereafter, I will introduce you to the charms of the belfry."

The priest finally stopped shoving, as Jake stood now inside what appeared to be a bathroom.

"Father?" Jake said, rather at a loss.

"Yes, my son?"

"All I want's a cigarette." He patted his chest. "I'm out."

The priest waved a dismissive hand. "That would be outside my Godly powers at the moment, because I'm out, too."

Jake sighed and thanked the priest, then turned for the bathroom and some silent time alone for the first time since he could remember.

~ ~ ~

After a rewarding hot bath, Dr. Caldwell redressed Jake's injured leg and set him free to partake in the unfortunate experience of downing a plate of the so-called Irish stew. He enjoyed several cigarettes called *Guards,* which he bummed from Shadrick. He also enjoyed a couple of brandy and Cokes with Father Burke before retiring to the belfry room, which proved aptly named. It was sparsely furnished with a twin bed, a sideboard, and a reed mat on the floor. In the corner of the room, a long rope hung through a circular hole in the ceiling. Jake gave it a once-over before going to bed. The motionless, dangling rope disappeared into the darkness of the bell tower of the church, where it was obviously attached to a bell high above.

Jake got undressed and slid into the rock-solid bed. For a time, he simply lay on the uncomfortable horsehair mattress, smoking a cigarette. The only light shone from a single low-wattage lamp resting on the cheap table beside the bed. Jake exhaled audibly, blowing smoke.

A soft creaking sound issued from the bedroom door. Jake lifted his head to watch as the door slowly opened. His heart leapt when he saw the familiar outline of Sarah.

"Sarah?" he whispered.

She held a finger to her lips as she tiptoed into the room. When she came fully into the light, Jake could see that she wore a long, snow-white cotton nightdress, buttoned right up to her neck. She crossed beyond Jake's bed and placed the flashlight she carried onto a rugged looking table in the far corner. Then, without speaking, she moved to the bed and looked down at him.

Jake rolled over and stamped his cigarette into the ashtray beside the bed. "Sarah, what are you doing here?"

"It's half past eleven, and the Sisters are asleep," Sarah whispered. "So is the Father . . . and I needed to be with you."

"In the Land Rover, you said you didn't know me," Jake warned.

Sarah gazed up at the ceiling, the light bringing her eyes to dance. "I also said we kissed in the boat and you said you didn't remember and asked me if it was good."

"That was a stupid thing to say."

The young woman held her head high, looking proud and maybe nervous. "Do you think I'm pretty, Jacob?"

Jake sighed. "You're stunningly beautiful, Sarah."

Sarah leveled her gorgeous eyes on him. "Then look at me, Jacob Fallon," she demanded.

Hastily, Sarah unfastened the buttons of her nightgown all the way down to her waist. The garb fell off her shoulders, landing at her feet. Without a word, she stood naked before Jacob and apparently unashamed. Jake sat up in bed. His eyes sparkled at the sight of her flesh. He lifted the sheet between them and she slipped in beside him.

The two lay for a time, facing each other. Jake's hand gently caressed Sarah's soft, chocolate skin. In time, Sarah reached down and found him. Jake sighed softly and kissed her.

Sarah broke from the kiss, whispering, "My Jacob Fallon. Nobody knows who you are, so I am claiming you for myself." She moved her hand slowly over him. "You don't remember now, but you will remember that we are joined in spirit. A spirit that includes survival in the bush."

Jake pressed his finger to her full lips. "Malumbo," he whispered, "you talk too much." He moved in to kiss her again, but she stopped him.

"This may be all I'll ever get out of life," she said passionately. "So love me, Jacob, if only for the moment."

Jake smiled into her glowing face. "For this moment, day, month, year, and the rest of my life."

Jake felt like sinking into the bed as Sarah kissed his cheek, then his ear.

She cooed to him in a crying whisper. "I love you, Jacob. I've got so much love. I don't know what to do with it. I will always—"

Jake stopped her once again, this time covering her lips with his own. She relaxed into his embrace. He threw off the sheet and rolled onto her. She opened her legs to welcome him.

CHAPTER 9

"You're kidding!" Bill paced his New York apartment, the phone pressed to his ear already warm beneath his worry.

"I just," his mother stammered. "I just don't know what to do." She began to sob into the phone.

"Mom, calm down. We'll think of something."

"Turn on the news," Patrick Fallon said, coming through from what Bill guessed to be the second line in the bedroom of the Bahamian villa.

He turned for his favorite chair, where he found the remote waiting on the arm. He flashed the remote at the television, the boxy unit coming to life. "What channel?"

"NBC," Patrick said.

Bill watched with wide eyes as David Brinkley delivered a report. The previous day, an Air Rhodesia plane had crashed near Kariba, Rhodesia. Not only had most of the passengers been killed, but guerrillas were blamed for slaying ten survivors and looting the passengers' belongings.

"I warned him not to go there," Mary said, sounding hysterical. "I warned him again and again."

"Calm down, Mary," Patrick said. "It's a big country. Who says that Jake was on that plane anyway?"

"Because I have a bad feeling about this," Mary said. "I always had."

"I need a drink," Patrick said.

Bill imagined his father setting the phone down on the bed, then going into the living room to pour what would likely be two stiff drinks. For a time, the young man listened to his mother sob.

"It'll be all right, Mom," he said softly.

The sound of clinking ice cubes could be heard over the line. Patrick had apparently returned in record time.

"What do we do?" Mary asked, after taking what must have been an epic swig of whatever booze her husband had prepared for her.

"Let me think, Mom," Bill said.

"Here, Patrick." His mother's voice came through distantly, as if she was handing over the phone. "You talk to him."

"You can listen in from the bedroom," Patrick said, equally distant.

"No, I think I have to lie down."

"Well, at least hang up the other line. I've left it off the hook."

Bill sighed as he waited for his parents to straighten things out.

"There's nothing we can do from here in the Bahamas," Patrick said at last.

Bill found himself nodding, his eyes still enthralled by the news broadcast – flames kicking up from a thick African brush.

"Maybe if we came to Manhattan," Patrick continued, "we could find some answers."

Bill tore himself away from the television, returning to his favorite window overlooking Central Park. The long cord from his phone allowed him to pace, which he did frequently as he talked. "The only way is to call directly to the airline in Salisbury," he suggested.

"Salisbury?"

"In Rhodesia."

"Huh," Patrick said pensively. Bill could imagine his father doing exactly as he was, pacing – only the older man would likely be running his fingers through the stubble on his chin. "What about the State Department?"

"There's no American embassy in Rhodesia," Bill explained. "I checked on that before Jake even left." Bill stopped pacing, closed his eyes, and rested his forehead against the glass as he explained to his father that the embassy had been closed from the time the minority white population declared independence. "I'll get on this as soon as we're done here, Dad," Bill said. "For now, you just worry about calming down Mom."

"You want us to come up?"

"Not just yet. I'll call you as soon as I establish something."

Patrick projected a long sigh over the line. "You're right," he said after a time. "Just hurry, all right, son? I'm not sure how long your mother can just sit here and wait."

Bill promised to hurry, ending the conversation with a heavy heart and a determined mind.

He hung up and immediately crossed to his desk in the living room, where he opened a drawer and pulled out a file. He sat at the desk and tossed the file down on its surface, where he immediately began to study the contents. In short order, he found what he was looking for, so he picked up the rotary phone on the edge of his desk and spoke to the operator.

After a terminal wait and being routed through several countries, he got through to Air Rhodesia in Salisbury, where there was finally someone with whom he could converse. He told the operator on the other end of the crackly line that he was seeking information on a man named Jacob Fallon. After spelling out his brother's name, he was told by the man on the other end of the line that he couldn't give out any information at that time. Bill explained that he was Jacob's brother and that Jacob was missing with his friend, Brian Wilson.

"Can you spell that name, as well?" came the properly British-Colonial voice.

Bill groaned, then spelled out Brian's name. "He and my brother Jacob were in the country on a hunting trip." He flipped frantically through his file before finding the brochure for the safari company. He passed the name on to the airline representative.

"You should call the safari company," the man said.

"But—"

"If you leave me your telephone number, I will get back to you as soon as we establish any information."

Frustrated, Bill gave the man his number and then hung up the phone. Immediately, he glanced over the brochure and found the number for the safari company, then dialed through to the US operator once more. This time the call went through quickly – almost as if the direct connection to Salisbury had been left open. Bill asked to speak to whoever was in charge of safaris with hunters from the United States. He waited impatiently for the other line to sort itself out. Finally, a voice came on the line asking if he could be of help. Once again, Bill explained that he was trying to track down his brother and his friend, Jacob Fallon and Brian Wilson.

"Jake and Brian?" the grizzled voice asked. There was a familiarity to the tone. Here was a man who knew Bill's brother.

"Yes!" Bill said excitedly. "Yes! You know them?"

There was silence on the line as it started to crackle. Bill continued to shout into the mouthpiece in an attempt to be heard.

The line became clear again as the voice said, "I'm here, man. And I'm afraid I've got bad news. They went fishing at Kariba and were scheduled on that plane that was shot down."

Bill fell silent, his heart thumping in his chest.

"It was no accident," the guide continued. "I'll bleddy well tell you that, man."

"Shot down?" Bill said, distressed.

"Bleddy shot down by ZIPRA, man," the guide said solemnly. "The killer wing of ZAPU."

"ZIPRA guerrillas?"

"Guerrillas to you, but bleddy terrorists to us, man."

"What about my brother and his friend?" Bill asked.

The guide told him that eighteen or more of the fifty-three people aboard had survived the crash; he believed that ten survivors, still dazed and shocked, were butchered by ZIPRA guerrillas before rescuers could reach the crash site.

"How can you be so sure?"

"Joshua Nkomo cemented the deed in a BBC interview, man. You should have seen him. Up there, looking all *proud* of the ZIPRA attack." The sound of a man spitting followed over the line.

The guide advised that twenty-four hours earlier, white Rhodesians had welcomed an official release on the news pertaining to ongoing negotiations between Ian Smith and Joshua Nkomo. Now there was uproar and demands to terminate any further negotiations. Apparently, if the Rhodesians had any false ideas that ZIPRA was fighting a war and not committing terrorism, that belief was totally shattered. Furthermore, they had waited in vain for any glint of condemnation of ZIPRA's action from Britain, the United States, or anywhere else. As in the past, they would clearly come to think that they were completely alone in their anguish and rage.

"Only eight survivors that made it back to Kariba, man," the guide said. "But I'm afraid your Jake and Brian were not amongst them."

A long silence followed.

"I'm really sorry, man."

Bill didn't know how to feel. Desperation came over him.

"If it makes any difference, this crash has really created a mess for the entire country, man. It's possible Jake and Brian just slipped through the cracks, you know? Security forces are sweeping the bush for more survivors, but it could be days or more before any news comes out."

"I understand," Bill breathed. He gazed at the far wall of his office as if it might contain a few answers, but all he saw was a white wall and emptiness.

He put his hand over his mouth as he listened to the guide speak his condolences. Only when the guide asked him for his telephone number did he come back to reality.

"Thanks, man," the guide said. "I'll try to get back to you with more information as soon as it comes in."

Bill nodded, feeling his eyes swell with tears.

"Hey, listen," the guide said. "You should contact the American embassy."

"I'd love to," Bill said, "but according to the State Department, we don't have an embassy out there."

"Ah, you're correct that there's no *official* embassy," the guide said, sounding almost conspiratorial. "But there are still people out here who believe that white Rhodesians aren't actually bent on the total suppression of the black population."

"What do you mean?"

"I mean that there's an *un*official American embassy."

Bill felt a sudden and small glimmer of hope flicker in his heart. "Who runs it?"

"It's operated by Robin Moore . . . along with his wife and a group of volunteers."

"Robin Moore," Bill breathed, trying to place the name.

"Yeah," the guide said. "Seems he didn't like the sickening type of terrorism we've got to live with out here. Plus, Moore's a big opponent of communism, which is rampant in one-party African countries like our neighbors, I'm afraid."

The line started to crackle. "Are you there, friend?" Bill shouted. Then, all at once, the line cleared once again. "Who's Robin Moore?"

"You should know, man," the guide said. "He's a famous American writer. *The French Connection*, *The Green Berets*, and others."

"No kidding," Bill said. "An author running an unofficial embassy in Rhodesia. Did I hear you correctly?"

The guide reiterated, explaining that the well-known writer had collected a mass of evidence on the terrorism employed against the Rhodesians, black and white, and that he'd taken this evidence to heart because he loved the country. Moore had spent a great deal of time in Rhodesia, the guide explained. The unofficial embassy was a couple of miles from the center of Salisbury in the suburb of Avondale.

"The American State Department is violently hostile to Moore's project, as you can imagine," the guide said.

"I can," Bill said, picturing his brother, bloodied but safe, trudging in to the embassy, giving a famous author all he could handle. This thought nearly brought a smile to his lips.

"If your brother's alive and hasn't yet turned up on state news, he's likely with Moore. Moore caters to something like six hundred Americans serving in the Rhodesian forces."

Bill thanked the man for his assistance and advised that he would wait with bated breath to hear from him, should he uncover any further information.

Bill placed the receiver on its cradle and walked back to his favorite window over Central Park. He placed his head against the aluminum frame holding the glass, where he banged his forehead three times in anger.

Collecting himself, he sighed and turned once more to the phone. He picked it up and dialed. "Dad," he said into the mouthpiece, "this is fast becoming a nightmare."

CHAPTER 10

I t was mid-December and late in the afternoon. The sky was a cloudless clear-blue over the quiet and slightly elevated little hamlet of Sinazongwe, nestled picturesquely on the edge of the calm Lake Kariba. Jake sat fishing by the water's edge when he was joined by Father Burke. The priest lit two cigarettes and handed one to Jake.

Jake wore his daily disguise: a Roman collar over a t-shirt and under a khaki safari shirt.

Father Burke smiled as he sat down beside him. "Feeling hot in that collar?"

"You know I do," Jake said through the side of his mouth. "But hot as this collar is, I have to admit that you were right."

The priest had suggested the collar almost from the moment Jake first set foot at the mission. He told him that such a disguise would be the only way to keep the police and the Zambian Army at bay whenever they came nosing around, which was often.

Father Burke nodded profoundly. "No, they'd have little interest in a man wearing a Roman collar." He chuckled. "Especially while in the process of extracting free vegetables from old Shadrick's garden."

"Sinners," Jake said.

The priest roiled with laughter. Then, after a time, he calmed and became serious. "I have to tell you, son; it's getting difficult to explain to all and everyone as to who you really are and why there's a need for another priest in such a remote place."

Jake shrugged.

"I'm not sure how long I can continue the charade, to tell the truth," the priest continued. "Particularly if word gets to the bishop of Monze. That would be an insurmountable problem."

Jake sighed, flicking his pole over the water and wondering why he had yet to catch a bite. "I agree, Father. And I have no desire to put you in jeopardy after all the times you've gone out on a limb for me."

Father Burke took a long drag on his cigarette, letting the smoke waft from his mouth slowly.

"And I understand that my loss of memory's not helping anyone," Jake added. "I just hope I'll be able to figure things out eventually."

Father Burke patted the younger man on the leg. "You will, son," he said. "You will."

"If I could only figure out who I am, I could get across the lake to Chete and give myself up to the Rhodesian authorities."

Father Burke opened his mouth to speak, looking as if he might protest, but Jake cut him off.

"I could tell them about the plane crash and take my chances with the white government."

"But, Jake—"

"Don't worry, Father Burke." Jake waved his hand dismissively. "I'm fully aware of what my fate would be if I were to get caught in Zambia by an army that can't protect me against the terrorists."

Father Burke raised an eyebrow. "Freedom fighters, son. They're awfully sensitive about that word."

"Terrorists?"

The priest shuddered. "Yes." Then he straightened up. "Anyway, never mind the army. If Kaunda's inner government cronies got hold of you, you'd be up to your arse in crocodiles."

Jake felt suddenly mournful. "If only I could remember who the hell I am."

Father Burke clapped a hand to Jake's shoulder. "Well, son, it's all moot, anyway. I mean, if you were to make such a perilous trip across the lake, what would become of Sarah?"

"Sarah?" Jake rolled his head back.

"Yes, Sarah." Father Burke's voice was lined with an element of animosity. "You remember: getting fat and pregnant Sarah. Forgotten about her?"

"I'm not ashamed of what Sarah and I did." Jake felt as indignant as his raised voice sounded. "The fact that Sarah's pregnant makes my idea all the more important."

Father Burke shook his head.

"I'm *certainly* not forgetting about her," Jake said. "I'm just at a loss as to what to do right here and now."

Father Burke sighed, clearly trying to calm the situation. "I'm sorry to have accused you of anything, son." He shook his head. "And you know I've come to like and even trust you. It's just that a great many white men like yourself have fornicated with colored and African women, only to leave mixed babies in their wake."

"I'm not—"

"Hear me out, son," the priest interrupted. "I've personally witnessed this kind of behavior more often than I care to admit. Desertion, son. It happens here all the time. And when it comes down to it, there's really nothing to stop you from running out on Sarah."

Jake sized up the older man's expression. He clearly meant what he said, but there was something else there, too. Something lying just beneath the sheen of his eyes. A secret.

"The only fortuitous thing is that you have nowhere to go," Father Burke continued.

Jake jumped up, his anger brimming. He shouted at the priest that he would never run out on Sarah. "You *have* to know that!" he barked.

Father Burke looked up at him almost peacefully. "I'm never sure of anything. And make no mistake, son. The only reason I continue to hide you at the risk of my ministry is *because* Sarah is pregnant."

"But how can you—"

"Look," Father Burke interrupted. He stood to look Jake in the eye. "I've known Sarah for many years. Since her birth, in fact. And given her . . . similar beginnings . . . I have no desire to see history repeat itself."

Jake was so angry that it took him a moment to realize what the priest had just said. "Wait a minute." He came down from his rage slowly. "Similar beginnings?"

Father Burke looked suddenly defensive. "Never mind all that." He began to stammer. "I just . . . a slip of the tongue, son. Nothing to worry about."

Jake sat back in his chair, leaning in to the priest. "No, this is important. There's something about Sarah's past. I've sensed it since the beginning."

The priest's expression melted to anger. "You'd do well to leave this alone, boy."

"'Similar beginnings,'" Jake repeated, leaning back in his chair. "Sarah was abandoned by her father, then."

"Jake, don't—"

"He's dead, she says. But when he was alive, was he someone of importance?"

"Jake, please—"

Jake's eyes grew wide. "Did he die and leave money to the ministry?"

Father Burke stood. "Jake, goddamnit!" He cast a fist in front of him, swinging at the air. "I told you to drop it."

Jake leaned back further. "Jeez, Father. Didn't realize I was on such thin ice."

The priest calmed some, lowering his hands to his sides. He shook his head as he stared at the ground. "We don't talk about Sarah's father, Jake, okay? It's unimportant. We just don't want her to . . . never mind."

"Okay." Jake did what he could to assuage the anger he'd stirred up in the priest so unexpectedly. But he held fast to his desire to pursue the matter further, when the time was right. Nothing that sparked this much outrage could be "unimportant." As soon as Father Burke let his guard down, Jake would do some digging.

Still, he put on his front of letting well enough alone, deciding it best to deflect the priest's attention. "When I'm well enough to travel, and when I can, she's coming with me."

Father Burke flailed a dismissive hand, then turned to go. He spoke as he walked away. "We'll see about that."

Jake caught up to him. "I want to marry her."

"Do you now." The priest smiled. He then nodded, the smile slowly fading from his lips. "Come . . . it's time for supper."

CHAPTER 11

On a clear fall day in Philadelphia, mourners gathered around the gravesite. After being identified by the Rhodesian authorities, Brian Wilson's body had finally come home and was being laid to rest in his family's lot. The mourners were silent as the casket was lowered into the earth. Bill stood solemnly beside his father, who held his wife's hand. Across the gloomy faces, the focus remained on one grieving couple, a visibly shaking and weeping pair named Albert and Susanne Wilson. Albert held his arm around the shoulders of his wife, who clung to the hand of a young woman in her early twenties. Brian Wilson's sister, Betty Anne.

Bill could scarcely imagine how the Wilsons could stand and watch their son buried. And it occurred to him that unless good news came soon from Rhodesia, he might have to do the same. The young man stood numb to the voice of the minister presiding over the final departure of Brian. He watched as the family members picked up some earth and threw it onto the casket as it disappeared into the ground. The Fallons followed suit, and were joined by the other attendees.

As Bill led the way past, he tried to listen as the minister closed his bible and spoke in hushed tones to the Wilson family.

He needed to know the counsel of a pious man in the face of unspeakable murder. But he could hear nothing.

Everyone began to disperse toward their cars, which were parked in a long, solemn line across the street. He heard over his shoulder as his parents consoled Brian's just outside the Wilson's waiting limo.

"Susanne," Mary said, her voice somewhere just above a crying whisper, "I'm so sorry."

Bill knew Susanne Wilson to be a sophisticated sixty-year-old woman with pale skin. So when he turned to see that she held a proud little frown on her face, he wasn't surprised. Her skin seemed to be much paler than normal on this devastating day. After a moment, she did something wholly unexpected: she broke down. She threw her arms around Mary's neck and wept.

"Why?" she said. "In God's name, why?"

Bill watched as his mother's shoulders began to quake, as well.

"Brian and your Jake survived the horrors of Vietnam," Susanne said through her sobs. "And then they go on an innocent hunting trip and this happens."

Bill hung his head, then turned to watch his father hug Albert Wilson, a tall, graying man in his mid-sixties. He listened in as Albert stepped back and looked Patrick straight in the eyes.

"He was butchered, Pat," he said with a quiet sadness.

"Butchered?" Patrick asked incredulously. "What do you mean?"

"I mean *butchered*," Albert said, clearly disturbed. "That's why there was no viewing; I couldn't allow Susanne to see our son. It would've killed his sister and our friends to see him like that."

Bill shuddered.

"It's better they remember Brian the way he was," Albert said. He appeared now physically and emotionally drained.

"See him like what?" Patrick asked softly. "Albert, Jake's still missing . . . please . . . anything you can tell me about what happened . . . "

"Oh," Albert said, hanging his head low. "I'm sorry, Pat . . . I almost forgot that you've been affected by this horror, too."

He slung his arm over Patrick's shoulder, trying, Bill supposed, to gain a little privacy. The young man edged toward them, feeling sorry for eavesdropping, but too curious to let this pass.

"Brian was butchered like a side of meat," Albert said through gritted teeth. "According to the report, Rhodesian forces found Brian in the bush. He was hanging naked by his legs from a tree."

Patrick gasped.

"You should have seen him, Pat," Albert continued, tears rolling down his cheeks. "His ears were cut off."

Patrick placed his hand over his mouth. For the first time since Bill could remember, he saw tears welling up in his father's eyes.

"There was a woman hanging beside him," Albert explained. "Also naked. I have no idea who she was, but the report said she'd been raped repeatedly."

Patrick's lips began to quiver so badly that it was visible, even from Bill's vantage.

"Like Brian, her arms were chewed off up to the elbows," Albert concluded, breaking into soft, long sobs.

Patrick took his hand away from his lips. "Oh my sweet Jesus!" he said. "*How*? Why?"

It took a while for Albert to calm enough to speak again. With obvious difficulty, he explained that the cutting off of Brian's ears was reportedly symbolic. "It seems that that's how they pay white mercenaries in Africa when they kill terrorists. They get paid by the ear."

"That's . . . *unspeakable*."

"So I guess the terrorists were retaliating . . . taking out their wrath on my poor boy."

"How barbaric," Patrick said, clearly aghast. "How fucking barbaric."

Albert continued to weep openly as he explained that the explicit report had stated that jackals, or maybe hyenas, had taken the victims' arms. "I guess half the woman's face was eaten, as well." He shook violently for the briefest moment. "The report said that Brian was shot in the side of the head at close range, and his face was visibly destroyed."

Patrick gasped.

"But I guess that, because he was hanging higher on the tree, he wasn't mutilated as much as the poor woman."

Patrick's eyes filled with tears once again. "I can only pray for Brian and pray to God my Jake got away."

"I pray the same for you, Pat. No family needs this." He paused for a moment. "Are you coming to the house?"

"Of course we are," Patrick answered. "If ever we needed each other more, it's at this devastating time." He grabbed Albert once more and hugged him tightly.

Bill hung his head as the man he admired most broke down with his friend. It was too difficult to watch.

He directed his attention, instead, to Brian's sister, Betty, who stood alone beside an oak tree. He strode to her, threw his arm over her shoulder, and tried to console her. She was nearly as tall as Brian, and an attractive twenty-five-year-old lawyer. Bill took her by the hand as they walked toward the limo, following the weeping parents away from the graveyard.

CHAPTER 12

Six months had passed since the funeral of Brian Wilson. Bill arrived at the Solebury home in a Range Rover. It had been snowing for several hours, but the road to the Bucks County farmhouse was well plowed. Bill got out of the vehicle and entered the mud room. Already, he could hear voices coming from the oversized family room. When he entered the room, he found that his parents were entertaining the Wilsons. The group sipped cocktails as they sat around a roaring log fire.

Patrick and Albert stood up and extended their hands to Bill. Bill gave both men a quick hug. Then he kissed his mother on the cheek and gave her a hug, repeating the gesture with Susanne.

As he found a spot in the comfortable armchair near the stone semicircle projecting out from the fireplace, Bill took the already prepared drink his father handed him. The music system projected soft classic rock through every room of the house. Bill strained to listen for a moment, hearing the end of "Message in a Bottle," by the Police fade into "Tragedy," by the Bee Gees.

"Tragedy," Susanne said – and for the first time, Bill noticed that she had taken on the same listening posture that he employed. "How totally appropriate for our families."

Without prompting, Patrick went to the Fisher amplifier and switched off the music. "Enough of that," he said gloomily.

Albert looked at Mary. "Hard to believe it's been six months since the funeral." He turned to Mary. "And still nothing about Jake?"

"Nothing," Mary said sadly. "Not a blessed word. I guess that part of the world is still in desperate turmoil." She dabbed at the corners of her eyes with a tissue. "I fear we'll never see Jake again."

"Better you never see the boy the way I saw Brian," Albert said with a sigh.

"I never got to say goodbye to my son," Susanne added with obvious remorse.

"I couldn't let you, sweetheart," Albert said – and he said it as if he'd said it dozens of times before. "It would've been too much for you." The old man sat back in his chair with a great, heaving sigh. "We've got to try and live with our grief and hope, and pray for Jake."

Bill took a moment to ponder the faces of the parents in the room. There was a devastating sadness, even now. His heart raced as he determined that he couldn't hold back any longer. "I'm going out there to find out exactly what happened to my brother," he blurted.

Everyone's eyes widened considerably.

"Oh no you're not," Mary spat. "I'm not losing another son to that stinking African continent."

Rather than speak, Patrick got up and crossed to the solid cherry bar. Bill watched as his father opened a couple of bottles of wine, presumably for dinner, examining the labels as he completed the task. With the eyes of everyone else in the room heating Bill under the collar, he watched his father top off his cocktail and draw a breath to speak.

"Anyone for a top up?" Patrick asked.

"Is that all you can contribute to the conversation?" Mary responded with obvious animosity.

"Well, no," Patrick said confidently. "I can contribute plenty."

The group by the fireplace all turned around to face him as if waiting for some kind of earth-shattering statement.

"For a start," Patrick said, "Bill's going nowhere near Rhodesia."

Bill felt his heart sink. He hadn't expected resistance from his father.

"I've been keeping a close watch on the place, and things have only gotten worse," Patrick added.

"What do you mean?" Albert asked.

"I mean that the boys were on a plane out of Kariba to Salisbury—"

"Pat," Susanne interrupted, "please don't talk about Brian as if he were still alive."

"I'm sorry, Susanne," Patrick said, his shoulders slumping. "I'm truly sorry."

"Patrick," Mary said, pursing her lips. "Sometimes your mouth gets ahead of your brain."

"I know, I know," Patrick said. "How many times did your old man tell me that?"

"Mom, Dad!" Bill admonished. "Please."

Mary apologized to the family's dearest friends.

"No apology necessary," Susanne said. "We just can't seem to get over this loss and . . . you know . . . move on."

"So go on, Pat," Albert said after a time. "What's happening over there?"

Patrick returned to his comfortable chair by the fire. "I'm sorry I haven't spoken about this sooner," he said, "but I didn't want to say anything to Mary, or for that matter, Bill. And since neither of them have mentioned anything to this point, I assume they never heard."

"What haven't we heard?" Bill asked, feeling a lump form in his throat.

Patrick looked down at the floor. "There was another news story out of Rhodesia last month." He turned to look his son in the eye. "It was February the twelfth, to be exact. The same thing happened again; another Rhodesian commercial airliner was shot out of the sky."

Everyone but Bill and his father gasped.

"The civilian Viscount was brought down by a heat-seeking missile just after taking off from Kariba Airport," Patrick explained. "All fifty-nine people on board were killed outright."

"Oh my God!" Mary exclaimed.

"Please, Dad," Bill said, breaking the stunned silence that followed. "Go on."

"I'm not sure that it would be—"

"Patrick!" Mary barked. "Tell us what happened."

The old man sighed, taking his drink in both hands as he rested his elbows on his knees. "According to the papers in southern Africa, the terrorists were trying to kill a Rhodesian general who actually took a later flight. There was outrage for revenge from white Rhodesians, especially when Joshua Nkomo, the terrorist leader, claimed credit and applauded ZIPRA for shooting down the plane."

"That's terrible," Albert said.

"He publicly laughed, I guess," Patrick said, shaking his head in obvious anger. "Reports had him stating emphatically that the white Rhodesian government was using the plane to carry soldiers, when they were really citizens or tourists."

"What about the conditions on the ground?" Mary pleaded. "When will things clear up so we can hear about our son?"

"That's all I know," Patrick said. "I'm sure there's more to still be learnt."

Bill felt the flush of anger in his face. "More to still be learnt? That's not good enough. That's exactly why I need to go find out what—"

"This is shocking information," Albert interrupted – and to Bill's eye, it appeared that his family friend cut him off to spare Mary. "To think that's what Brian and Jake faced."

Susanne looked at Mary. "Maybe there's a chance for Jake," she said in a tearful whisper. "They haven't found his body, have they?"

Mary shook her head tersely. The pain in her eyes was evident.

"They don't take captives, Mom," Bill said, wanting to take the reins even if it killed him. "That's why I should go out there."

Mary groaned, throwing up her hands. "You talk to him, then, Pat," she said to her husband. "I'm dead against it."

Patrick cocked a brow. "You heard your mother, Bill," he said. "I know we have no say in your life, but please don't put us through any further stress."

"Your father's right, boy," Albert added.

Bill sighed, shaking his head at the floor. He said nothing, not wanting to escalate the conversation into a full-blown argument. Still, he felt adamant that he would still open up his own inquiry, starting with the safari operation. He would just have to do it in secret.

Alice appeared in the doorway, announcing dinner. Bill was the first to stand, and in true gentlemanly fashion, offered an arm each to his mother and Susanne. The women looped their arms under Bill's, and the young man led the way to the dining room. He glanced back to see his father retrieve the two bottles of wine from the bar, and together with Albert, follow him into the dining room.

CHAPTER 13

Like most nights, it was still and breathlessly humid in the Zambezi Valley. Gathered around a table and playing cards in Father Burke's living room were Jake, Father Burke, and Dr. Caldwell. They all smoked cigarettes and enjoyed an after-dinner brandy and coffee. They played in silence, the only sound coming from the FM radio broadcast from the Rhodesian side of Lake Kariba. Jake paid little attention to the words emanating from the broadcaster – at least until the latest bulletin caught his attention.

Jake lost his breath. At the same time, Father Burke stopped playing and pointed to the transistor radio. All three men put down their cards and listened intently to the speaker.

"An agreement has been reached between the Ian Smith government and the UANC under the leadership of Bishop Abel Muzorewa," the broadcaster said in a tone that couldn't mask his own excitement. "I repeat, an agreement has been reached between . . . "

"Hot damn," Jake said softly.

Father Burke held up a finger to silence his guest. Jake listened intently. According to the bulletin, the agreement called for a power share between the two would-be rulers. This share would eventually lead to general elections. As of June 1, 1979, under this plan, Bishop Muzorewa would become the first African Prime Minister of Rhodesia. The British government had requested that all parties come to London for face-to-face meetings chaired by Lord Carrington. The meetings would include Nkomo and Mugabe and would attempt to thrash out a final settlement to the Rhodesian question.

"Well, well," Father Burke ventured. "This is a fine to-do. Smith has left Nkomo and Mugabe out of the deal with the UNAC. The Brits can't be happy with *that* outcome."

"Do you blame Smith?" Jake added sarcastically. "Two planes shot down. And Nkoma *admits* to shooting down the second one. I'd bet they shot down the one we were on, too."

Dr. Caldwell offered a curious look to Jake. "You *remember* the plane crash?"

"No," Jake said, picking up his cards again. "You know I don't. I'm just telling you what Sarah believes. Six months now, and she still won't stop talking about it."

Dr. Caldwell chuffed.

"You don't believe her?" Jake asked, his face darkening with subtle anger.

"I'm just a doctor," Caldwell said simply. "I've no mind for politics."

"Well," Father Burke said in his typically deliberate way, "there will be hell to pay in Rhodesia, regardless. Those two so-called leaders will be peeved, to say the very least."

All three men nodded, Dr. Caldwell even adding a little whistle. There would be retaliation. That much was certain. But where? And when?

It would only be a matter of time before the war in neighboring Rhodesia got worse. Vague though he was on most details about his life and his current situation, Jake had learned enough in six months to know that he could count himself lucky to be living in Zambia, rather than Rhodesia.

"We'll be playing host to even more of those damn freedom fighters," Father Burke said.

Jake grumbled through a nod. Father Burke didn't mean that they would be playing literal host, of course – only that every time the freedom fighters took a beating in Rhodesia, they would retreat back into Zambia and unleash their zealous wrath on the local population.

"You know, Father," Dr. Caldwell said, "lately, there've been reports that some of the guerillas found their way onto white-owned farms."

"Enough of this!" Jake interrupted. "This is all we ever talk about, man."

Both the priest and the doctor looked rather puzzled by Jake's outburst.

"What *shall* we talk about then, son?" Father Burke offered.

"Sarah," Jake said.

Caldwell clucked. "What *about* Sarah?"

Jake furrowed his brow. "She's carrying my *child*," he said. "Isn't it time I know a little more about her?"

"There's nothing to know," Caldwell fired back.

Jake felt the fire surge up from his belly and settle in his forehead. It was only a matter of time now before his anger got the best of him. For months, he'd been in love with Sarah Malumbo. For months, it had been made quite clear to him that she had a secret past. And for months, it had been just as clear that both Dr. Caldwell and Father Burke knew everything there was to know about that secret – and even clearer that neither was anxious to share it.

His anger building, the young man knew that he must leave quickly, or he'd cause a scene. So he stood from the table and downed his brandy. He then strode away, his coffee in his hand as he spoke over his shoulder. "You've said that for months, Caldwell. And I don't believe you."

The doctor watched Jake depart, a bemused expression plastered on his face. The last thing Jake saw as he turned the corner to exit the living room was the two older men exchanging worried looks. And for the first time since he'd arrived so many months ago, this didn't bother him.

~ ~ ~

Jake sat in a wicker chair, sipping his coffee. In his left hand, he held a fresh cigarette he'd lit from his previous one. He only had a moment to take in the silence, only a moment to stew in the growing anger he felt for being kept in the dark. It was Father Burke who joined him. The priest lit his own cigarette, nipping from the cup he held before sitting down beside Jake.

The younger man blew a stream of smoke toward the circulating fan on the ceiling of the verandah. As he watched the smoke swirl, he tried to capture a clear picture of the events of his life in Africa. "It's not that Sarah's having my baby," he said after a time. "It's not even that I'm grateful to her."

A puzzled look came over Father Burke. "What are you saying, son?"

"Father," Jake said through a long, slow breath, "I want to know about Sarah's history because I *love* her."

The priest rather snorted. "Love."

Jake moved to the edge of his seat, feeling furious. "You think I don't know what love is?"

Father Burke turned away. "No. Just that you don't know what it *means* to—"

"I'll remind you that I asked Sarah to *marry me* back in December."

The priest smiled, nodding. "I remember."

"So if I want to marry her, and she intends to marry me, how can you and Caldwell continue to keep things from—"

"We're just worried that history may be repeating itself, I suppose," Father Burke interrupted.

The suddenness of the assertion took Jake by surprise. But quickly, his surprise was overwhelmed by his malevolence. "I don't give a damn about who Sarah was," he said. "Whatever secrets are in her past, they don't matter to me. I only want to know what they *are*."

"Who's to say you won't just leave, my son?"

Jake looked the priest square in the eye. "Wherever I go, Sarah will be coming with me."

For the first time since sitting down, Father Burke smiled warmly. He took his grand time in gathering himself to speak again, offering at his brandy more than once before committing to voice. "I like a man of fixed convictions."

Something in the priest's demeanor suggested that Jake had finally crossed some unseen barrier. He felt that if he pressed the issue now, Father Burke might actually talk. But just as he opened his mouth to pry, the older man beat him to the punch.

"Well, I suppose you're right," he said. "And I guess I can tell Sarah's story the best I know it." He held a strange little smirk on his face. "It's funny how I came across this information, in truth. And it all came about because there are precious few white men to talk to in the Zambezi Valley." He chuckled. "If Willie Caldwell has more than a few brandies, he has the sweet voice of a lark."

Despite himself, Jake laughed at the homespun phrase.

Father Burke didn't miss a beat. "Son, we've been hesitant to tell you everything about Sarah because her father is white."

Jake sighed, immediately disappointed. "She and I both know that." He slumped back in his chair. But then something occurred to him. "Wait a minute . . . you're using the present tense."

The priest nodded so profoundly that his chin touched his neck. "That I am, my son. That I am." He sat forward, taking on a conspiratorial eye. "And before I go any further here, I need your word that this remains between you and me." He pointed over his shoulder. "I don't want the girl to get hurt."

"You have my word," Jake answered.

The minutes that followed felt like seconds to Jake as he hung on every word that Father Burke spoke. The priest said that Sarah's father was very much alive – and that he even knew all about Jake.

"How is that possible?" Jake asked.

"Oh, we keep him well informed," Father Burke answered simply.

Jake felt rather bewildered as Father Burke continued. The older man explained that a great deal of the Caldwell Mission's support came from a man named Samuel Cameron, one of the largest cattle and tobacco farmers in Zambia's southern province. Cameron's property was up near Monze.

"What's all this got to do with anything?" Jake asked.

"Cameron is Sarah's father," the priest said.

Jake shook his head, ruminating on all he'd just learned. He couldn't imagine a man abandoning his child – but to abandon his child and still remain so close to her? It just didn't add up.

"It's obvious Cameron doesn't want to know his daughter," Jake said.

Father Burke nodded. "Yes, that's true. Cameron has a wife, after all." He waved his hand dismissively. "Although, listen to me. Cameron's wife passed away a few years ago."

Jake put his head in his hands, absorbing everything he could.

"But you know," Father Burke continued, "Cameron also had another daughter named Rebecca."

"He's got *another* daughter?" Jake barked. "He abandon her, too?"

"No . . . he had her with his late wife."

"Oh, I see," Jake said incredulously. "Sarah's his big, black mistake."

The priest agreed with his eyes only.

Jake fumed. "Well, his mistake is my prize."

The two men sat in silence for the moment, only the sound of the breeze carrying through the open windows of the verandah.

"Someone should do something about this," Jake said finally. "You can't just abandon someone and get away with it."

"Now hold on there, Jake," Father Burke said softly. "I wouldn't say that Cameron abandoned her *entirely*. And nobody needs to do anything about it. We've got an arrangement, you see."

Jake shot him a confused look.

"He's looked out for Sarah by way of an education and establishing a job with the Sisters, which he arranged through Willie."

"But how could you sit by and just let this asshole pay to keep his indiscretion silent – pay to avoid seeing his beautiful daughter?"

"It was only after many years that I learned the full story," Father Burke said with a pensive nod. "It seems Cameron was actually in love with Sarah's mother. Otherwise, you see, he would have ditched poor Sarah, like most whites."

Jake looked on into the darkness, trying to imagine all the pain the White Man had inflicted on the continent and shivering when it occurred to him that it was too much to bear.

"Sarah's mother was a stunning looking woman, I'm told," Father Burke continued, breaking Jake's train of thought. "The daughter of an Ethiopian diplomat in Lusaka. Cameron met her at a cocktail party for the elite . . ." The priest fired a thumb over his shoulder. "And the rest is history."

"What about Sarah's mother's family? Couldn't they"

"It seems the family went back to Ethiopia. They left Sarah's mother here in disgrace with Cameron, proving the point that prejudice works two ways."

"So Cameron just had a one-night stand and—"

"You're misunderstanding me, son," Father Burke interrupted. "As I said, it seems Cameron loved Sarah's mother. Rumor has it that he even had her set up in Lusaka for a couple of years before she became pregnant."

"Where is she n—"

"Died in childbirth."

Jake sighed, trying to clear the images in his head. "So that's why the guy at the mission hospital and Caldwell were acting so strange. They have ties to Cameron."

The priest crossed his arms over his chest, saying nothing – but his eyes spoke volumes. *Everyone,* Jake guessed, had ties to Sarah's father. Save, of course, for Sarah herself.

Father Burke got up and went to the kitchen door, shouting for his old African cook. Almost instantly, Shadrick appeared.

"Madala (*old man*)," Father Burke said, "bring some more coffee."

"Yes, Makulu Baba (*big father*)," Shadrick replied.

Father Burke returned to his seat. "So now you know the story of Sarah."

Jake fumed for a moment, thinking on all that he had learned. In his experience, a man wasn't a man unless he owned up to his sins. What was worse was that the love of his life, Sarah Malumbo, would never get any true peace unless she put to rest the mystery of her father. He'd seen it in her eyes every day. When she spoke of him, she spoke of him as if he were dead. She longed to know him. Longed to understand her history – much as Jake, with his lost memory, longed to know his. The difference was that Jake's condition was medical while Sarah's was social. Jake didn't know which would be the worse fate: to be doomed to a life of no memory because of an injury or to be doomed to a life with no history because of the machinations of powerful men.

One thing was certain: now that he knew the whole story – and even where he could find this Samuel Cameron – he would not rest until he made Sarah's father face what he had done. He swore to himself right then that he wouldn't leave the continent until he had met Samuel Cameron, shaken his hand, and put things right. Sarah had saved his life twice. He owed her at least that much.

Sarah. How he loved her. How he wanted to make her happy always. He felt a calm smile form on his lips. "Will you marry us?" he asked the priest in earnest.

Father Burke raised his eyebrows. "You really *want* that?"

"I really want that. Sarah's been stripped of her true name, but I want our child to have *my* name." Jake looked down at the floor, feeling rather depressed. "For whatever it's worth."

Shadrick returned with a tray bearing two cups of coffee. He placed it on the table between the two men.

The priest looked up at him. "Shadrick, hamba lala (*go sleep*)."

Shadrick offered a toothless smile to Jake and then to the priest. "Hamba lala futi (*sleep well also*)."

The men watched Shadrick leave, but the moment he made it through the door, the priest turned to Jake, looking deadly serious. "I would feel irresponsible marrying the two of you, my son."

Jake opened his mouth to protest, but the priest cut him off.

"The fact that you have no identification is one thing. But there are other implications regarding the rules of the Church to consider, as well."

"The hell you mean?"

Father Burke chuckled. "Interesting choice of words," he said with a wink.

Jake was in no mood. He blasted air through his teeth, willing the priest to explain himself.

"Well, I assume that because you wear that crucifix around your neck," Father Burke said, pointing, "it must mean that you're at least a Christian."

The younger man felt absently for the cross hanging from his neck.

"But what else do we have to go on?" Father Burke said with a shrug.

"What about my last name?" Jake's eyes twinkled with the hope in his heart.

"Aye," Father Burke said, his Dubliner accent becoming more prevalent in that moment. "Fallon 'tis indeed of Irish origin."

"So I'm Catholic," Jake said. "Marry me already."

Father Burke turned away, but again, something in his eyes suggested that he might be close to cracking.

Jake reached out and grabbed the older man by the shoulders, taking the fabric of his cotton shirt in both hands. "Please, Father. Sarah's got no life here. And besides, I've already promised her that when I leave, I'll take her with me."

Father Burke sighed.

"All I'm asking is for you to help me do the decent thing," Jake pleaded. "At least Sarah would have someone who loves her and wants to care for her."

Father Burke looked up to the heavens as if sharing some vastly important information with his creator. "I'll talk to Sarah," he said after a time. "If she wants and needs to be with you no matter what, then I'll find a way."

CHAPTER 14

In the early evening, Sarah and Jake sat by the water's edge of Lake Kariba with fishing rods cast in the motionless water. They swatted the air about them, warding off the buzzing mosquitoes. Sarah was very visibly pregnant, with only two weeks to go until full term. The pair cast their lines silently, now and then offering an impish glance at one another. With every passing moment, Jake felt his heart grow warmer for Sarah. Even as the sun departed beneath the horizon, he felt filled with light.

"Jake!" came a voice from behind. It sounded as if it came from quite a distance. "Sarah!"

Jake turned at the waist. Out of the corner of his eye, he saw Sarah attempt to do the same, but she could not, given her condition. She was forced to throw a knee up on the dock and turn around fully. Jake squinted through the darkness. In a moment, he could see the source of the voice: Father Burke – and he seemed to be charging toward them at the greatest speed he could muster.

Finally, the older man came to a halt in front of Jake and Sarah, by now quite winded from the run.

"We have problems," he said, panting, his face flushed. "Big problems."

Jake blinked through his sudden worry.

"I've just got word from the bishop," Father Burke said, his breath coming back to him slowly. "Seems the Zambian authorities have been asking about the new priest in the Valley."

Jake jumped up, dropping his fishing pole beside his feet. "They're on to me!" he said. "Did the bishop squeal?"

Father Burke waved his hands dismissively. "No, man," he said. "No, of course not. I told the bishop about you a couple months back. Had to. He's aware of your circumstances."

"Well then what's the problem?" Sarah asked.

"The problem is that now it's out of the bishop's control," Father Burke said. "He can hide you, but he can't keep them from looking."

Jake clenched his hands to fists.

"We've got to get you out of here," Father Burke said.

"Oh my God, Father Joe," Sarah said, whimpering. "What's to become of us?"

The priest held up a hand to silence his charge. "There's more." His voice was solemn. With eyes only for Jake, he reached into his back pocket and pulled out a wadded piece of paper. Carefully, he unfolded it, revealing a tattered newspaper. "We never got to see this out here, given the remoteness of our location. But the bishop passed me this copy of the *Rhodesia Herald* from a few weeks ago." He handed the newspaper over to Jake. "Guess whose picture's in here?"

Jake glanced to and fro over the page, but was too excited to really take it all in.

Father Burke pointed out the ad. Jake found it in the upper right corner, comprising nearly a quarter of the page. It was an ad seeking a missing young man. As it stated, the ad was posted by the missing man's brother.

"Don't you *see*?" Father Burke asked.

Sarah moved in beside her lover. "Jacob?"

As the pair examined the picture and read in silence, Father Burke kept on talking. He told them that what they were reading suggested that Jake was indeed Jacob Fallon, called "Jake" by his friends, and that he was from Philadelphia.

"Apparently," he said, "this Bill's your brother. And by the looks of it, he's been seeking you out for a long time."

Jake felt puzzled. He wanted very much for this clipping to spark a memory, but nothing came. It wasn't even as if there was a light at the end of the tunnel. His memory was so dark that it scarcely seemed a tunnel at all. There was no end in sight to this fog.

"Well, no matter," Father Burke said, sounding rather disappointed. He snatched the paper from Jake. "Either way, we have to get back to the mission as soon as possible. There's a whole lot to do and many problems to solve."

Jake glanced down at the fishing poles, which Sarah had reeled in and taken out of the water. They rested well on the dock, so the young man decided that it would be safe to leave them. He took Sarah's hand. Together, the two followed Father Burke, the young man delicately helping his pregnant girlfriend navigate the rough terrain between the lake and the mission.

The priest rushed back to the mission through the door, followed as closely as possible by the pensive couple. Sister Margaret, a plain-looking woman in her late fifties, awaited them from within. Despite the heat, she wore a nun's shawl. Beside her stood Shadrick, who was too engaged in sweeping the living room floor to notice the visitors. Jake watched as the priest put his hand in his pocket and fished out a five kwacha note, dangling it under the old African's downturned chin.

"Shadrick," he said, "I want you to go to your village and buy two plump young chickens. Don't buy any old worn-out birds." He pointed at Jake, who adjusted his Roman collar. "Father Fallon here is leaving Zambia. He has to go to Lusaka tonight, and I want a nice, big dinner for all of us."

Shadrick nodded. He took the cash, and without a word spoken, propped the broom against the wall and left.

"Look where he left the broom!" Sister Margaret exclaimed. "That old fart's never doing things right."

"Nevermind the bloody broom, Margaret," Father Burke hissed. "Have you got everything ready?"

Jake felt rather perturbed. "What the hell's going on?"

"Well," Father Burke said, "you wanted to get married . . . and this is about the last opportunity you'll have before the both of you have a child." The priest offered an exasperated look at the nun, who blanketed herself with several runs of the sign of the cross. "Or before one of you gets arrested."

Sarah gripped her stomach and sighed mournfully. "Arrested?"

"Father Joe!" Sister Margaret admonished. "That's no way to talk."

Father Burke ignored the nun. "Look." His voice was gravelly and harried. "Here's the plan. I sent Shadrick away to his village for good reason: I don't want him talking to the police or the army. So, Margaret, let's get this show on the road."

Sister Margaret's tight lips set into a smile that looked more like a frown. Before her, she held a piece of glossy paper. "This document is your marriage certificate." She passed it close to Jake for a moment, letting him get a look. It was already signed and sealed, apparently cut in proverbial stone.

"How can we have a certificate?" Jake asked. "We're not even married yet."

"I aim to take care of that," Father Burke said.

Jake and Sarah looked eagerly at one another, Sarah's lovely face parting into a bright expression of joy. The corners of her big brown eyes seemed to hold tears. Jake couldn't keep himself from smiling.

"Not only is this a certificate certified by the Church," Father Burke said, passing his hand over the document as if it were sacred, "it's also the legal law of the land."

Sister Margaret pointed to the center of the document, where a set of names was listed, both of them ending in Fallon. "Time is of the essence. So I hope you don't begrudge us agonizing to concoct names for your parents."

Jake, beaming, examined the document more closely. He chuckled at the deeply Irish names the priest and the nun had chosen: "Paddy" for Jake's father and "Bridget" for his mother.

Before the young man could even sort out all that was happening, he felt himself shoved up closer to Sarah by Sister Margaret. When she had them in a position that apparently satisfied her, the nun nodded tersely, then scooted to one side. Father Burke shoved a Claddagh ring into Jake's hand. Without wasting even a moment, he began his speech about the significance of the ring.

"It's a Celtic friendship ring, admittedly," he said. "But it will be fine as a wedding band." He smiled at Sarah. "And besides, as long as you have a ring – *any* ring – it will be adequate."

Jake could see Sarah rather bobbing with excitement in the corner of his eye as he stood facing the priest. Indeed, he felt a great deal like bobbing excitedly, as well. This was something that he'd wanted for so long – and now here it was happening so suddenly, and in completely unexpected fashion. At this moment, it mattered little the reasons for the suddenness. That he would essentially have to run for his life as soon as Father Burke concluded hardly seemed relevant. All that mattered now was standing next to the woman he loved and listening to the vows as the priest recited them.

Father Burke carried out his duties loud and true. Jake and Sarah looked at each other and then back to the priest and nun standing before them. Sister Margaret stood with that same frowning smile. Jake, too, couldn't keep from smiling as Sarah began to well up.

It took both young people a few moments before they noticed that Father Burke was speaking to them – or more to the point, he was speaking to Sarah, trying to get her attention. By the time he said her name again, it must have been the third time unheard, judging by his tone.

"Sarah!" he said, grinning.

Sarah shook her head as if recovering from a dreamlike state. "Yes, Father?"

"This is the part where you say, 'I do,'" Father Burke said with a chuckle.

"Oh!" Sarah said excitedly. "I do. I do!"

"And do you, Jacob Fallon?"

Jake practically interrupted the priest, he was so eager to answer. "I do."

Father Burke instructed Jake to put the ring on Sarah's finger and to repeat a series of vows as he spoke them. Jake was so excited that he hardly heard them – still, he repeated them to the letter. When it came to Sarah's turn, it was clear that she was doing the same. The priest's voice was hardly audible to their ears as the couple stood smiling at one another, oblivious to the words and going through the motions like a couple of parrots.

"Therefore by the power vested in me and by the sight of God," Father Burke said, "I now pronounce you man and wife. What God has joined together, let no man put asunder. You may now kiss the bride."

Jake and Sarah stood staring at one another, both like statues constructed of pure joy. In a moment, it became clear that neither had truly heard the priest.

Father Burke leaned in to Jake. "Would you prefer it if I kissed the bride for you, my son?"

Sister Margaret giggled as Jake kissed Sarah firmly on the lips. For a long moment, the two young lovers held each other there, but after a time, Sarah pushed away. It was not a gentle push.

Jake looked over his wife, who stood in obvious pain. "What is it, love?"

Sarah gasped and held her stomach. She staggered a little, clearly trying to commit to voice. But before she could say anything in reply, she doubled over. Jake threw his hands under her, trying to comfort her and keep her on her feet.

"My water just broke!" Sarah wailed.

"Talk about timing," Father Burke said softly.

Sister Margaret took Sarah into a guiding embrace, attempting to sit the younger woman down.

"No," Sarah said, "we must . . . we must go."

Jake stepped over the pool of water on the floor and picked his wife up in his arms. Cradling her, he turned to the door, speaking over his shoulder as he walked. "Sister Margaret, can you run to the clinic and tell the doctor that I'm bringing Sarah to have our baby right now?"

Sister Margaret fired a questioning glance at Father Burke, who gave the go-ahead with his urgent eyes.

"Go, go," the priest said. "I'll clean up here and follow you."

Jake moved to one side to let the nun pass, then quickly followed her out the door.

~ ~ ~

Jake was seated on the veranda outside the clinic, chain smoking and awaiting his latest visit from Caldwell's nurse, the young black woman called Betty. Through her pearly white teeth, Betty's job was to report to Jake whenever something new happened in the doctor's office, as the father himself wasn't allowed inside. Jake had just begun to think that Betty had forgotten about him when he looked up to see someone else approaching. In time, through the darkness, he could see that it was Father Burke.

"Tis a strange effect I have on women," the priest said. "Marrying and birthing on the same day."

"She's in labor as we speak," Jake said, blowing smoke through his teeth.

Father Burke took a seat beside the young man. "Well, I didn't think she was having her appendix out," he said with obvious sarcasm. Then, the moment he settled in, he stood. "Let's go."

"Go?" Jake said, arching an eyebrow. "Where?"

Father Burke reached down and grabbed Jake's arm. "Out of sight, boy," he said. "Unless you want to chit-chat with the local constabulary, I would suggest hiding out down by the lake or in the bush."

"But Father, my *wife* is—"

"Give me time to get rid of them," Father Burke interrupted. "Shadrick will be back, and I'm sure he will volunteer that you, the new priest in town, are off to Lusaka to catch a plane out of the country."

"I can't leave her at a time like this!"

The priest was adamant, advising his young friend that they had just married, and instead of a honeymoon, they were having a baby. He told him emphatically that if the police or the army were to pick him up, they would take him away for questioning.

"In such a small and remote place," the priest said, "you'll surely be found. Unless you *hide*." And with that, he hauled Jake to his feet.

"But, Father, how can you ask me to—"

"Damnit boy! If you make me sacrifice my privileged position as a missionary priest, if you make me break all these rules for *nothing*, I might just have to renounce the cloth and beat the holy hell out of you."

Jake's eyes went wide. He made a turn to leave, but then hesitated, looking back at the priest.

"Get to hell out of here!" Father Burke urged.

Jake walked away in silence, like a scolded child as he left the verandah. Following the older man's directions, he wandered into the bush behind the priest's house and waited for what seemed to be an eternity.

The sun went down as he sat by a tree and pondered his unknown future. Only when he saw the lights go on in the house did he know it was safe. Gingerly, he made his way back toward the house. He peered through the window and found that there were no police or army personnel visible. Then he spotted Father Burke and Sister Margaret pacing the living room and speaking in inaudible tones. He gingerly approached the back door. Shadrick was not there. Quietly, he crept inside, where the voices in the living room became clear.

Sister Margaret was asking how all of this could possibly happen.

"The Lord works in strange ways," Father Burke said, shaking his head. "But they're married now. They can try again."

"But the child I saw looked perfectly healthy!" Sister Margaret protested.

"I'm sorry, Sister Margaret. I only know what Dr. Caldwell told me. The child took a turn for the worse right after you finished cleaning up Sarah."

"I can't believe it." Sister Margaret sounded as if she was crying. "That poor, sweet girl Sarah. All she ever did was to be born, and now this."

"Willie said he did all he could."

Jake appeared in the doorway. "Did what?"

Father Burke startled, letting out a little bleat. "I'm sorry, son," he said when he'd calmed. "The baby was as good as stillborn. Seemingly the infant breathed briefly, then passed away."

"What?"

The three stood in silence for a time, Sister Margaret crying into her hands.

"I'm sorry, my son," Father Burke said, placing a hand on Jake's shoulder.

Jake shook his head, unable to comprehend what he was being told. "Sister Margaret, what happened?"

The nun shook with sorrow for a moment before dropping her hands and facing the young man she'd failed. "I don't know," she said. "Your child seemed healthy when it first arrived. I just don't . . . I just don't know . . . "

Jake felt all energy leave his legs. He flopped back against the doorframe and buried his face in his hands. He began whimpering to himself. "Jesus, after all we've been through." He mumbled through short sobs. "How can you do this to her?" Before a priest and a nun, his only friends in the world other than Sarah, he cried.

Several minutes passed before he found the strength to stand and tell his company that he was leaving to be by his wife's side.

Father Burke grabbed his arm for the second time that day and spoke to him as softly as he could. He told him that Sarah was asleep and that the town was inundated with army personnel.

"Word is that they're trying to keep the peace," he whispered. "It's been reported that ZIPRA guerillas are wandering around."

"Father, I can't do this anymore. I can't just wait in the weeds while—"

"Boy, this isn't a joke," Father Burke interrupted. "Shadrick hasn't returned from his village. He's never done this before."

Jake tried to summon up sympathy, but all his emotion was left in reserve for his wife and his departed child.

"Well, I can't babysit you, I suppose," Father Burke said. "If you want to throw yourself into harm's way – if you want to ensure that Sarah loses *two* people she loves today – that's your decision. But I'm going to get the Land Rover and see if I can't find Shadrick." He took a step to pass Jake and head for the door, but stopped before he could build any momentum. "Come to think of it . . . it would be prudent and wise if you came with me. At least if you're with me, you'll have someone to lie for you."

Jake sighed, having no desire to go anywhere but to where Sarah lay. "Sister Margaret," he said slowly. "You said that the baby was healthy when you saw it last."

The nun suddenly looked less certain. "I'm sure I'm mistaken, Jake."

"She must be," Father Burke offered. "Caldwell's the best doctor in Africa."

Jake stood in confusion for a moment, swaying under the burden of his own mixed emotions. He wanted to believe Father Burke, but something just didn't sit right.

"I'll make sure Sarah is well," Sister Margaret said. "Don't worry, Jake . . . I will tend to her every need."

Jake opened his mouth to ask another question about the mysterious demise of his child, but was cut off when the priest flung his arm over his shoulder and dragged him toward the door.

"Come, my son," he said. "We must be off."

CHAPTER 15

I t was a clear and brightly moonlit night as the Land Rover rolled along the dust track toward Shadrick's village. Father Burke drove with one hand as he spoke with Jake, who wasn't listening. No matter how many times the priest told him that Sarah would be fine without him, that the prudent thing to do would be to remain on the move, and that the only focus should be on avoiding capture, Jake just couldn't stop thinking about Sarah.

What kind of a man goes on the run after his wife gives birth to a stillborn child? he thought. He resolved himself to the idea that he couldn't continue this charade – couldn't be concerned with his own safety when his wife was in such a state. He decided then that he must find a way to escape as soon as the opportunity presented itself. *The second Burke lets his guard down, I'm gone.*

He was snapped from his thoughts when, ahead of them, a small African boy appeared. The boy stood in the dusty track illuminated by the headlights of the vehicle. He looked no older than eight or nine years. At first, he waved his hands above his head in frantic fashion. Then he covered his eyes to protect them from the lights of the Land Rover.

The priest applied the brakes. "It's one of Shadrick's children," he mumbled to Jake.

"Old, decrepit Shadrick has children?"

The priest switched off the engine and they both climbed out. Despite his inkling to leave, Jake felt compelled to follow Father Burke down the track – at least for the moment.

The priest shouted over his shoulder to Jake as he walked. "Shadrick's got eight offspring, to be exact. He's a busy old Muntu."

The little boy came running up to the priest. "Father Joe! Father Joe! Mina baba, mina baba! *(My father, my father)*."

Jake joined Father Burke and the boy in the middle of the sandy track. The three stood silhouetted by the dust, the moonlight, and the Land Rover's headlights.

Father Burke took the boy's hand. "Hold on there, boy. Which one of Shadrick's mtwanas *(children)* are you, anyway?"

"Mena *(I'm)* Daniele."

Father Burke turned to Jake. "That's Daniel to you." He then turned back to the boy. "What's wrong, Daniele?

The little boy immediately launched into a frantic story, told mostly in English with a few words in the local Tonga language mixed in. He explained that freedom fighters had come to their village looking for a white man. They had beaten his father with a mbumbulu *(gun)* and taken away his stistela *(sister)* to the bush.

"Did he say they took his sister?" Jake asked, having a little trouble keeping up.

Father Burke ignored Jake's question. "Which one?" he asked of the boy.

Daniele held his hand above his head, illustrating the height of his abducted sister.

"He must mean Dorika," Father Burke whispered to Jake. "She's about sixteen years old. They'll rape her for damn sure."

Then the boy pointed at Jake and shouted, "Wena *(you)*!"

The priest shushed Daniele, then got down on his knee in front of him. In hushed tones, he asked the boy why he had pointed at Jake.

"He is the white man they are looking for!"

Father Burke turned at the waist to throw a concerned look back at Jake. "You see why I wanted you with me?"

Jake shook his head. He still didn't see the point. Wouldn't taking Sarah from the clinic and hiding in the bush make the most sense? He still couldn't figure the logic in the priest's plans, and he felt his resolve to escape renew all at once.

"The freedom fighters had a picture from a newspaper," the boy said. He leaned in to the priest, his eyes locked in a look of deep resolution. "But don't you worry. My father is very strong. He will not tell for a long time."

"Knowing the old codger, I don't doubt that, my son."

"But his head was bleeding when they were finished," Daniele added. "My mother sent me out for help."

Father Burke shuddered audibly. "We will go to the village and find him."

"No!" the boy said. "Mama said that I must find the doctor."

"I can help Shadrick if you just take me to him."

"No! Mama told them that no white man had come to our village." He pointed at Jake. "You can't bring this man to them now!"

"Finally," Jake said, tossing a hand to one side. "Somebody's making sense around here. C'mon, Father, let's get the hell out of here. The best place for me is—"

"Yes, I know," Father Burke interrupted tersely. "The only place for you is back at the clinic."

"Exactly."

Clearly reluctant, the priest took the boy by his hand and turned to the waiting Land Rover. "You're lucky we found this child," he said to Jake. "Or you'd have driven right into the teeth of the enemy."

"*I'd* have driven there? Seems to me *you* were the one doing all the driving."

"I will take you to the clinic," Father Burke said, grabbing the boy under the arms and lifting him into the back of the Rover. "We'll find a doctor." He then brought the vehicle roaring to life, turning it around on the path and heading back toward the town.

When they reached a rise overlooking the moonlit lake, he brought the Rover to a halt and looked to Jake. "You should get out and hide."

Jake groaned. "Are we running, hiding, or heading back to the clinic, old man? Make up your damn mind."

"Get in the bush," Father Burke said, clearly in no mood for joking. "I must check to ensure that the coast is clear."

Jake stepped out of the car, but protested nonetheless. "What will you do while I wait?"

"I must get the boy to the clinic. Then I'll phone the Zambian Army to inform them of Shadrick's daughter's abduction." The priest then stared up into the night, speaking as if to himself. "Not that they'll do anything about it, terrified as the bastards are of ZIPRA. Still . . . I have to make *some* attempt. I'm a priest, after all, and—"

"Father, are you done?" Jake asked, gritting his teeth. "Because I don't want to be out here all fucking night."

At the words, the Land Rover lurched forward. But as it did, Jake had a thought. He clapped his hand to the metal doorframe, willing the priest to stop the vehicle. "What about the girl? Daniele's sister."

"I'm afraid there's little we can do now," the priest said, looking sidelong at the trembling boy in the back.

"My God," Jake whispered. "We can't just sit back and do nothing."

"Jake, Jake." Father Burke shook his head slowly. "Welcome to the real Africa. There's nothing you can possibly do."

Jake gritted his teeth and gazed into the darkness behind the Land Rover.

"You've got your own problems with these terrorists," the priest said. "Keep to the bush. When I get back to this spot, I'll switch off the headlights. That's how you'll know it's me." And at that, he took off.

Jake stood in the swirling dust kicked up by Father Burke's vehicle. A thousand different things bounced around in his mind – and to this point, he would have guessed that nothing in the world would be dire enough to keep him from returning to his wife, regardless what the priest would say. But he hadn't considered this. A young girl, even as he stood there in the moonlight, was being brutally raped in the bush. And her attackers were after him. They would kill him on sight. As little as he knew about himself, he was no fighter. He felt certain of that. His only choice would be to wait for Father Burke to check on the clinic and return to him. From there, perhaps he and Sarah could find somewhere to hide.

Jake decided that the only course of action in the meantime would be to play sentinel. Here, he had the perfect vantage to view all incoming and outgoing traffic to the town. If anything headed from his left to his right, he could tear through the bush and charge for the town as the crow flies, hoping to cut the vehicle off before it could reach the clinic. If anything came from his right to his left, he would wait in hiding until he knew whether it was Father Burke.

Helpless and fuming, Jake sat once again against a tree in the bright moonlight, listening intently for any oncoming sounds. His only thoughts remained with Sarah and their dead child. Why did Jake feel like he wasn't getting the whole truth about his baby? And why would Father Burke have dragged Jake away in the Rover for no reason? The logic had been shaky from the beginning – and the more Jake thought on it, the more he felt the fool for going along with it.

But why would Father Burke want to distract him so? Why would he take him away from the one place where he belonged, regardless what had happened in Shadrick's village?

There were no answers. Only anger. And so Jake remained in this way for what seemed to be an eternity. Many long minutes bled into the hour. He shivered under a combination of frustration and the uncommonly chilly wind.

After a time, he could hear in the distance the reverberation of an oncoming engine. He crept closer to the dust track, doing his best to remain out of sight. As the vehicle approached, he could tell by the characteristic closeness of the headlights that it was a Land Rover, but could not be sure as to the occupants. The vehicle slowed down and switched off its lights, giving Jake the signal.

As Jake approached, he could see Sister Margaret sitting beside Father Burke. He felt angry at the moment he saw her, but then his anger was quickly replaced by surprise. Next to the African boy, Daniele, he saw Sarah. She sat gray-faced in the back, bundled up with a blanket around her shoulders.

His heart racing, Jake wrenched open the back door and climbed in beside Daniele. Immediately, he wheeled around to tend to his wife. Sarah held her head back and her eyes closed. The sorrow at the loss of her child was evident in her silence.

"What the hell's going on?" Jake asked the priest.

"I don't know," Father Burke answered. "But the army has gone. And according to the nurse, Willie's gone up to the club. Seems as if he's so upset with the loss of Sarah's child, he wants to get drunk."

"What the f—"

"And that certainly doesn't help Shadrick," Father Burke interrupted.

Sister Margaret motioned the sign of the cross.

Jake gazed back at his wife, seeing that she was still unresponsive. "What's Sarah doing here?" he demanded.

"I told you I would care for her," Sister Margaret said. "We couldn't stay at the clinic, and I sure wasn't going to leave her alone."

"I'm sorry for my missteps, my son," Father Burke added over the rumble of the engine. "I think it's time for you to go and take your wife with you. She's a strong girl, a child of Africa, and she'll be fine. Now that your brother's searching for you, the Rhodesians know who you are. And if you can get across the lake to Chete, you can go to the police."

"How do you expect us to get there?" Jake asked sarcastically. "Shall we swim?"

"Oh ye of little faith." Father Burke looked frantically over his shoulder, his eyes scanning the road behind. "I have a small boat hidden down by the lake a little way from here. It has a fifty horsepower Johnson and will get you the twelve miles if you toddle along." He looked at Jake with a hint of pride in his eye. "I've been planning this for a long time."

"Oh have you now?" Sister Margaret asked, sounding as annoyed as she was surprised.

"Indeed I have. The best kept secrets are your own, Margaret. Don't you know that?"

In another mile, the Land Rover rounded a sharp corner in the road before Father Burke brought it to a stop. Sister Margaret got out and opened the door for Sarah, helping her out of the back seat. In a moment, Father Burke had come around to take the burden off the nun's shoulders.

"I will take her." He ducked down, letting Sarah throw what appeared to be a thoroughly weakened arm over his shoulder. "I'm going to lead them down to the lake and show them where they'll find the boat."

Sister Margaret nodded.

"Stay with Daniele," Father Burke added. "If we don't return in ten minutes, take the Rover and find a place to hide for the night."

Jake watched as the nun quivered with fear.

"Don't you worry," Father Burke said, kissing Sister Margaret on the forehead. "We won't be long."

Sister Margaret threw her arms around Sarah's neck and hugged her close to her breast. "I'll miss you, Sarah girl. Come back and see me. Never forget your humble beginnings."

Sarah hugged the nun with her free hand, then threw all of her weight back onto Father Burke. "I'll miss you and love you always. And I will come home again."

Jake's heart leapt. It was the first he'd heard his wife speak since she'd been rushed off to the clinic, and the sound of her voice, though obviously weary, was like music to him.

Sister Margaret let go of Sarah's clinging hand. "I'm sorry about your baby, but you're young and you have your life ahead of you. There will be more babies in God's good time."

Sarah began to cry. Jake, meanwhile, kept his eye on the nun. There was something about her eyes that sparked of doubt when she spoke the words. What had transpired in the clinic? Why couldn't he get a straight answer about what had happened to his child? Was somebody hiding something?

"I want to see my child!" Jake called as Father Burke led the way down to the lake.

"Keep it down, boy," the priest said. He turned and passed Sarah over to her husband. "Here, you tend to your wife."

Jake looked into Sarah's eyes, wanting more than anything to be alone with her to discuss all that swirled in his mind. Instead, he could only help her gingerly along the path.

The trio made their way down the well-worn foot track until they arrived on a small hill overlooking the lake. The priest went down first. Jake followed, still holding fast to Sarah. When

Father Burke reached the waterside, he began picking at a bevy of branches arranged in a haphazard clump by the water. Slowly, his work revealed a thick sheet of tobacco sacking.

Jake brushed his hand over Sarah's gray cheek. She looked at him with watery eyes, but said nothing.

Jake turned his attention back to Father Burke, who had just removed the last of the branches. Without hesitation, the priest yanked the sheet back, revealing a small boat beneath. He shifted around, checking the fuel and then the spare tank, apparently to ensure that the fuel hadn't been stolen. Clearly satisfied that everything was in order, he turned and handed an envelope to Jake.

The young man examined the envelope, confused.

"It's your marriage certificate," Father Burke said. "And a hundred Rhodesian dollars. It's all I've got to give, I'm afraid. It's sealed in plastic, in case the contents get wet."

Jake took the envelope, folded it, and put it in his pocket. Despite himself, despite his suspicions, he couldn't help but feel grateful at the escape that the priest was offering. "Thank you, Father." He extended his hand. "Thank you for everything."

Father Burke took the hand offered him and shook it. "Don't speak anything of it, my son." A twinge of regret seemed to come to his eye, the same sort of look that had befallen the nun. Something strange had occurred here, and even the priest seemed to suspect it.

"When you can," Father Burke continued, sounding choked up, "and if you *legally* can, come back and see me. Something's not right here."

Jake's heart skipped a beat. He'd been correct, after all. "What do you mean?"

The priest leaned in close. "Willie always calls me to baptize any child, alive or stillborn," he whispered. "But he didn't call about your child. And that doesn't sit right."

At the words, a furious anger erupted in Jake Fallon. Suspicion had become certainty. Something strange had happened to his child, and he knew now that he couldn't leave the continent until he uncovered *what*.

Garbled shouting carried down the hillside from the direction of the road – from the area where they had left the nun and the boy.

The priest's eyes darted toward the sound. "Must be trouble. I've got to get back there."

"I'm coming, too," Jake said.

"No you're not," the priest barked. "Take the boat and get you and Sarah out of here."

"If something's happened to Sister Margaret, I'm not getting on that boat," Sarah cried hysterically.

Jake turned quickly on his wife. "Yes you are," he said, his voice laced with warning. "You've been through enough. And you'll only get in my way."

"You can't expect me to—"

"Hide in the boat," Jake interrupted. "I'll cover you with the sacking and branches. Just be calm and quiet and wait for me."

"Jacob!"

"Wait for me, Sarah." Jake looked deeply and adamantly into her eyes. "I mean it."

Jake fairly had to force his wife into the boat. When she finally lay down, he kissed her on the mouth, and then moved his lips in silence, telling her that he loved her. Her eyes welled with tears as she mouthed back that she loved him, too.

Jake covered her with the sacking and branches, and then turned to follow the priest up the ridge and along the path – all the while completely uncertain about what he was going to do if they did, in fact, encounter a fight. He'd heard Sarah's stories about his valor on the plane, of course, but a part of him still couldn't believe that he was capable of such things. If he found himself in a live or die situation, he wasn't sure he'd be able to defend himself. Still, he couldn't leave Sister Margaret to the defense of a pious priest.

Silently, the men moved closer to the road until they were within sight of the Land Rover. Jake could easily see the scene before him, bathed as it was in the light of the vehicle. On the road just in front of the headlights, Sister Margaret was being held down by two young terrorists in their early twenties. A third, slightly older man was unbuttoning his trousers for the coming rape. Daniele stood in front of the headlights, gazing helplessly at the scene.

The older man turned to the boy. "Get out of here!" he hollered in English.

Daniele screamed fearfully, then took off and ran for his life down the uneven track toward his village. Meanwhile, Sister Margaret screeched abuses at the men between prayers for God's mercy.

Before Jake could even calculate what he was doing, something snapped in him. Quickly, he picked up a thick piece of Mopani hardwood and charged out of the bush and into the lights of the vehicle. He leveled a blow first on the man with his trousers around his ankles. It was a calculated and precise blow, one that brought the hardwood to splinter in an explosion of shattered wood and blood, sending the man staggering sideways and toppling to the ground.

When the dust had settled, all eyes turned to Jake. The two men holding Sister Margaret released their grip. The nun immediately rolled to one side and curled into a ball.

Before the men could charge, Jake pounced, taking them by surprise. His fist found its mark against the ear of the man to his right, sending him face-first into the dusty track. The second man grabbed Jake's arm and swung him around, throwing him off balance and landing him flat on his back. Jake lost his breath. Before he could even roll to his side, his attacker leapt onto his chest, the knife in his hand gleaming in the headlights.

Jake fired his hands forward, grabbing the wrist holding the knife. He grappled with his attacker, who brought the knife to bear on Jake's sternum. Jake felt the blade pierce his shirt. He struggled, closing his eyes tight, all his strength concentrated on pushing the knife away. Then, all at once, the blade retracted. Jake opened his eyes, seeing a scuffle unfold above him. When his eyes adjusted fully to the light, he was shocked to see Father Burke with his arm wrapped around the terrorist's neck.

Jake surged forward again, grabbing the distracted attacker's knife and plunging it immediately into his chest.

The man went limp, and Father Burke let go. Without hesitation, Jake jumped up and rushed to the other man, who was only now staggering to his feet. Before he could get his bearings, Jake stuck him firmly in the heart. He then withdrew the knife and stuck him again.

"Did you kill the other one, too?" Father Burke called out with mild hysteria.

Jake wheeled around and checked the man with the trousers around his ankles. The man was already dead. The wood had split his head wide open, pieces of gray matter bulging out above his ear.

"Jesus," Father Burke said softly as he stepped in beside Jake.

"Watch your mouth, old man," Jake said.

A stirring sound came up from behind. It was Sister Margaret, her face wet with dusty tears. Father Burke darted over to help her off the ground. The young man watched as the priest slung the nun's torn clothing over her shoulders. He noticed that the priest was shaking from head to toe.

"This the first kill you've seen, Father?"

"You've done this before," Father Burke replied with a shaky voice.

"I guess I have." Jake felt almost as bewildered as the priest looked. "It seemed to come naturally, like from somewhere in my past."

"It came from your past, all right. And if I may add, it would seem a violent past."

Jake took a moment to observe his handiwork. Three men lay bleeding in the dust. All dead. All attacked with the precision of a man quite used to killing.

"What are you going to do about Shadrick?" Jake asked, deflecting.

"Don't concern yourself with that." Father Burke took the nun under his arm as he spoke. "I'll get Margaret back to the mission and seek help for Shadrick and his boy."

Jake nodded. As Father Burke watched, he collected from the nearest terrorist the sheath for the knife he held. He wiped the blood off on the dead man's shirt, placed the knife in the sheath, and stuck it in his belt. He then rolled the bodies into the bush. When he'd finished, he stalked around the site, picking up three AK-47s left in the dust by the men. He strapped each of them over his shoulder.

"Father, I have to go to Sarah." He looked to Sister Margaret, who had retreated to the Land Rover and was leaning against it, quaking violently with fear and shame. "Say goodbye to Sister Margaret. Now is not the time . . . for her or for me."

Father Burke grabbed Jake in a bear hug. "She'll be fine, my son. With prayer and time."

Jake pulled back and nodded.

"My address and telephone number are in the envelope you carry."

The young man checked the envelope in his back pocket. It remained.

"Go, Jake." Father Burke waved him away. "There are likely more ZIPRAs crawling the area. You must get to the lake."

Jake turned, but did not yet make tracks. "Where will you go?"

"I have yet to read the last rites for the gentlemen you dispatched."

Jake looked back at him, astounded. "The last rites for these animals? These men who would rape and do God-knows-what to a nun?"

"It's God's work I do, Jake. Always remember that."

Jake scoffed. "But they're probably heathens; or worse, they could believe in black magic."

Father Burke smiled. "All the better for them that I do this, then. And either way, it sure won't do them a bit of harm."

Jake shook his head in reservation, then did as he was told. The last he saw of the priest, he was helping Sister Margaret off the ground and into the Land Rover.

~~~

Jake climbed to the crest of a slight hill overlooking the lake. Hearing voices in the distance, he put his ear to the wind. Two men appeared, moving along the edge of the lake. Jake's heart raced. The men were heading directly to where he had hidden Sarah. With adrenaline flowing wildly, there was only one course now: he would have to intervene.

He crouched in the weeds, waiting for his opportunity. It came when the two men stopped to light cigarettes. Jake crept down the incline, careful to keep himself concealed in the bush. The men stood now between Jake and the covered boat. Jake kept to silence, moving along on his stomach, but the ZIPRAs did not. Twigs cracked underfoot.

"Jacob," came a voice from the underbrush, "is that you?"

Sarah, mistaking the terrorists for her lover, had spoken and blown her cover.

Jake watched as one of the ZIPRA fighters lifted his hand to silence the other.

Sarah whimpered again. "Jacob?"
~~~

They heard her this time. Jake was sure of it. He watched as, to conserve their precious smokes, they promptly stomped the top of their cigarettes against a tree and placed the unused portion into their pockets. Quietly, they slid their weapons off their shoulders and dropped their Russian-issue khaki military bags. They moved slowly toward the hidden boat, their weapons at the ready.

Jake waited again for the opportune moment. When it came, he charged without hesitation. From the bush he darted, hammering into both men, taking them into the dark water of the lake. By the time they surfaced, Jake had already planted his knife into one of the men. The terrorist floated away, face down, with the knife still protruding from the side of his neck. This seemed to startle the remaining terrorist, and Jake used the moment of distraction to get a grip with his arms around the man's neck. They flailed in the water, face to face, eyes interlocked as they struggled.

Jake, with the upper hand and in complete control, stared long and hard at the man he strangled. All at once, his mind flashed to the campfire in the bush. A lifeless body hanging from the tree came into focus for a couple of seconds. And then another flash: the face of the man he grappled with, sitting by the fire with an albino.

Jake shook the thoughts from his mind as he forced the terrorist's head under water and held it until there was no resistance. Finally, he let go. The second man drifted away into the lake.

Jake sloshed to the shore and picked up the weapons on the water's edge. He examined them, found that two of them looked clean, and threw them into the boat. The others he flung out into the deep water. He then turned to the military bags. Quickly he opened the bags, searching for food or medical supplies. But all he found was one bag nearly empty and one bag crammed with documents. He dispatched the empty bag into the lake, throwing the other over his shoulder. Then he stood and pulled the branches off the boat.

Sarah sat up with tears in her eyes and a look of terror on her face.

Jake comforted her with a stroke of her cheek and a soft kiss on her lips. "It will be okay. We don't have far to go now."

With that, he threw the document bag into the boat and pushed the craft into the water.

"Stay down," he whispered when Sarah sat up to see what he was doing.

She did as she was told.

Jake leapt into the boat and began winding the rope that would start the motor. When he had it wound, he yanked it back, listening to the thing sputter meekly. It seemed an eternity as he rewound the rope and repeated the action. He had to pull several times before the Johnson motor finally sparked into gear.

Shouting roared up from the distance as the engine echoed through the hot, still night. Jake hit the throttle full speed, and the light craft's bow lifted out of the water, skittering out toward the center of the lake. All at once, the shore line came alive with some twenty armed men, all of them firing at the speeding boat.

Jake turned, cradling an AK-47 in each hand, and wildly swept the night. The shoreline rippled with shouting and cursing from unseen men. Then there was silence as the men on the bank dived for cover. By the time Jake finished firing, the clips clacking empty, they had reached a point in the massive lake where he could ease off the throttle and settle into the seat.

After a few more minutes of cruising into the deep waters, Jake slowed the boat down further and turned to take Sarah in his arms. "I'm sorry I was terse. I didn't want to lose you."

She buried her head in his chest.

They sat there on the torn plastic seat in the moonlight, the boat keeping a steady line to a point directly across the lake: the Rhodesian town of Chete.

After a time, Sarah kissed him on the neck and pointed to the bag. "What's that?" Her voice was weak, weary.

"I took it from a dead terrorist. I'm not sure what it is, but it's crammed with documents."

"Let's see." Sarah leaned forward and fingered at the bag.

"Don't strain yourself. You've been through so much today."

"Don't worry about me." Sarah's eyes shined with a resolute strength as she looked up at him. "You just get us to shore."

Without a word, Jake turned back to steering the boat. He had learned enough about his new wife to know that arguing would be a waste of time. And besides, he knew it would be better for her to occupy herself in times like these – better to riffle through documents than think about collective misery.

Jake listened as Sarah rummaged through the bag. The sound of several heavy documents being flung to the floor of the boat followed.

"Look, Jacob," she said. "This is yours! And this!"

Jake wheeled around and took the items she handed him. "My Passport." He glanced over his name as if it were some long lost friend. "And my Pennsylvania driver's license."

He looked to Sarah in something of disbelief. He watched as his wife opened another passport similar to his. His heart leapt as she put her hand to her mouth, her face going pale. She sat frozen in apparent shock.

Jake reached out and took the passport from his wife's hand. He glanced down at the picture within. Horror erupted from the inside out. The photo he recognized. He screamed, dropping the passport to his feet.

Brian. He remembered the name. Brian Wilson.

Jake buried his face in his hands, his mind rushing with bright flashing lights. The white sands of the Bahamian beach. He walked along the edge of the calm Atlantic Ocean with his mother and father, all holding cocktails. A Saigon brothel. He laughed and joked with Brian, both of them stoned from the abundant supply of marijuana. Brian stood on the stairs with two girls, both of them dwarfed next to his tall, skinny frame. A Solebury farmhouse. Brian and Jake drank cognac and smoked his father's cigars. A Manhattan office. Jake's brother, Bill, joked with his secretary, whom Jake had freshly hit on. Bill turned and waved a disapproving finger through the glass partition, a wry grin forming on his lips. The savanna. A lioness charged as Jake took aim.

And then Sarah. The wreckage of the airplane. The bush. Brian's naked body hanging dead beside a horribly ravaged woman.

Jake wept into his hands. He could scarcely feel his wife's hand as it traced a comforting arc across his back – such was his pain.

Then every muscle in his face grew taut with anger. A new image emerged in his mind: the ZIPRA leader, the one with the scars on his face. In the vision, his enemy stood next to the fire in the bush. The albino sat beside him. Across the fire was the man Jake had just killed in the lake.

Jake collected the passports and his driver's license, placing them together inside the plastic bag in the envelope Father Burke had given him. He then sat back, looking up into the darkness, the drone of the boat's motor lining his ears.

"Are you all right, Jacob?" Sarah said softly.

For the first time in what felt like hours, Jake looked at his wife. She sat there, demure and wracked with worry. It warmed his heart, if only for the moment.

"I remember, Sarah," Jake said. "I remember it all."

CHAPTER 16

"I am Jacob Fallon. I was born in Philadelphia. I come from a wealthy home. My parents have a house in the Pennsylvania countryside and a villa in the Bahamas. I have a brother named Bill, who's a successful investment banker in New York. I have no sisters. I'm single and have no serious girlfriends." Jake paused for a moment to look at his wife's sorrowful face. "That was my past. But now I have a wife that I adore. Her name is Sarah. That's my life in a nutshell."

Sarah appeared suddenly mournful. "How can you kill so easily?"

He grabbed her close to his chest and kissed her on the forehead. "I don't kill for a living, if that's what you're thinking," he said softly. "I'm not a mercenary, either."

"Then, how—"

"Brian and I were drafted into Vietnam. We were forced to kill our fair share of Vietcong. I've been well trained."

Jake was startled away from his explanation by a loud and unexpected sound. An engine roared in the distance behind them; the motor of an approaching boat. Jake turned, but it was too dark to see anything. He leapt to the throttle, cranking it up to full speed once again. The hull lifted from the surface as the boat careened over the calm waters.

Gunfire rang out anew. It was reckless, wild. An untold number of automatic weapons screamed out, bullets skittering in all directions over the water. Jake made a hard turn against the fire, but it was too late. The Johnson motor took a series of rounds in the body of the engine and sputtered to a stop. A second volley hit the stern of the little boat so hard that the craft began to break up. The rear of the boat dipped beneath the surface, throwing Sarah into the murky water.

"Sarah!" Jake called, but she could not be seen.

He dived in after her, a third torrent of gunfire stripping the interior of the boat he left behind. Jake felt his senses assaulted by the cold water. The rumbling of the waves kicked up by the tumult above churned in his ears as he flailed to find his wife among the sinking wreckage. He moved his hands about, cracking against dropping iron and wood and pieces of the stern. Then, just as his lungs felt as if they might collapse, his hand grazed hers. He held her fast, surging for the surface.

When he breached, he shook the water from his eyes, checked on his wife, then scanned the lake all around. From his left, a single bright light streamed across the water – a Rhodesian jet boat starting up from a ghostly dark silence. The engines howled as the gunboat sped past their sinking craft and fired a barrage at the craft that had been pursuing and firing upon Jake and Sarah's sinking vessel.

Jake cradled his wife in one arm, and with the other sought something to cling to. He watched as the gunboat erupted into a deluge of continuous fire. The men on the pursuing craft dived into the water, the bullets riddling their hull. In short order, the boat exploded in a fiery wave, the smoke billowing up in a hot and flickering ball.

Just as Jake found a suitable handhold, the gunboat wheeled around. He called out to them, but they did not seem to hear. Instead, they let loose with their guns. Jake screamed, but it was no use. He could not be heard over the pounding fire that rippled all around him. He let go of his handhold and took his wife into his arms. Treading water, he looked into her eyes for what he feared would be the last time. She nodded understanding, gripped with fear though she was. He held her close.

All at once, the gunfire stopped.

Confused, Jake turned to the gunboat, where the silhouettes of several men could be seen beckoning to him. He could hardly believe what he was seeing.

"I'm American!" he called, unsure why such a thing would matter.

The men on the boat yelled out in a torrent of words Jake couldn't understand. Only when one of them pointed wildly at the water beside him did Jake see what was happening. The bodies of two dead crocodiles slid past on the water. The gunboat had shot them down, and the men aboard feared there would be more.

"Jesus," Jake said, now barreling for the side of the gunboat, his wife clinging to his back.

Just as he reached the boat, it fired a broadside into the water behind. Jake turned to see something shimmering black dive quickly into the water. Another crocodile. Maybe two. He gripped the side of the boat with one hand, lifting Sarah with the other, easing her toward a willing crewman, who took her from him and hoisted her on board. Then, dripping, he climbed and was helped to safety. From this vantage, he watched as several crocodiles resurfaced, slithering over the dark, bloody water attacking their own dead and dying kind.

Jake turned to the officer aboard the craft, who nodded once, then leaned forward on the throttle.

"Wait, wait!" Jake yelled.

"Can't wait here, man!" the officer yelled. "We're in Zambian waters."

Jake pointed emphatically into the debris of his boat. There, near the hull, he spotted the khaki army bag. "That bag!" he barked in protest. "That bag is loaded with identities of possible dead people. We *need* it."

"Identities of dead soldiers?"

"Identities of dead *people*. You'll have to figure out who's who."

The officer's thick eyebrows raised as he looked over to the man he must have called his first mate. Both men were tall and dark-skinned, both wearing red berets and stern looks.

"That's of great importance to us," the officer finally said.

He nodded to his first mate, who collected a grappling hook from beneath a gunwale and tossed it out to retrieve the bag. The moment it was aboard, the gunboat moved away and fired a volley into Jake and Sarah's sinking boat. The little craft immediately disappeared under the water.

"No evidence that bleddy piece of shit ever existed," the officer concluded.

The gunboat turned once again and launched into full speed toward the town of Chete and the Rhodesian bank.

Jake found a comfortable seat for Sarah, who nodded that she was okay. The first mate draped two blankets around their shoulders.

Jake looked curiously at the officer, the wind and spray whipping past his face. "How did you know?"

"Know what?"

"That someone on the lake was in need of help. It was like you were lurking in the dark. Not unlike those hungry crocodiles."

The gunboat officer broke into a hearty laugh. "In truth, you were lucky. We received a tip from a strange source."

"A strange source?"

The officer offered a profound nod. "The Catholic Archdiocese of Bulawayo. The message said that the fellow whose picture was in the *Rhodesian Herald* was trying to make his way across the lake."

Jake's heart leapt. Instinctively, his eyes darted to his wife. She gave him a knowing look.

"It stated that the guy was in one of the planes that was shot down by ZIPRA last year," the officer continued. "We take very seriously tips that can be authenticated from reliable sources as solid as this one."

"Father Joe," Sarah blurted.

"Father Joe?" the officer asked.

"The very reverent Father Joseph Burke," Jake said. He paused, considering all that had happened and all that stood to happen. The Rhodesians had them in their custody now, but at least they had escaped ZIPRA's immediate grasp. He leaned back and shouted to the heavens. "Joseph Burke! You clever, sneaky son-of-a-gun, you did it!"

The officer looked at him quizzically.

"You took care of Sarah and me to the very end!" Jake howled. "You are forever my friend and mentor!"

Jake grinned as he finished yelling, a grin that only grew when he turned to meet Sarah's gaze. Behind them, the town lights of Chete became brighter as the boat cruised to its destination.

CHAPTER 17

In the capital city of Salisbury, Jake was able to access his bank account and find accommodations at the Meikles Hotel, where the newlyweds would spend a glorious month together. Built in 1915, the Meikles Hotel was considered to be one of the best accommodations in southern Africa – owed mostly to the fact that it was still operated by the same founding family that had originally emigrated from Scotland. It was a superb colonial building with large verandahs and cupolas, and it offered timeless luxury and exceptional service.

Jake and Sarah stood together on the rooftop garden, looking out over the heart of the city. They stared out across Cecil Square, watching the day's activities unfold, the businesspeople on their lunch breaks and the Africans peddling carvings. Sarah wore new clothes in the form of a pair of jeans and sneakers and tight-fitting top. Jake was dressed nearly the same. Since the loss of their baby, still a mere month prior, Sarah had almost instantly regained her shapely figure, but neither had forgotten the pain of their loss. It was an almost daily burden, one that hung over Sarah's heart and kept Jake's mind altogether unquiet. For the former, peace would not come until some closure could be found with all that had occurred. For the latter, getting that closure would mean taking action. He had a plan. He simply hadn't told his wife yet what he intended to do.

Jake put his arm around Sarah's slim waist and kissed her on the cheek.

"Strange that people in the outside world do not know that blacks and coloreds can be in a so-called white hotel like this," she said. "It is unlike South Africa, where apartheid is the rule."

"I never thought of that."

"If you can afford it and dress correctly, there seems to be no problem here in Rhodesia."

"You've got an excellent point." Jake held her more tightly. He pressed his lips to her shoulder as she continued to gaze over the city.

"See that building to the right?" she asked after a time.

Jake looked in the direction she indicated. There, he saw a gleaming white modern building. "Yes."

"It's a well-known gentlemen's club called the Salisbury Club. They have strict rules regarding women and even Jews."

"That's wild," Jake said, not really paying attention. "Really wild."

"You're not interested in any of this, are you, Jacob?"

Jake backed away. "Actually, I'm wondering what's *really* on your mind. You've been brooding for days now."

She turned from him, furrowing her brow.

"See, that's exactly what I'm talking about." Jake reached in, taking her gently by the arm. "Come on. Let's go in and grab a seat in the bar. We have plans to make."

She sighed and followed.

Downstairs, they found a secluded table and ordered drinks from an African waiter wearing a fez. When the drinks arrived, they ceased their conversation until the waiter had withdrawn.

Sarah had been reiterating that she remained afraid about the idea of traveling alone to a strange country.

"It's almost the middle of June," Jake said the moment the waiter departed. "We have to get our lives together and move toward the future."

"The future?" Sarah chuffed. "Until a month ago, I was living with a man who had no past. It was so simple. So uncomplicated. Even when we were running through the bush for our lives, I at least had you by my side."

"I've spoken with my family." Jake offered a reassuring look. "As you know, they're well aware of you. I've told them at least a half-dozen times. They know that you're my wife and that you'll be traveling to the States ahead of me."

Sarah shook her head in obvious reservation.

"What is it?"

"I'm a child of Africa, Jacob."

He grinned. "And I'm a child of America."

"Don't make light of this." She scowled. "I mean to say that I am colored. Have you told your family of this?"

Jake sat back in his chair. He took a long sip of his beer, pondering what to say. "That's not going to be important to them, my love." He shrugged. "Besides, it's nobody else's business."

Sarah seemed frustrated. "Jacob, this is Africa. Men do strange things here that are overlooked or scorned – or worse, kept secret. You are throwing me into the big world of America, a simple African girl. How will I cope in your world without you?"

Jake chuckled. "You coped well enough in the bush while I was out cold. How many times did you save my life?"

"This is different."

"Listen, my parents' home is in the country. You'll love it."

She crossed her slender arms over her ample chest. "Not without you." She sulked for a time, staring into the corner of the bar. "You still haven't told me why you have to stay here without me, anyway."

Jake reminded his wife that he had promised the Department of Manpower that after they had taken their much needed sabbatical, he would be debriefed and allowed to bring them up to date regarding the entire time he had lost. "They need an eye-witness account of the crash."

"But I can provide that, too!" Sarah protested.

Jake ignored the point. "There's also Father Burke to consider. I have to find him and thank him for all he's done. Let him know that I know who I am now."

Sarah appeared ready to cry or to yell – one of the two.

"There's just so much more that I have to put behind me before I can leave Africa."

"I don't care about myself anymore," she whispered in sullen tones.

"Sarah, how can you say that?"

"I only care about *us*, Jacob. About you and me." She placed her hand on his. "And about a life of peace with no wars and dead babies." Her eyes began to well up in earnest as she spoke the words.

And for Jake, the true motivation came now to voice. As much as he would have liked to hide it from his wife, he knew that she understood his every whim, could read him like a book. The reason he would stay behind had little to do with the Department of Manpower or with Father Burke; the reason he would stay behind was the unspoken reason that Sarah so longed to do the same: something strange had happened with their baby – and until Jake got answers as to what, the ghost of his child would hang over him forever.

"Please don't make me go," Sarah said, her lips quivering. "Not without you."

Jake took both of her hands in his, holding them tight. "I promised my parents and my brother, Bill, that I would be on a flight out of Johannesburg as soon as I've been debriefed."

She nodded, crying.

"I will not be far behind. And besides, I've arranged for company to go with you on the plane. A woman from the American embassy in South Africa. She's traveling home to her family."

Sarah pressed her forehead to their interlocked hands. She cried, her shoulders shaking. She remained this way for some time before finally straightening up. "If I am to go alone and be without you," she said sadly into his eyes, "then, Jacob, take me to our room and make me another baby. I need part of you with me all the time."

Jake smiled and stood up. She tightened her grip on his hand and led the way out of the bar.

CHAPTER 18

Sarah slept – or pretended to sleep – for most of the twelve-hour flight from Johannesburg to London. When she wasn't actually asleep, her mind raced in several directions as to what the Fallon family might think of her. Occasionally, she would fall into a deep sleep, then awake in a jolt, remembering the Kariba flight and fearing that maybe she would be blown out of the sky.

She had been sent, as Jacob promised, with a woman named Rose, a pale-skinned, red-haired woman in her middle thirties. She was from the American embassy in South Africa and had been reassuring Sarah for most of the trip that everything would be all right – especially during the times when Sarah would wake in a panic at her surroundings, as if forgetting where she was.

The following day, the unlikely traveling companions changed planes in London, where they took off on their final leg of the journey to New York. Seven and a half hours later, the jet began to make its final approach into JFK. Rose shook Sarah awake, advising that they were about to land. Sarah was, of course, only pretending to sleep, nervous as she was that she would soon be in a land of strangers with a newfound family she had never met.

After deplaning, Rose, with all her State Department credentials, escorted Sarah with ease through immigration and on to baggage claim. Sarah followed her like a puppy, unaware of where to go and what to do next. When they passed through customs, Sarah saw something that made her heart skip. It was a tall, brown-haired man who looked like and unlike her Jacob. In his hand, he held a piece of white cardboard bearing the words, *Bill Fallon meeting Sarah Fallon*. The moment she saw the sign, he turned away, pacing as he was outside the customs hall.

"There," Sarah whispered to Rose, pointing in the direction of the man with the sign.

Rose nodded once, then moved confidently but slowly in the direction of the man – dragging as she was a giant suitcase, a bulky thing compared to Sarah's, which contained very little. Sarah followed nervously.

Without a word of greeting, Rose extended her hand to the man.

The man took the hand and shook it, looking confused. "Hello."

"Mr. Fallon?" Rose said.

The man nodded and offered a meek smile. "Bill."

"Pleased to meet you." Rose broke into a snorting little laugh. "I'm glad you had the card. You bear little resemblance to your brother."

In her heart, Sarah disagreed.

"Sarah?" Bill asked, an eyebrow arched.

The embassy woman cackled. "No, no," she said. "I'm simply delivering her into your care."

Sarah crossed one leg behind the other and looked to the ground the moment Rose pointed to her.

"This is Sarah Fallon," Rose said. "Your sister-in-law."

Bill stepped back for a moment, which made Sarah's heart sink into her stomach. All that while, she had been unsure as to what her brother-in-law would be expecting, and in spite of the long flight, she remained plenty alert to what his face was currently revealing. And she didn't like what she saw.

"You're disappointed that this is not a tan," she said softly.

Rose, looking uncomfortable, handed Bill her business card and a thick envelope, then awkwardly made to take her leave. Sarah watched in discomfort as Mr. Fallon pored over the envelope, taking a long while before he looked in her direction again.

"These are all of her documents," Rose said. "Everything you need is in here. I've even included a business card, so feel free to call me if you have any questions."

Bill offered a halfhearted thank you.

Rose then turned to Sarah, clacking her heels together. "Good luck to you, Sarah Fallon. Have a great life." Then she picked up her heavy suitcase and struggled away into the departing crowd.

Sarah gathered her meager little case into her hands. Without speaking, Bill took it from her and put it down on the floor where they stood. She felt utterly humbled, unable to even look up at him as he assessed her. But in time, she worked up the courage to look him in the eye again, and when she did, she saw something she hadn't expected: a broad smile.

"Let me start again." He offered his hand. "I'm Bill. Not Willie, nor William, Will, or Billy, but plain Bill. I'm Jake's older brother. And I'm very pleased to meet you, Sarah."

Sarah took the extended hand. "I'm Sarah Malumbo." She paused and returned the smile with an impish one of her own. "I mean, now it's 'Fallon.' It's hard to get used to that name."

Bill lifted her hand to his lips and kissed it softly. "I apologize for staring at you. I didn't realize. We obviously thought you were European."

"I'm half European; I believe the other half is Ethiopian."

Bill seemed content only to keep his eyes locked on her face. "Whatever it is, it's a delightful combination of perfection. Lucky old Jake."

Sarah smiled at the compliment. "You are very kind. Jacob told me you were a kind man and that you would look after me in his absence. I have a lot to learn, Bill. I do not want to be a burden on you or your family and be an embarrassment to my Jacob."

Bill smiled wistfully. "You're just like my mother, always calling him 'Jacob.'" He picked up her bag, turned, and waved that she accompany him. "Like it or not, from this moment on, we're all family."

For all of his foibles, Bill certainly did make Sarah feel welcome. He paused for a moment and shook her suitcase, apparently indicating her meager belongings. She smiled knowingly. He slung the cane he carried under the arm he used to bear the suitcase, then offered Sarah his other arm. Sarah grinned and looped her arm in his as they walked toward the exit of the terminal building. She had to admit that she expected a limp, given the cane, but he did not limp too badly. And he certainly seemed to be in good health when he slung her bag into the trunk of his BMW and strode around to open the passenger door for her. She thanked him and dropped into the waiting bucket seat, eager to see everything that her new life had in store for her.

Sarah was mesmerized during the trip from Kennedy Airport. Never had she seen so many vehicles as they traveled on the crammed beltway through Brooklyn and on down through Staten Island. Like a child trying to gain as much knowledge in the shortest possible time, she questioned Bill every mile of the journey. A terrified look came across her face as they crossed the Verrazano-Narrows Bridge.

"What is it?" Bill asked.

She chuckled cathartically, gripping the hand rest on the door beside her. "I'm frightened to be at such a height."

"Not to worry. It's perfectly safe."

She peered out the window, shivering. "I don't understand how and why a bridge should be built so far up in the air."

Bill laughed.

The final assault to her comprehension was when Bill drove onto the New Jersey Turnpike. There, Sarah witnessed the multiple lanes of traffic speeding along together.

"Unbelievable," she said under her breath.

"Yeah, the traffic can be terrible," Bill offered.

In seemingly endless fashion, questions leapt to Sarah's mind during the journey. And every time, she would ask them. And every time, she would find the answer in wise Bill. She kept her questions coming right up until Bill's BMW pulled into the turnabout in front of the Solebury farmhouse.

Sarah stared out the window, as nervous now as she was when she'd deplaned. There, beside a detached garage that looked something like a barn, crouched a couple who must have been her Jacob's parents. They appeared unaware of Bill and Sarah's arrival, given that they continued to tend to the plants lining the overlarge garden some sixty yards from the farmhouse. The woman appeared to be giving instructions to a much younger man – perhaps a landscaper – who stood above her like a scolded schoolboy.

Only when the arriving pair got out of the car were they noticed. The older man was the first to do so, and he sauntered in their direction with a rather blank look on his face.

The man shouted over his shoulder to the woman as he walked toward the vehicle. "Mary, they're here!"

Looking around, the woman named Mary continued to address the landscaper. Then, in a moment, she shouted back. "One moment! I'll be right there!"

Sarah looked at Bill, the pang of fear in her heart showing clearly on her face. "I'm scared."

Bill smiled. "Of what?"

She sighed. "Jacob's parents."

"Well, they're also *my* parents," Bill said, talking now through the side of his mouth. "So I can tell you there's nothing to be scared about."

Still, Sarah felt her palms begin to sweat.

The man finally arrived before them. He eyed Sarah for quite some time before speaking – much in the same way that his son had done. Whatever his feelings, he hid them well as he took Sarah's hand and kissed her on the cheek. He then gave her a bear hug that almost took her breath away. By the time he'd finished, she was smiling hesitantly.

He stepped back, holding her hands and looking her square in the face. "So this is Jake's Sarah. What a pretty thing you are. I can see why Jake swept you up."

"Thank you, Mr. Fallon," Sarah said nervously. She looked down at her simple frock, feeling the weight of the fact that she hadn't slept properly in what felt like days. "I don't feel so pretty right now."

At that moment, Mary came into view, having approached in remarkable silence. Her face was easier to read. She wore a bewildered and startled look. Sarah's heart sank as her mother-in-law put her hands to her mouth and her eyes got larger. It was a look of distain.

Without a word, Sarah turned and ran. She was so upset that she didn't even think about where she would go – she just knew that she had to get away from the hateful expression in the eyes of the mother of the man she loved. Her feet pounded heavily on the gravel driveway, and her eyes began to water. She got only twenty yards or so before she felt a hand on her elbow. She turned mid-stride and saw Bill there, the young man panting from the exertion. She came to a stop, resting against an ancient oak tree as she stared up at Bill.

"What are you doing?" he asked, clearly confused.

Sarah broke into tears. Instead of answering, she merely threw herself into Bill's embrace. The wind brought the reason to her ears, however. On it, she could hear snippets of the conversation unfolding between Mr. and Mrs. Fallon.

". . . not surprised she's running, Mary," came Mr. Fallon's voice. "The look on your face said it all."

"For God's sake, she's black," Mary snapped. "Why didn't that little shit tell us?"

Sarah sobbed into her brother-in-law's chest.

It took a great deal of convincing from Bill – particularly with random barbs continuing to float down the driveway: "What will our friends say," ". . . she must have weaved some black magic on him," ". . . what the hell was Jacob thinking?" But through it all, Bill comforted Sarah by the oak tree. He advised her to come back and face his parents, as running never solved anything.

"All she can see is just a black African Umfazi (*wife)* from the bush," she said tearfully. "God, I just want to go home to Africa and be with Jacob."

Bill sighed, holding her closer. "It's too late for that now." Then he pulled away, giving her a look that did quite a lot to reassure her that she wasn't alone here. "At least for now. In the meantime, the two of us will just have to grin and bear it."

Sarah looked into his face. "You said the two of us?"

Bill smiled. "Yes, the two of us. I'm in your camp all the way."

Sarah glanced down at his bad leg. "Why are you not limping?" she asked quietly. "I saw your cane."

"Probably you." He beamed. "Magical you. Magical Sarah."

She offered a smile.

At that moment, Mr. Fallon arrived, smacking his son on the shoulder in playful fashion. "Hey, you two. What's going on?"

"She's a little upset, Dad," Bill explained. "And can you blame her? You saw the look on Mom's face."

"Taken by surprise, my boy." He clearly meant well, but something in Mr. Fallon's voice suggested that he was merely trying to cover for his wife.

"Bill," Sarah whispered, "you mean Jacob didn't tell any of you?"

"No," Bill said.

"He should have," Mr. Fallon admonished. "Or at least you should have called ahead, Bill."

"You and I both know it wouldn't have made a difference, Dad," Bill said through his teeth. "Prejudice is prejudice, whatever way it's cut."

Mr. Fallon ignored his son and took Sarah's hand, leading her back toward the house. "I don't believe we finished our introduction earlier. My name is Patrick Fallon."

"Pleased to meet you, Mr. Fallon," Sarah said, still feeling quite reserved and uneasy.

"Please call me Pat, young lady."

Sarah nodded. She then looked back to find Bill bringing up the rear, following closely. As they walked, Patrick apologized for any behavior that made it appear as if the Fallons were demeaning their guest. He comforted her in the notion that she was his son's wife and that that was good enough for him.

"And her?" Sarah asked, watching the woman who only just now had traversed the steps leading into the front door of the house.

"Let me worry about Mary," Patrick said. "She's just suffering from a multitude of emotions, I'm afraid. Given time and experience, you'll learn that it's just a matter of the fact that you've taken away her baby boy."

Sarah placed a hand to her heart, feeling wretched and apparently showing it on her face.

Patrick chuckled. "I don't mean it like that, sweetheart. I only mean that when a woman has to give away her son to a wife, there's an automatic immediate resentment. But it'll eventually elapse."

She exhaled, shuddering.

"Although I've never had the experience," Patrick pontificated, "I imagine that it must be pretty much the same if a man takes away a father's daughter." He patted her hand, still held firmly in his. "It'll take a little time for my wife to fully accept, appreciate, and understand you, young lady. But rest assured, she'll come around."

Sarah looked up at her father-in-law. "Jacob and I had our baby taken away," she said in a crying whisper.

"You and Jake had a baby?" Bill asked, sounding shocked as he stuck his head in to the conversation.

Sarah sighed, looking mournfully into the distance. "Our baby was stillborn."

Both men were silent as they arrived at the front door. There, Mary waited patiently on a small stone bench. She wore a rather forced-looking smile, one that Sarah had heard her husband describe as a "Philadelphia Main Line smile," whatever that meant.

"Mary," Patrick said, "I would like to introduce you to your new daughter-in-law, Sarah."

After another long, cold, appraising look, Mary stepped in to give Sarah what felt like a guarded hug. "I'm so sorry for my reaction, dear. I was taken aback. Jacob – and for that matter, William here – neglected to inform us." She pulled back. "We were expecting a white colonial girl. I apologize. I'm not a racist. Really I'm not."

Bill chuffed, but when Sarah looked at him, he shrugged off any appearance of disbelief at his mother's claims.

"Well," Sarah said cautiously, "I'm half a colonial girl."

Mary apparently ignored the unintended sarcasm, as she took her daughter-in-law by the hand without addressing it. "If

Jacob loves you, then I love you, also." She turned, leading her guest up to the door. "Come, let me show you to your room."

The women were first into the house, the men following diligently behind. Sarah sent one last pleading look at Bill, who winked, urging her onward.

~ ~ ~

The Fallon men sat around the bar in the living room, both of them cupping drinks in their hands. In time, Mary came down the stairs and joined them. Bill watched as his father handed her a drink, which Mary accepted, climbing quickly onto a bar stool.

"I need this," she said with a sigh.

"Where's Sarah?" Bill asked.

"Having a shower." She fired a frustrated look at her son. "Did you know that that girl's got virtually *no* decent clothing?"

"I carried her case. I know."

Patrick shrugged. "Well, you should take the girl to the mall, then, Mary. Buy her a wardrobe."

Mary scoffed.

"It's the least you could do for your son's wife."

Mary scoffed harder. "Stop calling her that."

Bill felt his heart sink as he watched his mother chew on her misguided disgust.

"It's hard enough to comprehend that Jacob's married," Mary said, "let alone his choice of wife."

"Give her a break," Patrick said, standing to refill his scotch. "She's your son's wife, whether you like it or not. And besides that, she's a stranger in a strange land. You can't keep hitting her with all this animosity or she'll wilt."

"Damnit, Patrick, I'm fully aware that that woman is now Jake's wife. I just never suspected that a son of mine would do this to us."

"Do *what*, Mother?" Bill asked scornfully.

Mary made a face as if she'd just tasted something bitter. "Send home an African."

Bill felt his face boil. He stood, readying himself to yell, but his father stopped him with the usual anticipatory wave of his hand.

"I'm sure she'll change her mind in time," Patrick said with a note of warning.

Bill calmed, though he continued to seethe as he returned to his seat beside his father.

"In time, I suspect our Sarah will tell us more about that baby she and Jake lost."

"Baby?" Mary said, clearly astounded enough to nearly spill her drink.

"She just mentioned it," Patrick said. "She and Jake had a baby. It was stillborn."

Mary stood, her hands clenched to fists. "So *that's* why he married her! He did what was the proper *Catholic* thing to do."

"Mother," Bill said incredulously. He paused for a long while, massaging the bridge of his nose. "People don't *do* the proper Catholic thing anymore. Times have changed since you were her age."

"The boy's right," Patrick said. "Besides, Jake could've just made a run for it if he knocked her up. He's got no ties to the middle of dark fucking Africa."

Mary was spiteful as she jogged the men's memory regarding the story Jacob had told them on the phone; how he had lost his memory and that Sarah was his guardian angel who had literally saved his life.

"Maybe she's wicked," she added. "Evil. Maybe she *conned* Jacob into marriage."

"Mother, that's ridiculous!" Bill said, pushing away from the bar and stalking to the other corner of the living room. He simply couldn't sit near his mother anymore. Such was his anger at her hate.

~~~

Sarah, her hair still wet from the shower, stood at the top of the stairs, listening to the conversation driving up from the room below. Her face was flushed with anger, and there was deep sadness in her eyes as she tried to hold back the tears. She listened as her mother-in-law continued to spew hate. And she listened as her brother-in-law admonished her to not be so quick to judge without any facts or input from Sarah.

"Why are you standing up for a colored girl?" Mary asked.

"Jake made me promise I'd look out for her," Bill snapped.

Sarah's heart sank. Even her ally was only doing this because he felt bound to do so.

"I just never believed I'd have to start in my own home," Bill added softly.

"Come now, William," Mary said. "Don't be so sensitive. All I'm saying is that we have to be cautious. We have to really find out about her and Jacob and this so-called lost baby."

A long silence followed. Sarah wept silently as she thought about her husband running alone through the bush, thought about the jungle of torment that seemed to be facing her now, and above all, about the child she had so recently lost.

"Either way, I like her," Patrick said after a time. "And I'll bet if you were to take her to a hairdressing salon and get her a decent hairstyle and some modern clothing, she'd look terrific."

Sarah shuddered, wringing her hands. Then she tentatively began the journey down the stairs.

Mary sighed. "I'll take her to the mall this afternoon." Still, she sounded reluctant. "We'll see what we can muster up."

At that moment, Sarah entered the room, making her presence known with a soft clearing of her throat. As all eyes turned to her, she reflexively took her shoulder-length ponytail in her hand, feeling the moisture drip down to her neck. She wore no makeup,
~~~

but suddenly felt sorry that she hadn't taken the time to apply any. The jeans she wore were the same that her Jacob had bought for her in Salisbury. Under the scrutiny of the Fallons' gaze, she fought back the tears and tried to act normal.

"Come in, girl," Patrick said, standing. "Come in."

"A shower always makes one feel better," Mary added with another forced smile.

"Yes, Mrs. Fallon," Sarah answered with respect.

"You can call me 'Mother,'" Mrs. Fallon said in a rather demanding tone, "but never 'Mrs. Fallon.' It's far too formal."

"As you wish," Sarah said, trying to mask the chill she felt in her heart.

Bill moved in, whispering into Sarah's ear. "You didn't hear any of our conversation, did you, Sarah?"

"No," Sarah lied.

"Good," Mary said, leaning in to eavesdrop. "Listeners never do hear anything good about themselves. Not that we were talking about anyone in particular."

An uncomfortable silence followed.

It was Patrick who once again came to the rescue. "Mary, why don't we have some lunch and you girls can get out and do a little shopping."

Sarah sighed, nodding and trying to return the phony smile of her mother-in-law.

~ ~ ~

Later that evening, everyone was seated on the verandah, coffees and cognacs in hand. Sarah slowly swung back and forward on the creaky porch swing. Patrick and Mary were seated opposite each other. Bill rested on one of the verandah rails, intent on firing passing glances at Sarah. Patrick had already inquired as to whether the women had found anything worthwhile at the mall, and Mary had abruptly ended the line of conversation by explaining in frustrated tones that there was nothing too exciting. She had noted that Sarah was a petite girl, and that they were thusly limited to finding anything decent in her size. All they could muster up, she had explained, was a selection of underwear and a couple of skirts and tops.

At that moment, Sarah had looked at Bill, and for the first time held a slight smile on her face. She revealed that she thought there was a great selection of clothing and that compared to the shortages in Africa, anything would seem good.

So now they had come to another of the uncomfortable silences that seemed to rule the evening.

"What about the Wilsons and the Fourth of July?" Patrick asked of his wife after a time.

"The Wilsons?" Bill asked, confused.

"They have their yacht down at Cape May," Patrick explained. "They've asked us to take a trip with them down to the Keys over the Independence weekend."

"Quite a trip," Bill said.

Patrick nodded. "It would be a good seven to eight weeks in all." He turned to his wife and smiled. "We sort of committed before we knew about Sarah." He then fired an apologetic look at his daughter-in-law. "But no worry. We can cancel."

"That would be very disappointing to them," Mary said.

Bill sighed, shaking his head at his mother's snarky attitude. "You shouldn't change your plans," he said, nevertheless. He then offered a subtle look at Sarah. "If it's all right with Sarah, she can come back to New York with me. At least until Jake returns."

Sarah's eyes widened.

"Not to worry," Bill explained with an outstretched hand, "I've got a three-bedroom apartment with acres of room."

Mary, for all of her terseness on the evening, appeared suddenly relieved. "That would certainly solve the problem."

Bill glanced over at Sarah, who simply kept swinging as she locked eyes with him. Just as he thought she would shrug it off, she spoke.

"It would solve a lot of problems." She sounded more than a little sarcastic.

Bill chuffed. It was uncanny: he could see his brother in her more and more all the time.

"What exactly do you mean by that, young lady?" Mary asked, her animosity evident.

Sarah shrugged. "I simply meant that if I go with Bill, then I can continue my studies right away."

Everyone blinked through their bewilderment.

"I was taking a correspondence course in Africa," Sarah explained. "I seek to be a journalist. I want to shed light on all the truths about the Africa that *I* know."

The men smiled at this. The mother rolled her eyes.

"How noble," she said sardonically.

"Thank you, Mother," Sarah said, clearly learning the game quickly.

Just as Bill was about to yell at his mother, the definitive mediator, Patrick, changed the subject.

"I was telling Mary that you and Jake lost a baby," he said. "Can you tell us about it?"

"It's too painful to talk about," Sarah answered softly.

Bill shot a look of disappointment at his father, who appeared suddenly sullen.

"I'm sorry," the older man said.

Sarah stopped swinging and directed her lovely eyes on Patrick. "Don't be. There is no place for sorrow in my or Jacob's life."

"Pat, stop prying," Mary added.

Sarah, looking restless, stood from the swing and took a cigarette out of the pack lying on the table next to her. She accepted the light that Bill offered her, then spoke softly, explaining that it was all right to pry and that eventually the pain would subside. She had tears in her eyes as she explained that sadly, she had never even seen their baby.

As Bill listened, he would occasionally watch his mother. Mary appeared genuinely remorseful as she told Sarah how sorry she was for their loss.

"Why didn't you get to see the baby?" Bill asked.

Sarah shrugged.

"Did Jake see the baby?"

Sarah shook her head slowly. "It was pretty chaotic. There were terrorists and police and army everywhere when I gave birth. We weren't safe."

"That sounds terrifying," Mary said – and to Bill's eye, she appeared to be warming up for the first time to her daughter-in-law.

Sarah nodded. "All I know is that Sister Margaret got me out of the mission hospital a few hours after the baby was born, and that Jacob and I escaped in a small boat across Lake Kariba." She took a long drag of her cigarette before exhaling slowly. "That was when Jake got his memory back. He saw a picture of his friend, Brian."

Mary looked shocked. "But walking around after delivering a baby is crazy. You could have bled to death."

"I had no choice."

Silence reigned as Bill tried to envision the horror that Jake and Sarah faced on the day that Sarah gave birth.

After a time, Bill looked at Sarah inquisitively. "You met Brian?"

She strode over to her seat and stamped out her cigarette in the ashtray beside the pack of cigarettes. "Not in life. I saw him murdered in front of me. And I don't want to talk about it. Not now, not ever."

Bill looked to his mother, who appeared ready to cry.

"I would like to go to sleep and forget all these memories," Sarah said. "May I be excused?"

"Of course, my dear," Mary said – and she said it so warmly that it startled Bill.

Sarah stood and made her way to the door. Once there, she stopped and turned to face the others. "I'm sorry if I have caused you pain. Or that I may possibly become an embarrassment with your friends."

Bill felt his stomach flutter with embarrassment of his own.

"I don't ever have to meet any of them," she added. "I can hibernate like an old bear and wait for my Jacob to come and get me. Goodnight, everyone."

She then left the verandah, leaving Bill to glare at his tactless parents.

~~~

The following morning, everyone stood beside the garage as Bill placed his and Sarah's suitcases in the trunk of the BMW. Patrick hugged Sarah. It was clear that he had a soft spot for her as he kissed her lightly on each cheek. She smiled warmly at him before turning to Mary. The matron of the house, to her credit, gave her daughter-in-law what appeared to be a genuine hug, as if she was starting to melt. She also kissed her on one of her cheeks. It was a kiss that Sarah did not return.

With a wave, the young lady stepped around to her side of the car and got in beside Bill, who was already in the driver's seat.

Mary spoke to them through the open window. "Don't forget Christmas and the New Year party. You *have* to be here." She shot a sidelong glance at Sarah. "And remind Jacob about it when he arrives, please."

Bill confirmed that they would be there. "When you finish your trip with the Wilsons, come out and see me in New York.
~~~

Sounds like Sarah and Jake will be taking root there, too." He offered an appraising glance at Sarah, who nodded.

"Get going, boy," Patrick said over his wife's shoulder. "Or you'll catch traffic at the Holland Tunnel."

Bill chuckled, knowing that his father had always hated the long and particularly grueling Irish goodbyes that Mary was used to. The younger Fallon agreed, starting the car and moving slowly away. Sarah and Bill waved through the now closed windows as Patrick and Mary turned away in conversation. Whatever they discussed, Bill felt glad to be rid of them for the time. Now he could enjoy a few days alone with his brother's wife, getting to know her while they waited for his brother's return.

CHAPTER 19

Having spent a full four weeks in New York, Sarah stood facing the heavy drapes in Bill's luxury apartment. The living room was still semi-dark as she opened the drapes to reveal a large window overlooking Central Park. It was early in the morning, and it appeared to be a typically hot and humid day in mid-August Manhattan. She held a lit cigarette in her hand and wore an overlarge dressing gown belonging to Bill. Her hair was uncombed and she looked disheveled.

Sarah heard a sound behind her – the sound of Bill's feet on the hardwood as he walked from the direction of his bedroom to the kitchen – but she ignored it, preferring instead to take in the remarkable sight of his view. The aroma of coffee reached her smoky nostrils.

"The dead has arisen," Bill shouted from the kitchen. "Care for some coffee?" Sarah didn't turn around to answer. "Thank you."

"You really meant that hibernation thing when we were at my parents' house, didn't you?"

"Did you read Jake's letter?" she asked with a sigh.

"I read it."

Sarah continued to look mournfully out the window. "Jacob," she said, feeling almost angry with her wayward husband. "He gets us out of harm's way, sends me to America, and is now fighting with the Rhodesian forces."

Bill returned with the coffee, offering a smile that seemed odd to her. "I told you when you got here that he's always been the rebel son."

Sarah sighed again, preferring to change the subject from the man who had apparently been willing to stay in Africa and maroon his wife alone in New York – and for several months, at least. "You have your own little piece of Africa right out there." She nodded at the view. "I miss it so much." She turned to face him then, running her hands through her hair in an attempt to look presentable.

Bill frowned, apparently dwelling on the subject of his brother.

"Why didn't he leave well enough alone?" Sarah asked. "They want Jacob to identify the terrorist who killed all those people, and we really don't know who was actually in charge."

Bill handed her a cup of coffee. "I know my brother. He couldn't save Brian when you were witnessing the whole massacre, so he's hell-bent on avenging him. Like I said, the rebel son."

Sarah sighed. "I don't think he's ever coming back. It's a war of horrible circumstances."

Bill took her by the hand and led her to the comfortable leather couch. "Jake will be fine, Sarah." He spoke in comforting tones. "You'll see. He'll be back."

Sarah sighed again, thinking about whether it would be appropriate to tell her husband's brother that she had no more tears to cry, or that she had nowhere else to go. She didn't even know if and where she was considered legal. She and Jake had broken so many laws.

Bill suddenly smiled and took her arms in his hands. "You know what? I think it's time that I 'Pygmalion' you."

Sarah arched an eyebrow. "Pygmalion me?"

Bill edged closer to her. "Have you ever read George Bernard Shaw?"

Sarah smiled. "In Africa, when the sun goes down, all one does is read. You're talking about the *My Fair Lady* story, aren't you?"

"Yes I am."

She cocked her head back, grinning suggestively. "Do you want to transform me, Bill?"

"Very definitely."

Her heart sank and she frowned. "Into what?"

Bill appeared taken aback for a moment, as if he was just now realizing the subtle insult laced beneath his good intentions. "Into a more beautiful woman than you already are," he managed.

Sarah pursed her lips. That would do.

"You're two weeks overdue to start your journalism course, and you look like hell cooped up here day and night. You need a makeover."

Sarah giggled, despite herself. "Maybe you're right. What if Jacob saw me like this?"

Bill got up and took her mug and placed it on the coffee table in front of them. He then grabbed her by the hand and dragged her to her feet. "First," he said, dripping with enthusiasm, "we'll hit Fifth Avenue. There's Saks and a whole world of high-end stores."

She nodded once.

"Today you take back your life, Sarah Fallon. I am taking control until Jake comes home. Go put on those overworked jeans of yours. We have shopping to do."

Sarah grinned, turned, and complied. She was glad to have Bill. He always knew how to make her feel better – always knew how to draw her mind away from Jake. And besides, he was right. Jake would be fine.

~ ~ ~

Jake sat by a small fire in the African bush in the company of six other men on a damp late afternoon in mid-November. These men were regular Rhodesian Security Forces, known as RSF, and they had been tracking ZIPRA terrorists for several days. On this day, they finally found themselves close to an encampment that intelligence had confirmed was a temporary ZIPRA base.

Jake closed his eyes and listened to the crackle of the fire. His mind flashed back to the last sortie, where he and several of the RSF soldiers had crept up on an advance ZIPRA guard. With silenced automatics, they had systematically eliminated the advance lookouts. One of the soldiers' automatic rifles had jammed and Jake had charged a terrorist lifting his AK-47. The terrorist, not knowing who to shoot first, turned back to the soldier trying to eject the bad round. Jake had dispatched his enemy with a knife plunged deep into the eye.

Jake sat now beside Brendan Morrison, the Rhodesian Security Forces officer. Morrison was a thirty-two-year-old home-grown Rhodesian. He was lean, well built, and tanned and had the rugged look of a man who had worked the land all his life.

Just as Jake drifted into the dreamy region before sleep, Morrison grunted and raised his hand. The American snapped out of it and stood with the rest of the RSF forces. They followed Morrison in a straight line in the direction of the purported ZIPRA camp. The bush was thick here, visibility low. And a dank smell hung over the air.

Not a half-mile down the path, gunfire sprang out. It took the men by surprise, as intelligence had put the camp at least another mile to the west.

Morrison barked to open fire, then took cover behind a tree. Jake did the same, unloading with his rifle whenever the carbines downwind lulled in their crackling. Morrison kept shouting rapid orders. "Don't back down!" he hollered. "We don't want any runners!"

Jake thought about what he had seen of the ZIPRA in his short time enduring this conflict. There was always a first onslaught. And those men almost always ran to warn the others. When that happened, it was best to have a full magazine ready.

"Take out the legs!" Morrison shouted. "We need some of them alive!"

Morrison was referring to the need for information. Without information from survivors, they would stand little chance of finding the man he sought.

"I got it!" Jake hollered back. He fired a few bursts into the tree line, about two feet off the ground. "Loud and clear."

The line of security forces fired discriminately at the terrorists. The coordinated sweeping of their weapons clearly caught the ZIPRA off guard. Twenty terrorists fell before the others started to run. The soldiers' weapons swept at a lower level. Soft thuds of bullets ripped into the legs of the fleeing terrorists as men fell moaning and dying onto the damp ground.

When the battle had ended, the RSF found four men in the bush. They all screamed in agony, bleeding into the dark soil, some of them holding one leg and some of them holding both. Morrison ordered that the bleeding men be brought together and set by a tree. As Jake carried out his orders, he listened to the screams of the wounded men, crying out for the help of their comrades. Once he had set his men up with his back against the tree, he stood beside Morrison.

"Do you want some help there, ndoda (*man*)?" Morrison asked sarcastically. "Those legs are bleddy finished for playing soccer, man."

The terrorist pleaded hysterically. "Helepa mena, Bwana *(help me, sir)*."

Jake looked at Morrison. "He said Bwana, not Nkosi (*sir*). That's Northern Rhodesian, not Southern."

Morrison smiled. "Boy, you learn fast for a Yank. But Northern Rhodesia is called Zambia."

Jake was defiant. "I know what it's called. I learned the hard way."

Morrison turned back to the hysterical terrorist. "My God, he's only a pickanin (*child*). He's no more than fourteen years old." Still, he knelt down in front of the boy and put pressure on his wound.

The boy winced terribly.

"Where's your number one Impi (*commando*)?" Morrison asked through his teeth.

The boy's voice cried out in a childish manner as he pointed in the direction where the rest of his group had run into the bush. "Gone to the place by the lake. Please, Bwana, helepa mena."

Jake was in no mood for patter. "What fucking place by the lake?" He glared down at the boy. "Pickanin or no pickanin, I kick your fucking brains out."

Morrison looked taken aback. "Bleddy hell, man. Hold on there, Fallon. Honey always gets you more than vinegar."

Jake kicked at the dirt beneath his feet. "Guess I'm getting impatient killing these creeps and not getting any answers."

Morrison pulled two folded hand-drawn sketches from his pocket and shoved them in the face of the young African. "Do you know these Impi?"

The boy closed his eyes, but the man beside him shook his head from side to side. When he opened his eyes, the young boy did the opposite, nodding. The older man, furious, brought his fist down on the boy's bleeding legs. The boy screamed and Jake reacted. His Uzi blasted a quick burst. The man flopped over against the other two injured men.

Ignoring what Jake had just done, Morrison continued. "Where are they?"

The young terrorist whimpered. "They are my leaders. We have a safe village about six miles north of where you can see Spurwing Island. We meet there every week after dark."

"When do you meet again?" Jake demanded.

The boy grew even more jittery. "Tomorrow night, maybe tonight after this attack. Helepa mena, please. Don't kill me. I don't want this war, but they make many ndoda *(men)* join in or they kill your baba *(father)* and mame *(mother)*."

Jake spoke scornfully as he pointed to the picture of the albino. "Will this white kaffir be there?"

The boy shivered. "He's a feared one."

Morrison then pointed to the picture of the terrorist leader with the scars. "And will this number one Impi be there?"

The boy nodded. Tears streamed down his face.

Jake and Morrison turned and left the wounded men behind. Morrison shouted over his shoulder to his radio man to call for help for, "the poor wounded buggers."

"Their war's over," he said. "Need to get them out of the bush."

"You mean you won't kill them?" Jake asked, surprised.

"No."

"But they would have most certainly terminated any RDF soldiers they had captured." Jake was emphatic. "I've been there. I've seen it."

Morrison stopped and grabbed Jake by the shoulders. "You have to remember, Jake." He spoke deliberately. "You're with Rhodesian Security Forces. We are soldiers. We do not kill prisoners."

Jake furrowed his brow. "I've heard otherwise. There are stories of men who collect ZIPRA ears as trophies."

Morrison shook his head. "I can't speak for the mercenaries we employ. They are not soldiers. They're simply on a cash-fueled killing binge."

The American pondered the words, and decided that Morrison was right. There needed to be a moral high-ground, even in wars against terrorists.

"Come," Morrison said. "We'll make camp."

~~~

With the mid-afternoon sun beating down, Jake sat across a makeshift table – a wooden plank set atop two gathered stones – from Morrison, sipping tea and thinking of Sarah. His wife. His beautiful wife. She was so far away from him as he sat with his compatriots in the African bush.

"We'll have a short walk tomorrow," Morrison said, snapping Jake from his trance.

"How far do you reckon?"

"We're no more than a mile from them now. According to the pickanin, the place we're looking for is an old white fishing camp that's become too dangerous."

"Dangerous?"

Morrison smiled. "Dangerous with all these armed bleddy bastards running around. What you fail to understand, Mr. Fallon, is that if one abandons anything in Africa, someone else will take it. Or live in it and eventually fuck it up."

"When do we move out?"

"At dusk. I want to be in place when the sun is going down. Need to time the attack so that we'll have light until we're maybe a hundred and fifty yards from the spot."

Jake lit a smoke, more excited about the plan than he cared to admit. "I'm having a hard time waiting to reunite with the man who killed my friend."
~~~

"Salisbury wants them alive, Jake," Morrison warned, wide-eyed. "That's the mission priority. You'd do well to keep that vivid in your mind."

Jake waved his hands dismissively. "I remember."

A casual silence followed, Jake smoking and Morrison sipping his tea. It would be the latter who would break it.

"What are you doing here, anyway, Jake? You don't look like the mercenary type. And this isn't exactly your war."

Jake pondered the question carefully, figuring the best way to justify his position without revealing too much. "I'm here because these motherfuckers killed my best friend. And they almost killed me and Sarah."

"Sarah?"

"My wife."

Morrison nodded knowingly. "That's right, man. I was told that you married a black."

Jake scowled. "She's colored."

"Bleddy same."

"As you say, bleddy same to you." Jake was annoyed and mordant. "But not to me. I owe her my life. And I'd appreciate it if you didn't talk about her in such a derogatory fashion."

"Sorry, man." Morrison lit his own smoke. "But like I said, this is my war, not yours. You're an American. You can go home."

"Fine," Jake said through his teeth. "What about you, then?"

"This is my bleddy home, man." Morrison sounded rather hopeless. "And it's been my family's home for a couple hundred years. Where do the fucking blacks and all the world government arseholes think we should go?"

Jake nodded and took a drag of his cigarette. "Hell, I guess."

"What a way to treat the descendants of colonial settlers. My ancestors built a beautiful piece of God's earth out of this land. They placed it on the world's map for all to see."

"You're right there, my friend." Jake looked toward the entrance to the tent, imagining the untamed continent beyond. "I wonder how long it'll remain the breadbasket of southern Africa."

Morrison scoffed. "Well, I'll tell you this: the new government sharing power idea of Muzorewa's is a nonstarter. Just a last-ditch attempt by Ian Smith to hold on."

"What do you mean?"

Morrison explained that for a start there were two terrorist groups that were totally different in their expectations of the future. They never did and never would agree to anything in the end. The original inhabitants of Rhodesia were bushmen. The two groups of terrorists were mainly made up of two tribes, the Matabele and Mashona. They had always been enemies, Matabele calling the Mashona "dirt eaters."

"Dirt eaters?"

"They've been calling them that for a hundred years, at least. It has to do with the Matabele standing on the heads of defeated enemies, making them eat the dirt."

"It was the Matabele that shot my plane out of the sky."

Morrison nodded. "They are Nkomo's people, yes. But make no mistake, the Mashona are just as hard-headed. They follow Mugabe, and have been trained in North Korea and China. Even if the whites left Rhodesia, these two clans would war indefinitely. Their tribal history goes back a long way."

"What a pisser," Jake said, exhaling smoke.

Morrison's eyes went wide. "It's a bigger pisser than that. We get attacked here by terrorists set up in our safe-haven neighbors. Meanwhile, those same neighbors are starving. The real pisser is that if Rhodesian farmers were allowed to raise their crops unabated as they used to do, they'd produce enough maize, tobacco, and cattle to feed not only our own population, but those of Zambia, Malawi, Botswana, and Mozambique, as well. We've managed such exports in the past, anyway."

When he'd finished speaking, he looked quite disgusted. But he stood up and stomped out his cigarette. "Whatever happens, I wager that by January of next year, the Rhodesian War will be over."

Jake didn't bother asking Morrison why he felt that way. He'd heard the gossip himself – the gossip that there would be another shaky treaty, yet another new government made up of the two warring factions.

"It's all a bleddy joke," Morrison added. He then looked to his men. "Let's move out! It's time."

They all stood, one of the men dousing the fire outside the tent, several others deconstructing the haphazard camp.

When they'd finished, Morrison waved to his men and put a finger to his lips. "I want total silence. I don't want to hear even one stick break underfoot. Keep alert at all times. Not a sound. And God bless the man who doesn't switch off his fucking transistor. Don't worry about any newscasts or rock music. No news is good news until we make some explosive music ourselves."

CHAPTER 20

Bill strode out of his favorite Manhattan restaurant, an expensive place near the park. Sarah staggered behind, looking a little flush from wine but certainly stunning in her new designer clothing. Her hair had been styled in a short crop with a natural wave. The transformation from a simple African to a New York sophisticated girl about town was evident as she stood by Bill's side, waiting for the hailed cab. In no time, a cab pulled up and they stepped in. After Bill gave the driver instructions, there was a long period of uncomfortable silence, both Bill and Sarah taking in the roaring traffic all around.

"Did you enjoy the show?" Bill asked after a time.

"It was terrific," Sarah said, her speech a little slurred.

"And dinner?"

"As always, it was equally amazing and the wine was absolutely wonderful. Not too dry with a delightful hint of blackberries." Her unsteady eyes then trained upon him, as if she was concentrating all her will on the effort. "Mr. William Fallon, you have taught me well about the finer things in life and totally spoilt me into the bargain."

Bill blushed. "I like spoiling you, Sarah." His heart raced and he fidgeted with his hands. He thought hard about whether he should say what he longed to say, but in the end, he left it unspoken.

Sarah either didn't notice or ignored his shifty demeanor. "Tonight, now *that* was a celebration. To think I actually got the position!" She placed a delicate hand on Bill's wrist. "And it's all because you believed in me, Bill."

Bill chuckled, reveling in the touch of her hand. "Well, don't thank me until you see what you'll be doing."

"I never would've even been invited in the door, if you hadn't pulled the strings."

Bill's smile broadened. "You're starting at the bottom, Sarah. Don't expect to be covering the travesties in Africa just yet. Expect a little more of the mailroom kind of stuff in the early going."

"I don't care," Sarah said, her head falling back in a comical show of apathy. "We've all got to start somewhere!"

Bill drew a sharp breath to speak, to tell her now in this flourishing moment how he felt about her, why he wanted to help her find a job and fit in the city. But before he could get out the words, the cab pulled up to the curb and the driver announced their arrival. Bill took a ten dollar bill from his clip and handed it to the driver. Then he watched her slender form exit the cab. He followed closely behind.

"I can't believe we're here already," Bill said. "We could have walked it."

Sarah looked down at her ultra-high heels and giggled. "Not in these shoes. You would be carrying me, Bill Fallon, bad leg or not."

The two approached Bill's apartment building, arm in arm. The doorman opened the main street door to the foyer and welcomed them. Bill felt his hands begin to sweat as they took the elevator. He wondered if she could tell, given that his hands still held fast to her arm. If she could, she didn't show it. Instead, she hummed through the entire elevator ride to Bill's floor, only stopping when the doors slid smoothly open.

Bill jangled for his keys, then opened the door to his apartment and stepped to one side, allowing his guest to enter first. Sarah immediately kicked off her shoes, which flew across the room and thwacked against the opposite wall. She laughed aloud, clearly not trying to hide her own intoxication.

Bill took a quick look around the apartment – a place that no longer looked so much like a bachelor lived there, thanks to Sarah's influence. The framed picture of Amanda no longer hung on the wall. It had been replaced by a Matisse print that Sarah had chosen. He stared at it for a moment, wondering what in the hell he was supposed to do now. There was no denying the longing he felt for Sarah, but there was no way to act on it without destroying something beautiful.

She stumbled into him at that moment.

"You need coffee, girl," Bill said with a frown. He headed for the kitchen.

Sarah chuffed. "I need another drink is what I need."

"Haven't you had enough?" Bill called sternly from the kitchen. "A happy buzz can soon become a thumping headache."

When Bill returned, carrying a pair of empty glasses and a corked bottle of champagne, he found his company in lesser spirits than when he had left her. Indeed, Sarah appeared to have become drunkenly morbid.

"What if Jacob's *dead*," she said, accentuating the last word with surprising darkness. "Why would he want to go back into the bush?"

Bill said nothing. He looked down at the empty glasses in his hand like a rebuked child.

"It's *asking* to be killed. I'm so scared he's never coming home, Bill."

"Jake knows how to take care of himself, Sarah." Bill shook his head, wanting to change the subject. "You called the US 'home,' I noticed." He smiled as he said it, offering a little wink.

Sarah did not back down from her apparent sadness. "Where else am I supposed to call home?" She stalked toward the window, pulling the curtain back just far enough to look down on what had clearly become her favorite view. "I feel as if I'm drowning in my sorrows and rejoicing at the same time."

Bill felt his heart sink. "What do you mean by that?"

Sarah's shoulders began to heave as if she was crying. Bill took a step toward her, wanting to embrace her, but then realized with a start that he was still carrying champagne and glasses. He wheeled around to set them on the coffee table before striding over to Sarah. By then, Sarah had stopped shaking and had turned around to rest her back against the heavy glass.

"I've been here in New York for months now," she said. "And apart from that one letter, I still haven't seen or heard from my husband. We may as well not be married."

"But you said—"

"As for rejoicing," Sarah said, interrupting Bill as if she had read his mind, "I rejoice because you have brought about a transformation in me." She held her arms outstretched, looking down at herself as if inviting Bill to do the same. "You have made me what I am today, Bill Fallon. A confident, capable New York woman with a good job and a good home."

In that moment, Bill longed to take her into his arms, longed to kiss her. He felt wretched for feeling this way, but there was no two ways about it. It didn't matter whether this woman was married to his brother. He wanted her. Now and forever. He knew, though, that he would have to avoid this feeling. And so he deflected.

"You've been more than paying your way with your cooking. I tell you, Sarah, I've never eaten so well."

Sarah grinned, roiling up his desire once more. But just as he culled together the will to do as he pleased, she snapped him from his focus with a simple request.

"How about that drink?"

Bill smiled, despite the fact that he felt like screaming frustration from the inside out. "What would you like?"

"That champagne looked fine to me, garçon," she slurred.

Bill worked on uncorking the bottle while Sarah moved to sit silently on the couch. She watched him go through the motions with deep and inviting eyes. He poured two glasses to the brim and returned to where she was sitting, handing her one, careful to ensure she didn't spill it on herself. She took the glass and immediately sipped at the bubbly champagne. He sat down opposite her in an armchair.

Sarah took another sip before speaking again. "I have to apologize, Bill, because I'm not usually so forward, but I can see in your eyes that you want me."

Bill felt himself swoon. All at once, he loathed himself. How could he ever think that this beautiful thing, this lovely woman married to his brother, would want him? And how horrible he was to want it.

"I, I, uh," he stammered. "I'm sorry." He said the words in a tone that toed the line of ambiguity between statement and question.

"Don't apologize, Bill. I want you, also."

Bill felt short of breath. He practically fell to his knees in setting his glass on the coffee table between them. He felt rather ready to crawl on all fours to her, so reduced by her words to the state of simple beast. But before he could even set his glass on the table, she stoked his fires.

"You have done so much for me," she said, her eyes brimming again with tears as she looked away. She took a long swig of her champagne. "You have looked after me, taught me this world, held me when I cried for Jacob. You kept my spirits up when I was lost in self-pity and truly you made me feel like a part of the Fallon family. You are like my Rock of Gibraltar, Bill. Always there. Always helping me."

Bill projected a shuddering sigh. He didn't know what to think. He remained rooted to the edge of his chair, his feet supporting his weight in an unnatural position. He felt frozen, like the only thing that could reanimate him were the words of the woman who sat across from him.

Sarah looked him squarely in the eyes. "Bill, I have known for some time how you feel about me. If there was no Jacob in my life, you would be the only life I knew. Can you see how confused this makes me?"

Bill nodded. "That makes two of us."

Sarah suddenly stood, staggering a little. Bill stood just as quickly. He grabbed the glass from her, and then took her hand. In this way, he walked her to her bedroom. She flopped backwards onto the bedspread. Bill took the cover and pulled it down under her body. Sarah unzipped her skirt, apparently trying to wriggle out of it. Both excitedly and reluctantly, Bill helped her, sliding the fabric gently over her alluring curves and down over her slender legs. Her hips aloft, she unbuttoned her blouse. Again, she needed help, and she accepted it with eyes half-closed, half-inviting. Bill stared down at her. She lay on the bed now, stripped down to her lacy underwear. He seethed through an inaudible moan, then leaned over to pull the sheets down behind her and lace them up over her legs. In this way, he covered her – but beneath the silk, she appeared no less alluring.

She wriggled around under her cover, and in time, Bill realized that she must have been removing her bra and panties. There was no avoiding the swell he felt in his pants. If he didn't leave now, he would do something they would both regret. He turned, flailing for the door like a drunk lost in foggy darkness.

"Bill?" she cooed after him.

He turned heavily, but did not reply.

"Thank you for not taking advantage of me."

He shuddered and hoped she did not see it. "Yes," he said softly. "Yes."

"I will not tempt you again."

Her tone. The way she said the words. It was like a stake through his heart. He'd never felt so depressed in his life. And here he'd only done the right thing – done what good men do.

CHAPTER 21

Dusk was fast approaching as the company of eight men silently waited in the bush. The sun had gone down and the moon was rising. Jake could hear talking in the distance. Around the camp, an inconspicuous African village had been developed. Given that the village had been unknown to him, Morrison had suggested that he should be the one to run reconnaissance prior to the raid. Jake had protested, wanting to take on the mission himself. After a quick spat, Morrison finally caved, allowing Jake to go.

"I guess this vendetta of yours is serious," he said with a smile.

Jake merely nodded. He could practically feel the blood of his enemy – of the man who had mercilessly slaughtered his best friend in the world – warm upon his face.

When he had reached a line of sight with the camp, he crept on his belly for the final hundred yards. At the edge, his breathing slowed to a near stop, Jake came across an advance guard sleeping against a tree. Without sound, he crept up to the man, his knife clutched between his teeth. He would simply wake up dead. The guard slipped sideways to the ground, blood oozing out of the gash Jake had slit quietly into his throat.

The guard had died easily, and for this, Jake was thankful. But the gurgling sound that issued from his throat would be too loud. A second guard stood up to investigate just as Jake ducked back into the bush. Jake watched as the guard, apparently mindful of the possibility for a trap, fell to the ground and began to crawl toward him. Jake lay in waiting, his automatic gripped firmly in both hands. When the guard came within range, Jake fired a single silenced shot, hitting his crawling enemy squarely between the eyes.

Jake waited until there was no further movement before pressing forward, crawling along the ground until the camp came fully into view. He was now less than fifty yards from the village and the old game fishing camp. He refocused his night-vision binoculars for a closer look. He panned the tree line, moving past a tall figure before stopping and moving back again. The albino. He stood there in the night-vision lens as clear as day. Even as Jake watched him, he took a seat by a fire that crackled next to an old thatched fishing hut.

Jake removed his binoculars and drew a breath through his teeth. Calmer now, he looked through the lens again, scanning the camp. In short order, he found the man he had come for – the man with the scarred face. Jake swallowed, but there was no saliva. In his excitement, the adrenaline flowed freely. It was all he could do to settle down and count the complement of men flanking him. He noted that the tatty African village surrounding the camp had not been abandoned, despite its terrorist element. Women and children came and went freely, all of them passing a mindful eye to the scarred man at the edge of the lake.

Jake longed to cup his rifle's sight to his eye and take aim, longed to kill this man on his own, regardless of the consequences, but he knew that he could not. He had a mystery to unravel once this score had been settled – and a wife to return home to, after that. Running suicide missions wouldn't help anyone. So he finished doing his head count, finished gathering information on potential cover and strike directives, and crawled away as silently as he had arrived.

~ ~ ~

"I count fifteen," Jake said to a bleary-eyed Morrison. "But there could be more. They're all holed up near the old fishing camp, just like you thought."

"*Fifteen?*" Morrison repeated, sounding incredulous.

"Well . . . there were seventeen. But I, uh, encountered a couple of them in the bush as I approached camp."

"You didn't—"

"Silent kills, Morrison," Jake interrupted. "Relax."

"Jesus, man. You learn that shit in 'Nam?"

Jake nodded. "There are women and children in the village. It's possible there are more targets hiding in the mud huts. We could be dealing with more than fifteen."

"And there could be some serious peripheral casualties." Morrison sighed. "Did you see the designated targets, at least?"

"They were both there," Jake said through his teeth. "Larger than life."

"Fine." Morrison made a few military motions over his shoulders, signaling his men to fall into their flanking positions. "Let's go find your friend's killers."

Jake grinned hungrily, something that apparently gave Morrison pause.

"Hold on, man." He looked Jake squarely in the eyes. "You're not invited to this party unless you can remember the rules."

Jake rolled his eyes. He knew what was coming.

"Scarface and the albino – they get shots in the legs only. You got it?"

Jake nodded, furrowing his brow and turning away.

"No kill shots," Morrison urged. He grabbed Jake by the bicep and pulled him back to attention. "You got it?"

Jake groaned. "Jesus, Morrison." He shook off his commander's grip. "I got it."

Morrison looked genuinely relieved. "Good. Then we follow the path you cleared for us. Once we get by your dead lookouts, we'll spread out in a fan like wild dogs."

"Wild dogs?"

Morrison let out a mirthless chuckle as he led the party deeper into the bush. "Just another African wildlife strategy. You and I will be in the center, man. And we'll fan out and attack like wild dogs, driving our prey exactly the way we want them to run. They'll have a one-hundred-eighty-degree semicircle coming at them, and we're protecting all our troops by knowing exactly where all our guys are. This will give the enemy the feeling of being surrounded, all without us having to worry about friendly fire."

Jake grinned a bloodlust grin. "Sounds like fun."

Morrison turned and issued whispered orders that he and Jake would make the initial burst and that this would be the signal for open fire. Then the men, Morrison included, followed Jake in single file along the path he had created, each soldier ensuring he placed his foot on the exact spot as the man ahead of him.

When they reached the optimal point, an especially dark corner beside a rusted shed, Morrison waved to his men and they crept away in a semicircle, two of them on one side of Jake and Morrison, three on the other. Jake watched them take their positions in the bush through the green and semi-dark light of his night-vision goggles. He turned back to Morrison, who brought up his Uzi to waist level and nodded. With his eyes, he seemed to say, "Ready," and he fired a burst into the terrorist camp.

Instantly, the rest of the squad opened up with rapid fire, all of them advancing slowly as they retained their continuous hail of bullets. The camp came alive with screaming men and women.

Many ZIPRA returned fire without hesitation. Still, they fell back slowly from the continuous onslaught dealt by the RSF.

Women and children ran out of the huts and attempted to disappear into the bush. Terrorists continued to fire at anything that moved. The albino, clearly frustrated and angry, turned his fire on the fleeing women and children as if they were deserters. Bodies of women and children fell over each other as the explosive bursts of his AK-47 stripped the flesh off their backs. A dozen or more ZIPRA fighters already lay on the ground, moaning and dying as Morrison's force continued its advance in fan formation. The trained soldiers honed expertly and only on the terrorists in the camp, their guns turning disinterestedly away from the women and children.

In less than a minute, the ZIPRA fighters had been turned back. They ran for the bush, some of them dropping their guns as they scurried away. The younger of the RSF soldiers started to sweep the legs of the fleeing terrorists, bringing them down with constant fire. Left and right, men fell flat on their faces, then rolled onto their backs and held their legs in agony.

Only four of the remaining terrorists continued to return fire.

"I'm down! I'm down!" one of the RSF soldiers screamed.

Jake took one quick look to his right, but couldn't see who had fallen. A lull came in the firing, then. The soldiers moved hastily toward the old fishing camp. Jake felt his legs moving rapidly, but could feel nothing – the kind of adrenaline wave he had become used to in his years of conflict. He could see the valley now, muddied in the center, with sparse patches of brown-red grass waving on the perimeters. To the right, the dark waters of the lake twinkled with the light of the moon. Standing in silhouette was the old fishing hut. Jake could sense that if he could just reach this valley, he would find the man he'd been looking for all these months. He began to sprint, his finger still tense on the trigger.

His foot caught an exposed root and he tumbled to his knees. A small burst erupted from his Uzi, but no damage was done. He had simply fallen behind the rest of the pack – he had broken the rank and upset the formation of the wild dogs. He leapt to his feet, and just as he did so, he saw Johnson, the soldier who had been flanking him to his immediate right. Johnson had his eyes elsewhere, had his gun trained on the valley. He didn't see his attacker. Didn't see as the albino himself jumped out from behind a tree to engage him from the back. The albino fired a burst that ripped into the young soldier. Johnson fell to his knees in agony, his arm and shoulder shattered. The albino charged with a machete held high above his head. He brought the blow down, bearing on Johnson's neck. Time froze for Jake, but he felt his finger easing down on the trigger, felt himself taking aim on the albino's head.

Sound returned to him in the form of gunfire from his left. It was Morrison. His spray of bullets had relieved the albino of his head. Jake charged up to him, his heart pounding with surprise.

"I thought—"

"No more casualties," Morrison interrupted. "We've still got Scarface. We leave him alive."

Jake beamed, then got back into rank and moved on the camp. In only a few steps, he heard rustling in the trees beside him – right where he had left Morrison only moments ago. Instinctively, he ducked down into the brush.

"Put the guns down or I'll kill this ngulube (*pig*)!"

The voice was wretched, coarse. It made Jake's blood boil. He crawled through nearby brush, trying to get a view of its source. And there, around the next tree, he found it: the man he had stayed behind for, the man who had killed his best friend. Viewed through the night-vision goggles, the scar stood on his face in stark contrast. Scarface pressed the muzzle of his automatic into Morrison's ribcage. Morrison winced, but did not cry out.

His face remained contorted in a look of defiance that would chill most men to the bone. His hands gripped the arm slung round his throat.

Jake realized that the scarred terrorist was not looking in his direction. He only seemed to have eyes for the gunfire.

"Throw down your weapons!" Scarface repeated.

"Do no such thing," Morrison shouted. "Remember the orders. We want him alive."

"Alive!" the ZIPRA leader shouted incredulously. "Alive?"

"Salisbury wants to talk to you about the shooting down of a commercial aircraft," Morrison gasped through the tight grip around his neck.

Jake crawled soundlessly through the bush. In a moment, he would be behind the man who held his leader at gunpoint.

The scarred officer was now laughing. "A wonderful moment in history for our freedom fighters. So I am famous and they want me alive? That's mushe (*nice*), maningi mushe (*very nice*). Ngisi (*Englishman*), in another few months, this war will be over and we will rule. So take me alive. I'll see you kicked out of the new Zimbabwe."

Morrison struggled now for the first time. "I'm no Ngisi. I'm a bleddy fucking Rhodesian, you jovela buso (*gonorrhea face*). Remember that, kaffir."

As the confrontation got hotter, Jake slowly edged forward to within striking distance. The ZIPRA officer, clearly insulted by Morrison's remark, fired a single round into the RSF leader's arm. Morrison let out a scream as his bicep seemed to explode.

"Remember that, wena mhlope makanka (*you white jackal*)," the ZIPRA leader yelled.

Jake leapt out of the bush and charged toward the back of the large baobab tree behind the two warring leaders. Without sound, he swung around to the front of the two men, slashing his eight-inch knife in an upward backhand motion, burying it into the terrorist's mouth. He could hear the sound of breaking teeth and feel the knife penetrate the soft flesh, glancing only briefly as it pushed through the back of the skull. By the time he let go, the knife had come straight through the back of the terrorist's head, affixing him to the tree.

The ZIPRA officer, still clinging to life, looked at Jake with deep surprise. His weapon fell to the ground and he let go of his grip on Morrison. Then he slumped, the blood gurgling from his mouth, the knife holding him fast against the tree.

Morrison staggered to his feet. Holding his bleeding arm, he stared at the dying terrorist.

Jake retrieved Brian's passport from the front pocket of his military vest and shoved it in the dying man's face. "Have a good look, you son of a bitch! This guy had a name. He was Brian Wilson. He was here on vacation, and you butchered him, you piece of shit."

Morrison was clearly in extreme pain, but that didn't hold back his anger. "We wanted the fucking kaffir alive!"

"Not as much alive as your family wants you, Brendan," Jake snapped. Then his fury left him and he became respectful. "Sir, I couldn't stick with orders that allowed this prick to take another shot at you."

Morrison winced, staring down at his mangled arm. "Salisbury will be pissed," he said through his teeth.

"I could give a fuck."

The young soldier serving as emergency medic – Donald was his name, if Jake recalled correctly – approached Morrison and started to work on his butchered arm. As he did so, Morrison shouted orders to look for the wounded.

Jake stared with satisfaction at the dying ZIPRA officer. "This prick is still breathing and gurgling his ass off."

"Put him out of his misery," Morrison grunted. "You'd do that for a dog."

Jake took the ZIPRA's hands and put both of them on the handle of the knife sticking out of his mouth. The man was still alive enough to attempt to pull it out. Jake taunted him. "That's a boy. Pull it out. And when you do, you'll fall like a rock and bleed to death, just like Brian and the woman you raped to death."

Morrison stood and yanked the knife out of the man's mouth. He threw it to the ground, where it stuck between Jake's feet. "You learnt your shit in Vietnam, all right. You can be as cruel a bastard as he is, Jake. Enough is fucking enough. I'm a soldier."

The terrorist fell to the ground, gasping for air, his life's blood oozing out of his mouth and the split in the back of his head. Morrison fired a single shot into his forehead. The sound of his weapon echoed in the now silent bush, and in the distance, they could hear a helicopter panning the clear, still night, searching for their flares.

CHAPTER 22

It had been three months since she had heard any word from her Jacob, and three weeks since that uncomfortable moment with Bill, in which their mutual attraction had been made known. Things had been awkward between them for longer than she would have liked, but they sat now in a cab on the way back from the opera. Sarah had opened up to Bill for the first time in weeks, laughing at his jokes, leaning into him, even reaching up to caress his cheek at the end of the second intermission.

The opera had been insufferable, of course. She had never been one for the stage, but she always found the intermissions entertaining. They afforded her the opportunity to laugh at the affluent from a distance, and then pretend to be interested in their conversation whenever she was introduced. She could watch sweet Bill work the room. He always seemed to know everyone. And then, of course, there were the drinks.

Before coming to America, Sarah had never been much of a drinker and never smoked. But for whatever reason – whether it was the stress of being in a new country or the confusion of her feelings whenever she was around Bill – she now drank like a fish and smoked like a chimney. This opera had been no different.

The pair of fifteen-minute intermissions had proven ample time for her to choke down four martinis, and she still swayed in her seat, even now, as they rode home following the final act.

Bill's hand had graced hers. She had felt warmth rise into her face, but she was happy. And for the first time, she'd looked into his eyes and seen nothing of Jake there. Only Bill. What she saw pleased her. She saw a handsome man, an excellent provider, and perhaps the kindest man she had ever known.

And then he'd said it.

"I love you."

Her heart fluttered and dropped as she turned away. She felt a tear come to her eye, but then immediately disappear. She bit her lip, wishing that he hadn't said what he did, wishing that it didn't make her feel the way it did. She wanted to be offended. Disgusted. Upset. But what she felt was very different indeed. What she felt was joy. Conflicted joy, but joy nonetheless.

"That was some third act, wasn't it?" she asked. She dared not face Bill, for she knew the look of dejection she would find on his face would cripple her.

~ ~ ~

Her head began to swirl a little as she prepared for bed. She brushed her teeth, let her hair down, and began to remove her dress. As she unlaced the straps over her shoulders, she felt a presence. She gasped as she turned to find Bill there. He stood in the doorway, sheepishly staring at the floor.

"I'm sorry to startle you," he said. "It's just that I was wondering why you didn't respond to what I said in the cab."

"Oh," she said, placing a hand to her chest. She wasn't embarrassed or angry, simply confused and overwhelmed.

"Maybe you didn't hear me. What I said was—"

"I heard you, Bill."

He stopped and drew a breath, which he held in apparent excitement. "And?"

She sighed and went to him. She knew it would be a mistake, but she threw herself into his tender embrace. "Bill, you know I love you, too."

Against her cheek, she could feel his heart beating in his chest. They held each other for a long while, Bill's hands working up and down her back. She dreaded the question that she knew to be coming, because she still didn't really know how to answer it.

"What about Jake?" Bill asked, sounding dejected – as if the fact that this woman was married to his brother had only just now occurred to him.

She pushed away, looking him in the eyes. "I will always love Jacob." She watched him as he seemed to shrink several inches in height. "To the day I die, I will always love that man."

He appeared almost ready to fall backward.

"But I love you, too," she added quickly.

He straightened up. "What the hell does *that* mean?"

She looked at her feet, so small entwined with his. She wasn't sure how to answer that question, but she found herself piecing things together even as she spoke. "You are here and Jacob is not. Who else *can* I love?"

"Oh!" he said, tossing his arms in the air. "This is love out of sympathy, then."

She darted back into him, feeling his arms wrap slowly around her. "Of course not, Bill. I love you very deeply."

~ ~ ~

Bill left the bedroom and crossed the hall to his own room. She could hear the door close behind his en suite bathroom. Sarah semi-staggered and went into her own bathroom, removing her dress and her underwear en route. She focused on her nude reflection in the bathroom mirror as she took off her make-up. She brushed her teeth, then used the bidet, and finally put on her dressing gown. She left the bathroom, the cold water sobering her somewhat and stared for a moment at her empty bed. Damn her eyes, she had hoped to find him there – waiting impishly in the half-dark. But he had remained in his bedroom, a man of principle, if not one who could control his heart.

She sighed. She had to be with him now. There would be no sleep unless she submitted to her desires.

Barefoot, she entered his bedroom and slipped silently into his bed. She giggled softly as she listened to Bill gargling as a finale to his ablutions. Just as he opened the bathroom door and flipped off the light, she settled down in the bed and turned on her side as if going to sleep. It was not long before Bill made it known that he had noticed the lump in his bed. He crossed to her side and looked down at her. She did her best to look asleep.

"Sarah," he said slowly, "what are you doing here?"

"I am going to sleep."

"In my bed?"

"In your bed." She drew the comforter over her shoulder. "I'm lonely."

Out of the corner of her eye, she watched Bill get into bed. He appeared to be wearing only his shorts. She waited for him to take her into his embrace, but instead, he turned away from her and faced the opposite direction – an honorable man, even in the face of the ultimate temptation. She sighed as though she was settling down for the night, but she turned at the neck to keep an eye on him. Bill continued to stare in the opposite direction. Even without seeing his face, she could sense that he was worried and confused. She wanted nothing more than to alleviate these worries, to make him feel better. And so she snuggled up behind him, draping an arm over his neck, pressing her nude form into his back.

Finally, he turned and faced her, his eyes closed as he whispered, "Goodnight again, Sarah Fallon."

Sarah waited for him to open his eyes before she spoke again. "Love me, Bill," she whispered. "Love me like the woman I am." She kissed him on the lips. "I need you."

Bill seemed to collapse into himself as he returned the kiss. Sarah immediately responded, pressing into him and running her fingers through his hair. She rolled onto her back, her fingers sliding down into his underwear. Bill winced as she found him.

She sighed. "Nkospezulu (*god in heaven*) forgive me."

Bill removed the sheet, exposing her firm body, her erect nipples. He cupped one of her breasts and leaned in to kiss her. Sarah moaned slightly at the touch, but didn't resist. Bill pulled down his shorts with his free hand, Sarah still holding him. He kicked them off in the bed and rolled over on top of her.

"God forgive me."

CHAPTER 23

Jake and Morrison sat in the departure area of Salisbury Airport in late December. They were smoking and waiting for an early-morning Victoria Falls flight to be called. Morrison wore civvies, his arm in a sling. Jake wore jeans, sneakers, and a t-shirt with a picture of Victoria Falls plastered on the front.

"No, there's not much the Department of Manpower can do now, my friend," Morrison said, blowing smoke. "You just shouldn't have killed that bloke. He was under the impression he'd outlast the conflict, become a hero of the revolution."

"Oh, I know that." A stream of smoke escaped through Jake's pursed lips. "But when he plugged you in the arm, it gave me the opportunity to avenge old wounds."

Morrison shook his head incredulously, a little smile forming on his lips. "Well, I guess you're happy now, Jake. And it's all over for you. For us, it's only just begun."

Jake sat back and thought about Morrison's future. He imagined his brief commanding officer watching the new and inevitable independence come to life.

"So tell me again why you're going to Zambia," Morrison said, breaking the silent reverie.

"Well, you don't want me here," Jake said sarcastically.

"Fancy that."

Jake became suddenly serious. "Doesn't really matter, anyway."

"Another score to settle?" Morrison asked.

Jake squinted his eyes shut. In the short time he had known this man, he'd gotten to where he could read him like a book. Still, he deflected. "Zambia's a country that I can legally go to now, since nobody ever knew I was there in the first place."

"That hasn't answered my question."

Jake sighed, realizing he'd never get around this one, even if he tried. Morrison was too stubborn. "I have to see some people who helped me. Right a wrong. And . . . do a little digging into local history."

"About the country?"

Jake looked his friend squarely in the eyes. "About my wife."

Morrison offered a knowing smile. "Ah, personal stuff. My father always said to stay away from the personal." He stood then and offered his free hand. "Good luck, Jacob Fallon. It wasn't always fun to be in your company, but it sure was bleddy interesting."

Jake smiled and shook Morrison's hand. When the handshake broke, the injured man paused and looked at the piece of paper he'd been slipped.

"Your address in the States?" he said, confused. "Are you sure you want a so-called white Rhodesian racist to visit you one day? What would the rest of the world say?"

Jake chuckled. "I learned a lot in my time here, Brendan. You're no more racist than the terrorists I've killed."

Morrison nodded with a smile.

"Not everything's black and white, my friend. There are other colors in the rainbow. You're welcome in my world any day, any time."

The public address system sounded, announcing the boarding of the Victoria Falls flight. Jake turned and took Morrison's hand once more. They shook hands, then gave each other a quick embrace. Morrison turned and headed toward the exit door as Jake departed in the opposite direction.

~ ~ ~

The phone rang in Bill's apartment. Sarah lay beside him in his bed, asleep. He put the receiver to his ear and listened as he placed his arm on her bare back. She stirred and turned to face him, lying silently, watching Bill do all the listening. After a moment she got out of bed and started to put on her dressing gown. He kept the phone to his ear and concentrated on her naked body from the rear as she finally fastened the gown. Then she strode from the room. Bill had slept with her enough times now to know her routine – here she was slipping into the kitchen to pour two cups from the automatic coffeemaker, a black one for Bill and one for herself doused with sugar and cream.

Bill went through the motions of talking with the man on the other end of the line. And with every passing turn of phrase, he became more confused in his emotions. By the time the conversation had come to an end, the source of his confusion sashayed back into the bedroom with two hot cups in her hands.

Bill hung up the phone and sat up in bed.

"What's wrong?" Sarah asked as she placed the cups on the bedside cabinets.

"That was my father."

"So?"

Bill had trouble looking her in the eyes. "You'll be pleased to hear that Jake's very much alive and well."

Sarah gasped in what looked like sheer joy – a surprising amount of joy, from Bill's perspective. Hadn't she just woken up next to him, after all?

"My father got word from our bank that Jake accessed his account from Barclays Bank in Livingstone, Zambia," Bill said. "My father wants to know if we have any idea as to what's going on."

Sarah jumped up and down like a child.

"You look . . . pleased."

"Pleased?" Sarah squealed. "I'm elated. Are you not also pleased, Bill?"

Bill ignored her excitement. "Livingstone. What the hell's he doing in Zambia?"

"I've no idea. How can we find out?"

"Questions, questions." Bill took a quick sip of his coffee. "We're asking each other questions and have no answers. How the hell can I find out?"

"More questions."

Bill felt himself take on a certain degree of animosity, and it was reflected in his scolding tone. "We'll have to wait. I'm sure there's a reason."

Sarah looked deflated. Sad.

"And for your information," Bill continued, "I'm *overjoyed* that my brother is all right. What concerns me is what the hell we're going to do about us."

"Us?" Sarah said softly.

"Sarah, for more than a month now, I've been sleeping with my brother's wife."

Sarah took on a defensive posture. "You think I don't know who is the brother's wife here?"

Bill chuffed.

"And as for what to do, I have no idea." She paused for a moment, apparently thinking deeply. "I love you, Bill. But as I've said so many times before, I love Jacob and always will love him."

"We'll be like freaking Mormons," Bill said sarcastically. "Except, instead of two wives, it's two husbands. My mother will be charmed."

"This is no time for sick humor." Sarah's lovely eyebrows grew taut over her tearful eyes. "We have problems that you and I as adults have to address."

Bill chuckled darkly. "My God, you've come a long way with your dialogue."

"You taught me well." Sarah sighed. "Bill, I'm moving back into my room. It's the only thing to do. By Christmas, Jake may be home and we can sit down and discuss this."

Bill felt furious. "I'm not discussing this with him. How can I discuss what a heel he has for a brother? If I told him I slept with his wife, it would kill him."

"Bill, I love him."

"Yeah, and it seems you love me, too."

Frustrated, Bill jumped out of bed and pulled on a track suit. He sat on the edge of the bed, fastening the laces of his sneakers. When he was finished, he got up and headed toward the bedroom door. Sarah asked where he was going.

Bill felt awash in conflicting emotions. He could fight for his position in her life or he could lose the woman he loved. "I'm going out to get some fresh air. I'm annoyed, confused, upset, and angry and I fear I can only lose you in the end."

Sarah reached out to him, but he refused the contact and left the bedroom in a hurry. He stalked to the front door and slammed it behind him, leaving Sarah in his wake. In his mind's eye, he could see her weeping into her pillow, but it didn't bother him any. He wanted her to hurt in this moment. He felt that she deserved it.

CHAPTER 24

Due to the Zimbabwe war for independence, the Victoria Falls Bridge had been closed in protest by the Zambia government. Access to Rhodesia, either by road or by air, was disallowed. Jake had established that if he took a flight, it would have to be routed via the diminutive Botswana airport of Selebi-Phikwe, an equally small mining town which was situated in the northeastern part of the country, as there were no restrictions between Zambia and Botswana. Thus, at this semi-desert location, a Zambian plane would land and either a South African Airways or Air Botswana aircraft would take over for the completion of the trip into Rhodesia. In keeping with British government sanctions against Rhodesia, this was yet another farcical endeavor designed to isolate Rhodesia from the rest of the world.

With the severance he had received from the Department of Manpower, Jake would outfit himself as a tourist working his way through Africa as inexpensively as possible. He bore the appropriate equipment to suit the purpose, down to the overstuffed knapsack on his back. After striking out several times in hitching a ride from the Victoria Falls Hotel, he finally was fortunate enough to meet an Indian store owner from Livingstone willing to offer Jake a lift.

The ride was uneventful over a route of frequent use, many landlocked families and friends having beaten it down over the years of overcoming government rulings on sanctions in either Zambia or Rhodesia. When he was dropped off at his location, Jake thanked the driver, declining the invitation to the Indian trader's home to indulge in a homemade chicken vindaloo. He stepped out of the cab of the rumbling truck and made his way into Barclays Bank. There, it seemed to take an eternity to solicit the manager's help in transferring a quantity of his US dollar funds. He was advised that he would not be able to gain access to any cash until the following day, and was thus forced to spend the night at the small casino hotel and wait out the transfer.

The next day, funds in hand, he rented a Mazda pickup truck from Duly Motors. Following his map on the Great North Road, Jake passed through the village of Zimba, then the small towns of Kalomo and Choma until finally he found the Batoka turn-off to Sinazongwe, the same road he had first travelled with Sarah. Morning bled into afternoon before he finally pulled the pickup into the dusty road beside his ultimate destination.

He went straight to the back door, where he knew he would find the kitchen.

"Father Bwana Jacob!" came a voice the moment he made his presence known. It was Shadrick, and by the look of him, he was quite excited.

Jake smiled and shook Shadrick's hand vigorously. "Shadrick, you old fox! Looks like Sister Margaret stitched you up well and you've made a great recovery."

"Yes, Father Bwana."

"And your matwana (*child*)?"

The old African hung his head. "She has not come home."

"I'm very sorry, Madala," Jake said sadly.

Father Burke, apparently overhearing the conversation, came into the kitchen. He stood in his usual attire of shorts and a t-shirt, his face pressed into a broad smile. "Jacob Fallon! A sight for sore eyes, you are!"

Jake smiled. "Father Burke . . . my man of the moment with far-reaching arms. Through the intercession of the archdiocese, Sarah and I were plucked from a certain death." He rushed forward and grabbed Father Burke in a bear hug.

The priest returned the hug, and then they stepped back from each other. "Think nothing of it. How's our Sarah?"

Jake explained the fight on the edge of the lake, how he found the bag full of private documentation and regained his memory. He informed that Sarah was in the United States, safe with his family, and made it abundantly clear to Father Burke that she would never have been there without his help.

"And why aren't you in America with your new wife, my boy?" Father Burke asked.

Jake gritted his teeth. He hadn't planned on getting right down to it, but there was no sense in beating around the bush. "Loose ends," he grunted.

Father Burke nodded his head back as if sensing a coming storm. "Bring us some tea," he said to Shadrick. "No, no, wait a moment; let's have a brandy and Coke. Okay with you, Jacob?"

"Okay," Jake said with a nod. "And it's 'Jake.' My mother calls me Jacob. Sarah calls me Jacob. And that's enough with the Jacob. I'm Jake."

The priest clapped his hands and rubbed them together as if in agreement.

"My memory is so clear, Joe. I come from a wealthy family in the Philadelphia area. I know who I am and what I've done. And I've done a lot."

"Such as?"

"I got the bastards that killed my friend."

Father Burke performed the sign of the cross and said a silent prayer. Then he clapped Jake on the back and led him into the living room. "Come. Let's keep things simple. At least until we've had a few."

~ ~ ~

"Have you forgotten the last thing you said to me?" Jake asked, now halfway into his second brandy and Coke.

"What was that?" Father Burke said, but it was clear he was quite certain he remembered. "Remind me."

"You never got to baptize our baby. That's unusual, right?"

"Ah." Father Burke took a healthy swallow of his drink – his third, the older man being quite an efficient drinker. "That, I do remember. But I've had time to think on it these past six months and have decided that Willie Caldwell's explanation suits me just fine."

"Which was?"

"Your baby was very badly deformed . . . and I'm not sure if you're aware of this, my son, but that kind of birth is considered a bad omen for the locals."

"Is that so?" Jake didn't believe a word of it.

Father Burke, oblivious, rocked back in his chair. "I'm afraid so, Jake." He took another good slug of his drink and then motioned for Shadrick to fetch another. "These drinks are so weak." He looked down into his empty glass, then with his thumb, motioned in the direction of the kitchen. "The old bugger helps himself to my brandy and waters it down so it looks okay. When it really gets light in color, I jump all over him."

Jake nodded, but didn't tear his mind from the subject of his child. Father Burke seemed to notice.

"The locals wanted to bring in a Nyanga *(witch doctor)*, you know," he said almost defensively. "But Willie wasn't having any of that kind of unchristian nonsense at his hospital. So he took the body up to Mazabuka and had it buried there."

"But, Father—"

"I don't want to speak of this matter anymore, Jake. It's not healthy to rehash such things."

Jake sighed. He knew that there was more to this story. There was a lie in there somewhere. Not from Father Burke. No, the kindly priest's eyes suggested that he, too, had a hard time believing some of the things coming out of his mouth. But that made it all the more frustrating to Jake Fallon. He was close to the truth, but not even the man he could trust the most was capable of unraveling it for him.

In any case, Jake decided to change the subject. "Well, that's not why I came here, anyway, Father," he lied. "I came here because I wanted to reimburse you for the boat we took. And for all your covert assistance. I'd like to send a check to the mission once I return to the States, but I wanted to make sure it was all right with you first."

Father Burke offered a humble smile just as Shadrick returned with a full tray of brandy, Coke, and ice. "That's mighty generous, son." He leaned forward to prepare his own drink this time. "I'm sure that any donation would be gladly welcomed at the mission."

Jake grew suddenly tired of talking to his friend. He had come here for answers about his baby, and to this point, had gotten none. So he figured he would turn the attention of the investigation to someone else who had been present at the birth. "Where's Sister Margaret? I'd like to thank her, too, for all she did."

Father Burke sighed. "I'm afraid that after all that happened to her that night you escaped, she felt compelled to leave. She's back in Dublin for a spell. At least until she can get the memory of the attempted rape out of her mind."

Jake's shoulders slumped with regret. "I understand."

"We've got a new old maid assigned to us now," Father Burke said. "A real peach of a woman."

Jake nodded.

"Well, hell." Father Burke raised his glass. "To Sister Margaret!"

Jake clinked his glass to the priest's, a slow smile forming as he watched the older man down his fourth drink of the evening.

"It is a Saturday, after all," Father Burke said, his face growing red. "The night's still a pup, but with some serious drinking, it'll be a full-grown bitch tomorrow morning."

Jake chuckled.

Father Burke prepared another drink for himself and for Jake, then held up his glass, laughing. "Well, sláinte *(health)*. And when we finish drinking, you can retire to the infamous belfry bedroom."

Father Burke's jovial face brought another smile to Jake's lips. They lifted their glasses and toasted each other and continued to consume brandy and Cokes late into the humid evening.

~~~

Jake dreamt of Sarah for what seemed to be the entire night. He smoked several cigarettes alone, as if waiting for her to creep into his bed. But she was several thousand miles away and he wondered what she was doing. It was an uncomfortable and restless night until he finally awoke the following morning in the belfry bedroom with a sharp hangover pain behind his left eye. He lifted his bleary head off the coarse pillow to see Father Burk's catechist, a dwarfish little man going up and down with the rope, ringing the church bell with gusto. It was loud and intolerable, and through the mist of a previous night's drinking, he recalled Quasimodo. He shook his head and held his hands on his ears until the catechist was finished.

The little man dropped to the floor, and without saying a word, mischievously smiled at Jake and left, passing Father Burke in the doorway. Father Burke, apparently hardened by his years in Africa, did not have the appearance of a man who had just woken up from a night of drinking. He was dressed for business in a pair
~~~

of dark trousers, a white shirt, and a Roman collar. Jake threw his legs out of the bed and pulled on his jeans. With his bare feet on the polished concrete floor, he sat there on the edge of the uncomfortable horsehair mattress, smiling at Father Burke's attire.

"Join me for a coffee before you go?" Father Burke asked.

"Will I ever," Jake said. "I forgot about the bells and your crazy-ass catechist."

Father Burke smiled. "Jonas."

"Jonas. Anyway, after that shit, I could really use coffee. Lots and lots of coffee."

"It's Shadrick's day off, I'm afraid." Father Burke turned and beckoned for Jake to follow. "So you'll have to help yourself to the coffee in the kitchen. As for me, I've three masses today, and must be off."

Despite what he'd said, the priest did indeed stay for a cup of coffee. Two, in fact. He tarried there in his comfortable wicker chair right up until the point where his parishioners would be cooking in the hot morning sun and his converts might have a change of heart. So with a start, he stood and took his leave. The two shook hands through the open window of the priest's Land Rover.

With Father Burke now out of sight, Jake didn't waste any time. He stalked back to the belfry room and collected his belongings. He returned to the main house and took a welcome shower in the priest's bathroom. Then he dressed and ensured that he had all his belongings. He would visit Dr. Caldwell today. To hell with what Father Burke thought had happened the day Sarah gave birth; he would find his answers today. He would find the truth.

And then, as if in answer to an unspoken prayer, a familiar woman appeared in the doorway. He knew her as a nurse from Dr. Caldwell's hospital – a young woman who had been kind enough to provide him with updates on the birth of his child, despite the chaos all around at the time. Still, he could not quite recall her name.

"Oh, hello," he said, squinting at the sun that poured in behind the young woman with slight shoulders and tight, curly hair.

"Betty," she said, pointing to herself as if sensing his confusion.

He nodded. "Betty! You're the nurse from the hospital. What can I do for you?"

The young woman took a quick glance over her shoulder, then spoke in a voice just above a whisper. "Bwana, I need to talk to you."

"Come in, Betty." He stepped aside and motioned toward a chair in the corner of the kitchen.

Betty entered, but instead opted to stand behind the door. "I have to tell you something." She sounded quite nervous.

"What's wrong? You look like you're hiding behind the door."

"I don't want to be seen."

Jake's heart skipped. "What's going on?"

Betty shivered through a sigh. "Nobody knows I'm here. Not the Father or the Sister. Not even Caldwell. But I heard through the vine that you were in town. Bwana Fallon, I'm a Christian and I can't be quiet any longer."

Jake's breathing slowed to a near stop. "What's wrong, Betty?"

"The baby," Betty blurted. "Sarah's baby . . . that baby did *not* die."

Jake staggered backward and flopped into one of the kitchen chairs. He'd long suspected something like this, of course. He'd stayed behind in Africa for just such a possibility. But to hear it now – spoken aloud in no uncertain terms – was almost more than he could take. Betty did not move from her hidden position. Her dark face was lined with sorrow. It seemed to grey with fear as tears filled her eyes.

After a time, Jake lifted his head as if it was made of lead. "Where is my son?"

"Daughter," Betty corrected.

He buried his face in his hands and started to whimper. "A daughter. I have a daughter."

"Yes, Bwana."

"Where is my child?" He lifted his head again, anger now in his eyes.

"Please, please, Bwana. Don't shout and don't blame me. It was the white one, the doctor. He was to blame."

"Dr. Caldwell?"

"Yes."

Jake could hardly contain his anger now. "Why?"

Betty seemed to grow more upset with each moment. "I cannot tell you that. He will kill me."

Jake's mind reeled. Only one name came to mind. One name that could be responsible for such a dark thing. But he would need confirmation.

~ ~ ~

Jake drove like a man possessed. He had his destination, and he had his vendetta, thanks to Betty. En route, he thought about all the things he had learned from the poor girl: about how she had been threatened into silence by Caldwell; about how she had wept openly in fear even as he stood and comforted her, forgave her; about how she had quaked and run away like a little girl scorned by her mother even after the truth had come out – but not until she'd given him the next bit of information he would need to exact his revenge on the men who betrayed him. With quivering lips, she told Jake exactly where he could find the birth and death records in Caldwell's hospital. And it was here where Jake now drove.

Around the next bend, the building stood. It flashed into Jake's sight like a distant memory. He pulled up beside it and threw the pickup into park. Then stepped out and made his way into an office that he hadn't seen in what felt like decades. He found the entry hall empty. He assumed he had either beaten Betty here or she had gone home to avoid the confrontation she suspected to be coming. In any case, Jake had to knock on the door of the office in back.

"Who is it?" came a familiar voice.

Jake pushed through the door and stopped in front of the desk with his hand outstretched. "Dr. Willie, how are you?" he asked with a smile.

Caldwell was clearly astonished as he took the extended hand. "Jacob, what are you doing here?"

"I got my memory back and was visiting Father Burke." Jake kept his tone cordial and genuine. "I just wanted to say hello and thought perhaps you could have one last look at the leg where you removed the stitches."

"How wonderful!" Caldwell stood up from his chair. "You know, getting one's memory back is no small thing. I'd like to hear all about it." He then turned to the overcrowded shelves behind him and took down a box of swabs. He placed the box on his desk. "But first, we'll check the leg, so drop your pants and sit down."

Caldwell placed both of his hands flat on the desk to steady himself as he stood. With speed and exacting action, Jake grabbed a fistful of swabs in a ball, and with his other hand, brought his knife down on the back of the doctor's hand, slicing through to the wood and pinning the hand to the desk. As Caldwell's mouth opened to scream, Jake stuffed it full of swabs. Caldwell flopped back in his chair, blood oozing from his hand, his eyes rolling around in his head.

Jake grabbed the knife by the hilt. "I'm taking this out now. So don't touch the swabs in your mouth. I don't want to hear a sound from you."

Caldwell nodded in silence as his face grimaced in agony. Jake swiftly withdrew the knife, and the blood pumped profusely out of the back of Caldwell's hand.

Jake continued in a cold, calculating tone. "You asked me what I'm doing here. Well, I'll tell you. I'm here because you owe me a daughter."

Caldwell's head moved from side to side in denial. Jake snatched the doctor's other hand and slammed it down on the desk. Caldwell's eyes were red, filled with terror, the tears of pain flowing freely. He spat out the swabs at the sight of the knife in the air.

"Please, God! No more, no more! I'll tell you everything."

Jake turned the knife over and held it, business end up. "If I suspect one lie comes from your rotten being, I'll impale you on this blade right up the ass. And then I'll sit and watch you bleed to death."

"Please," Caldwell whined as he shook his head. "No more."

Jake stuck the knife back into the desk and picked up the bleeding hand. He went behind Caldwell's desk and took a bottle of peroxide off the shelf. He then poured peroxide directly onto the wound. The doctor moaned at the bubbling liquid on the back of his hand as Jake put a bundle of swabs on the wound and bandaged it.

"There. All better. But I suggest you get that stitched later."

Caldwell moaned.

"Now it's answer time. Where's my child?"

The doctor blurted out through his pain. "Samuel Cameron. He has the child."

"You fuck!" Jake screamed. "What did you do, sell our child?"

Frantically, Caldwell explained that it was not like that. He said that Sarah was Cameron's daughter and that Cameron had always supported her, unseen. Jake listened intently as he heard the entire story once again of how Cameron was madly in love with Sarah's mother, but remained married and even had a daughter – a pretty blonde girl named Rebecca. According to Caldwell, Cameron's affair with Sarah's mother sent his marriage into a spiral, and only a few years ago, his wife had passed away.

"She never could take his fraternizing with the natives," Caldwell said through his teeth.

"He may have supported Sarah, but he never loved her."

Caldwell clutched his hand. "In his way he did. But only because of her mother. He promised in my presence that he would look after her."

"So that includes stealing babies?" Jake barked.

Caldwell simpered. He seemed now incapable of looking Jake in the eye.

Jake found this curious, and his mind flashed to something he hadn't thought of before. "What's he got on you, Caldwell?"

The doctor began to cry fitfully. "I'm a gambler! The casino in Livingstone knows me only too well. I have run the mission hospital into almost ruin a couple of times. Cameron always pulls me out . . . at a price."

Jake stepped forward, brandishing the knife threateningly. "What does he want with my child?"

Caldwell balled up in his chair, turning away from his attacker. He explained that Jake had nothing to do with it. That Sarah was the beginning and end of the story. "Cameron's known about you from the first time you set foot in Siavonga." He sounded almost as if he were laughing through his tears. "He could have had you picked up by government immigration officers, or worse, by the army and at any time he chose."

"The baby!" Jake demanded.

Caldwell shook his head as if righting himself. "Cameron wanted to continue controlling a piece of Sarah's life. He knew you couldn't do anything about it because you're here illegally."

Jake fumed. "And what about Sarah? She wasn't here illegally. He must be one warped fucker to take away a woman's most cherished creation."

"That's Cameron. The ultimate ruler of his own domain."

Jake sat down, already planning what he must now do. He thought for such a time and at such depth that he practically forgot about Caldwell.

"What now?" Caldwell whimpered. "Before I bleed to death."

Jake leaned forward, wiping the blood from his knife with a cloth he retrieved from the doctor's desk. "Here are the rules. And so help me God, if you break any of them or repeat a word of this to anyone, here's what will happen, and I have no qualms." He stopped cleaning the knife and looked Caldwell coldly in the eyes. "Firstly, understand that since last we met, I have killed some thirty to thirty-five terrorists and would give their comrades all they would need to believe that you are the man with whom they should seek revenge. All it takes is a little evidence, and I have it. Secondly, I'll make sure nobody's in your family home in Charlotte, North Carolina, before I burn it to the ground. Do you understand me, Doctor?"

"Yes, yes, I understand."

"If you even hint that we've met or I hear that Cameron gets wind of this, you're a dead man."

Caldwell was a beaten man. "What do you want?"

"Where do you keep the birth records?"

The doctor pointed to the cabinet beside the door. Jake smiled at the thought that Betty was right. He walked over to the cabinet and pointed to a drawer, looking around at Caldwell for confirmation. Caldwell motioned that it was the next drawer down.

Jake opened the drawer and fumbled amongst the files. He turned once more to Caldwell for help.

"The file is under the letter 'M,'" Caldwell said. "That's for 'Malumbo,' which was Sarah's mother's name. I don't even know if that was her real name. That's what I got from Cameron."

Jake withdrew the file and read the content. "It states here that the baby's father was unknown. I should stick you like a pig, you piece of shit."

Jake returned to the desk with a blank birth certificate document in his hand. He threw the pad on the desk in front of the doctor. "I stuck you in the left hand so you'd still have your good hand to fill out a new certificate. One with the child's true parents, true names."

Caldwell didn't offer any resistance. Jake stood over him in an intimidating fashion as he began to write clearly and slowly. When he had completed the task, he stamped the document and handed it to Jake.

Jake examined it, then, satisfied that it was in order, folded the document and placed in an envelope he retrieved off the desk. "Remember what I said, old man. One word is all it'll take."

The doctor nodded, clearly still in pain.

"I may call you from the American embassy. If I do, you will confirm the contents of this document and the fact that you delivered our baby."

"I promise you I will," Caldwell whispered. "I'm glad it's over."

Jake broke into a crooked smile. "Oh, it isn't over yet."

Caldwell's eyes widened as he seemed to cower further into his chair.

Jake's eyes went from threatening to kind in an instant. "We've got to take care of this hand."

Caldwell sighed with clear relief.

"You have a bottle of scotch?"

The doctor offered a weary sigh. "In the second drawer of my desk."

Jake withdrew the bottle from the drawer and took a deep swig. He then put the bottle to Caldwell's lips. The doctor gladly gulped down a couple of strong gulps. Jake pulled the bottle away, and with a quick swing, brought it crashing down on the edge of the desk. He then picked up a piece of broken bottle and jammed it into Caldwell's hand. Caldwell screamed.

"That's with compliments from Sarah Malumbo," Jake barked.

Caldwell searched for clarity with his eyes.

"We had an accident with the bottle," Jake said tersely. "Have you got that loud and clear?" Then he started to shout for help. "Nurse, nurse come in here quickly! We've had an accident!"

Betty, apparently having arrived sometime during the fray, appeared at the door and looked knowingly at Jake. Jake ushered her to the doctor's side.

CHAPTER 25

The small town of Monze had little to offer, with the exception of a couple of fuel stations, useful as a refueling spot on the Great North Road from Lusaka to Livingstone. Roughly ten miles to the west of the town was the old site of Fort Monze, one of the first police posts established by the colonial powers in the old Northern Rhodesia, now Zambia. There was, of course, the local social country club, which kept many of the town's rich quite happy. And there was a neglected graveyard, a monument in the shape of a cross, a farmer's co-op, a bevy of Indian supply stores, and Barclays and Standard Banks.

It was less than a week from Christmas as Jake followed a white Mazda pickup – this one in much better condition than the one he had rented – into town. As he watched the taillights ahead of him flash on and off, he remarked to himself that it was going to be yet another strange Christmas with no possibility of snow and nothing but continuous African heat. He assumed that his parents, and likely Sarah, would be at the Bahamian villa, but he always missed the snow.

The vehicle he followed pulled up alongside the Indian general store. A full two days of reconnaissance had told him that the woman who stepped out of the driver's seat was Rebecca Cameron, an attractive twenty-five-year-old blonde with a well-sculpted figure and long, slim legs. She wore short shorts, sunglasses, a tight t-shirt, and flip-flops. She fumbled in the cab for her bag, slammed the door, and went into the store.

Jake waited from his vantage point just up the road, passing the time by sharpening his knife on the wheel wrench of his rented Madza vanette, the local name for a pick-up truck. In a few minutes, Rebecca returned to her vanette, followed by two tall Africans. The men loaded sacks into the back of the vehicle. Rebecca talked and laughed with them, then got into the Mazda and drove away. Jake started up his vanette and slowly followed.

Rebecca's own Mazda Vanette turned into a fenced yard containing tractors, ploughs, and other farm equipment: the local farmer's co-op. She parked the pickup and headed for the building. Jake waited until she was out of sight before he parked beside her and got out. He opened the hood of his vanette and unclipped the distributor cap, removed the points, and started to file them. When he was satisfied with his intent, he checked underneath his vehicle. But his intentions were less than noble. Certain that he was unwatched, he rolled under Rebecca's Mazda and slit the fanbelt. He then got up and coolly wandered into the building.

His only hope now was that Rebecca wasn't the kind of woman who read the paper. Many months had passed since his brother had run the search ad for him. Only an avid reader of the *Rhodesia Herald* would recognize him now.

Rebecca was being served by an African clerk as Jake walked up beside her, a slip of paper in his hand. Another African came up to serve him.

Jake handed the African the slip. "Would you happen to have these points for a Mazda?" He pointed to the slip now in the African's hand. "Here's the part number."

The African scanned the slip and then walked away without responding.

Jake turned to Rebecca and greeted her with a smile. "Hi."

"Hello back to you," Rebecca said with a smirk. "Or should I say 'Hi?'"

"Hi it is," Jake said smoothly. He examined her out of the corner of his eye, waiting for recognition. When none came, he assumed he was in the clear.

"You're obviously an American. They always say 'Hi.'"

Jake fired his hands to either side. "Guilty."

She broke into a wide, hungry smile – exactly the smile Jake had been hoping for. Here was a woman attracted. Here was the perfect in.

"What brings you to Zambia, especially Monze?" she asked suggestively.

"Just passing through. I think the points are acting up and could die at any moment. Didn't want to break down on the way to Livingstone."

"Don't blame you."

The African came back, shaking his head. "Sorry, Bwana. Out of stock. Come in next week. Or you could try Choma."

Jake played dumb. "Choma?"

Rebecca took over. "It's the next town down the Great North Road to Livingstone."

"Hell," Jake said, taking the paper back from the African. "They probably won't have then there, either. It's four days to Christmas. But I guess I'll have to take a shot."

"Going home for Christmas?" Rebecca asked, clearly trying to keep the conversation going.

Jake smiled warmly. "To Philadelphia? No, no. I thought I'd hang around in Livingstone and see in the New Year."

Rebecca looked at him suggestively. "Have a great time, then."

"Good talking to you." Jake turned to go. "Have a great Christmas yourself."

He left the building, his heart pounding over a job well done. He felt like cheering as he hopped into his car and drove slowly out of sight – just far enough that Rebecca would think he had departed, but not far enough to lose sight of the road he knew she would be traveling down.

Several minutes later, Rebecca's truck passed Jake's location. Jake waited until she was three hundred yards ahead before firing up his battered rental and starting slowly to follow her. Rebecca's Mazda sped out of town and along the tarred road. Jake followed for a short distance, but pulled over periodically in order to stay far enough out of view. He remained aware of the fact that the points he had just altered might collapse at any moment, rendering his vehicle inoperable. He held his breath and followed slowly for twenty minutes or so. Then, around a bend, he found her along the road. The fan belt he had cut had done the job he intended.

He rumbled up alongside the broken down vehicle. The hood stood open and the engine steamed. Rebecca was lying under the front end of the Mazda, apparently checking the engine, when Jake climbed down from his rental. Only her long, slim legs protruded from beneath.

"Need any help?"

Rebecca scurried out, coming to rest on her backside. "The American?"

Jake extended his hand, helping her off the ground. "Jack Dillon at your service."

Rebecca took the extended hand. "Rebecca. Rebecca Cameron."

Jake nodded.

"I repeat: 'Rebecca,' not 'Becky.' Not 'Becks,' not 'Reba,' but 'Rebecca.'"

"Got it, Rebecca." Jake smiled. "It's a nice biblical name."

"My father loves biblical names."

"So what's the problem with the Mazda?"

She jerked a thumb over her shoulder. "Fan belt. Totally buggered."

Jake looked down at the young woman's lovely legs. "Unfortunately, you're not wearing tights."

Rebecca gazed down at her legs with a start. "Aren't we getting personal? Think I need to wear tights in this heat?"

Jake laughed. "No, it's just something I learned in Vietnam. I had a Jeep with a busted belt, and I used this Vietnamese girl's tights, tied them tightly around the generator and fan, and made a makeshift fan belt to get the Jeep back to base."

"So you were in Vietnam," Rebecca said cynically. "Shitty war. Got your arse drafted, no doubt. You don't look the warring type."

"Yes, yes, and yes," Jake quipped.

Rebecca raised an eyebrow. "So did the tights work?"

Jake beamed. "Sure as hell did."

The young woman turned and put her hands on the frame surrounding the steaming engine. "Vietnamese girl wearing tights. What's that all about?"

Jake came up alongside her. "Actually, she was a hooker."

"Well, Jack Dillon," Rebecca said derisively, "I have no bloody tights and I'm no bloody hooker, so don't ask me for my knickers."

Jake laughed. "Can I take you home?"

Rebecca cocked her head to one side, apparently fretting that Jake was hitting on her. "I'm not a—"

"A hooker, I get it," Jake interrupted. "I mean can I give you a lift back to your house?"

Rebecca sighed, then informed him that her father's property was six miles down a gravel road less than half a mile away. "I'd be grateful for the lift. Just don't try anything."

Jake lifted his hands reassuringly and then trotted around to the driver's side of his idling truck. Shortly, Rebecca hopped in on the passenger side.

"Okay to leave your truck here?" Jake asked.

"Daddy will send some farm boys with the tractor to pick it up."

Jake threw the less than pristine rental into gear and took off. Rebecca gave instruction for Jake to make the turn onto a gravel and sand road. From here, the truck wound its way along an uneven surface to the Cameron ranch.

"So your father . . . " Jake said, trailing off.

"Yes?"

"You don't know if he subscribes to the *Herald*, do you?"

Rebecca chuffed. "Him? Hell no. He wouldn't read that rag."

In his mind, Jake cheered his luck. "Then where's he get his news?"

She raised an eyebrow. "Why, the *Scotsman*, of course."

"Ah, he's a Scot."

"As Scottish as they come."

"I thought I heard a little hint of the accent in your voice."

Rebecca stared ahead then, apparently pondering Jake's words. But in a moment, he could see out of the corner of his eye that she was looking at him again.

"Why do you ask, anyway?"

"Ask what?"

"About the *Herald*?"

Jake shrugged, doing his best to look dismissive. "I just haven't read the news in a while and was hoping I could trade him a daughter for a copy of today's paper."

Rebecca laughed, but there was no mirth in it. "I'm sure he'd be happy to offer up the Scot, if you'll take it."

Before Jake could answer, his truck's engine began to sputter. They had gone no further than three miles before the thing began to smoke and come to a standstill. Jake acted surprised at the engine failure he knew to be coming. He got out and opened the hood, peering inside. Rebecca was smiling when he came back to the driver's door with the dead points in his hand.

"So much for the lift home," she said. Unfazed, she got out of the vehicle. "Looks like we'll have to walk it, and we'd better be quick or the sacks of chicken feed back in my truck will disappear the moment the first Munt comes along."

Without waiting for Jake, she led the way, taking a few steps northward on the gravel road before squeezing herself between two strands of barbed wire fence to her left. She smiled as she looked back at Jake, who remained standing by the side of his truck.

"Come," she called with a wave. "It's less than a mile this way through a section of the farm." She stopped and put both hands on her alluring hips. "Or are you like most of the Yanks that come to Africa hunting – afraid of the bush?"

Jake scoffed, but smiled.

"A brave soldier like yourself shouldn't worry," she urged. "I'll protect you."

Jake followed her through the barbed wire fence. "That's good to know."

After an uneventful trek through the bush, they arrived at the Cameron residence, which proved to be a tall and elegant homestead on the hill. Jake followed Rebecca down a cement walkway. Wooden poles were spaced every four feet, running the entire length of the pathway. Overhead, slats had been nailed into the wooden uprights. The entire length of the construction was adorned with a massive creeping bougainvillea in brilliant purple and red.

"This is beautiful," Jake remarked.

"But a great home for the boomslang," Rebecca said. "We had one here and it took forever to shoot the bastard."

"What's a boomslang?"

She stopped walking and looked at him as if she was about to tell a campfire ghost story. "The boomslang is a large highly poisonous tree-dwelling snake." Her voice was lined with tension. "It's greenish brown in color and is deadly. It's a fan of our pagoda, with its thick shrub coverage." She walked on, and Jake followed. "It likes to live in an aerial position, where it's harder to see. As far as I'm concerned, the boomslang is the original camouflage king. It strikes without warning, and delivers potent venom to its victim through large, deeply grooved folded fangs in the rear of its mouth." She shook her head mournfully. "Fatal, if left untreated."

Jake chuckled cathartically, his eyes scanning the foliage above for any sign of movement.

"Anything else you want to know?" she quipped.

Jake shook his head as he quickened his pace. At renewed speed, the two followed the path up to the verandah of Rebecca's father's home. Rebecca excused herself, stating that she wanted to freshen up from the heated walk through the bush. She departed the verandah, leaving Jake to enjoy the view from the elevated position of the home. He gazed out over the expanse of the African bush, enjoying what seemed a never-ending view. The verandah was rectangular with one long side missing. A square pool sunken in the center appeared to be full of tropical fish and plant life. There were several doors leading off the verandah, all designed to give easy access to any part of the property.

As he took it all in, an African servant wearing a fez appeared through one of the doors and approached him. He smiled without uttering a word and placed a tray full of liquor bottles on an overlarge sideboard beside him. The servant then returned to the door, where he was greeted by a taller, whiter figure. This was a man Jake knew only from pictures, and he gritted his teeth to remind himself that he was here for trickery, not for brute force. He must keep his composure if he was to meet his aim.

The figure approached with a confused little smile. Jake looked for any sign of recognition in the old man's eyes, but found none. This was Samuel Cameron. He wore a safari suit and carried the ruddy face of a Scotsman in his mid-sixties. He was a tall man, with the ever-brown arms of white men in Africa. His legs from the end of his shorts down were also a golden brown.

He extended his hand for Jake to shake. "Samuel Cameron." His accent was thickly Scottish.

"Jack Dillon," Jake replied.

Cameron gave him a long, appraising look. "Thanks for assisting my daughter."

"My pleasure, sir."

"Well, it looks as if you're also buggered. Rebecca said your Vanette broke down with dead points."

Jake nodded. "You wouldn't happen to have a spare set?"

"No, laddie. I mostly use Land Rovers. For those, I have lots of spare parts, but not for a Mazda. But that reminds me, I should order a set for Rebecca's Vanette."

Jake smiled. "Well at least you're forewarned. As for me, I'm royally screwed."

Cameron smiled back. "You're certainly buggered for now. Besides, it's getting late. Have dinner with us and spend the night. We'll see what we can do tomorrow."

Jake's heart leapt. His plan had succeeded. He was in. "That's very generous of you."

"It would be my pleasure." Cameron winked. Then he turned toward the door he'd come out of, motioning for Jake to follow. "I'll send a couple of tractors to tow the vehicles back to the farm. As soon as they arrive, I'll have your suitcase delivered to one of the spare rooms." He pointed to a room off the verandah. "Take this one. In here, you won't be disturbed."

Jake peered into what looked like a lavish and well-adorned room.

"Have a shower, laddie," Cameron said. "I'll arrange some clean clothing for you in advance of your luggage. When you're refreshed, you can join us for a sundowner before dinner."

Jake thanked his gracious host once more, then left the verandah for the room to which Cameron had directed him. As he settled into the room with the magnificent view of the African landscape, he felt rather traitorous in his intent. But that feeling soon faded when he remembered why he was here. He quickly showered, and upon exiting the en suite bathroom, he found a clean change of clothing neatly laid out on the bed.

CHAPTER 26

Jake dressed quickly and came out of the guest room wearing one of Cameron's borrowed overlarge safari suits. He found the man of the house sitting on a sofa in the central drawing room, sipping on a scotch and soda. Cameron waved for Jake to join him.

"What's your poison, laddie?" Cameron asked.

"Brandy and Coke."

Cameron rose and fixed Jake his drink at the little bar in the corner. "Brandy and Coke. Spoken like a true Rhodesian." He turned and offered Jake an appraising look. "And looking like one, to boot."

"Rhodesian?" Jake asked.

"Well, 'Zambian' I suppose. But up here, it used to be Northern Rhodesia, and with that safari suit, you fit right in."

"You look like a pansy in that outfit," Rebecca's voice echoed with a loud laugh.

As Cameron finished stirring Jake's drink, his daughter appeared through the double doors at the head of the drawing room. She had made herself up and was now wearing a short red dress with ribbon straps over her shoulders. It had been a long time since Jake had enjoyed the touch of a woman, and the vision of this one seemed to exude the kind of sex appeal that he could only remember as if in dreams. Her long, slim legs were tanned so well in the evening light that it looked as though she was wearing the tights he had suggested earlier in the day. She crossed to the tray where her father was standing, picking up the drink he had just prepared. Cameron scoffed as his daughter looked squarely at Jake. She sniggered and joined the young man. Her father started pouring a second drink to replace the first.

"I think he looks good," Cameron said, returning with Jake's drink.

"Daddy, he looks out of place."

"Well, I'm not changing," Jake said. "I like it."

"Well said," Cameron said with a snort. "Let's take our drinks and head on into dinner."

Reflexively, they all stood, drinks in hand. Jake immediately took Rebecca's drink for her and followed Cameron. Cameron quickened his pace, apparently unconcerned about participating in the conversation that would carry between his guest and his daughter.

"Quite the gentleman," Rebecca said, nodding at Jake's hand, which held her drink.

"You look amazing," Jake whispered. "Some transformation. Third World to First World in a matter of hours."

Rebecca giggled flirtatiously as she took the lead into the dining room. "Thank you, kind sir."

Jake sighed and watched her form as he followed. *Keep it together, Jake,* he told himself. *Remember Sarah. You're here for your daughter. Not to chase tail.*

~ ~ ~

Later that evening, the trio was seated back on the verandah, all of them enjoying after-dinner drinks and coffee.

"If you're staying for the New Year," Cameron said, "you should try the local country club instead." He offered a wink at his daughter. "We have one hell of a New Year's party. I always pipe in my homemade haggis for a traditional Hogmanay."

"Hogmanay?" Jake asked.

Rebecca sighed. "Hogmanay is Scottish New Year." She pointed to her father. "He makes this foul-tasting ball of animal innards, cooks it forever, and sets it alight with a bottle of scotch."

"Aye, and the entire Country Club eats it," Cameron added, elbowing Jake in the ribs.

"Probably because they're so drunk they can hardly stand up," Rebecca fired back.

Cameron laughed. "Anyway, forget Livingstone," he said to Jake. "It'll take you a couple of hours to see the falls, and then you'll be pulling your plonk for the rest of the time."

Rebecca groaned. "Daddy!"

Cameron ignored her. "Join us, Jack. You'll be our guest over the festive season. I work every day with my cattle and crops, so Rebecca can entertain you. You can get in a bit of fishing and perhaps fire off a few rounds at the plentiful game on the farm. I'll even let you walk with the piper as we pipe in the haggis. What do you say?"

Jake beamed. "That's the best offer I've had in months."

"Then it's settled," Cameron said with finality.

A voice was heard at one of the verandah doors, and they all turned to face the direction of the sound. There, Jake saw an African nanny standing in the doorway, holding a baby in her arms. Jake's heart raced as Cameron beckoned her over.

The nanny walked over to the threesome and handed the baby to Rebecca. Rebecca smiled at the child and kissed it softly on the cheek. The woman then took the child and stood in front of Cameron. Jake sat breathlessly as the older man moved the blanket so that he could see the baby. He never touched the infant, but nodded his head to the African woman. The woman started to move away.

It took every ounce of Jake's self-control not to leap from the chair. Instead, he stretched out his arms and suppressed a little whimper. "May I?" he asked meekly.

"Why sure, Jack," Cameron said, sounding surprised.

Jake held out his hands to receive the child. The nanny looked at Cameron, who nodded in approval. Jake was nervous as he took the little bundle into his arms and gazed in wonderment at his daughter for the first time. He was fearful of the delicate little human in his nervous arms, and entirely overjoyed, but knew he must endeavor to remain totally divorced. Still, his eyes began to well up. He thought of Sarah and how she should be here to share the moment with him.

He knew that if he held her for much longer, there would be no hiding his tears, so he handed his baby quickly back to the nanny.

Cameron looked at Jake curiously. "Scared of babies, laddie?"

Jake smirked and responded quickly. "I'm sorry." He dabbed at his eyes with his fingertips. "A little over a year ago, my best friend's wife lost a baby about this age to meningitis." He paused as he looked at Rebecca. "You're right; babies scare the hell out of me."

Cameron laughed heartily. "Nothing to be scared about. They're only babies."

He then stood, taking his time to look back and forth between his daughter and Jake, who sat opposite each other. "Well, it's goodnight for me. I've a farm to run. You young people enjoy this beautiful African night."

Jake immediately stood. "Goodnight, Sam," he said enthusiastically. "And thank you for the invitation. And for your hospitality."

Cameron directed himself to Rebecca. "It'll be our pleasure, Rebecca, won't it?"

"Yes, Daddy," she responded coyly. She held a soft little smile until her father disappeared into the main home and closed the door behind him.

"Yes, Daddy; no, Daddy," she said bitterly to Jake. "Three bags full, Daddy."

"Wow!" Jake said, taken aback.

"Wow is right!" Rebecca shook her head. "He's a miserable old bastard, and as much as we keep up the friendly faces, it's all bullshit."

Jake chuckled.

"I'm convinced he's a woman hater," Rebecca continued. "He certainly hated my mother and drove her to her grave." She paused and seemed to ponder something deeply as she looked at Jake earnestly. "Now my brother, Robby, that's another story. The sun shines out of his arse." She got up and went to the liquor tray. "Want something stronger than port?"

"Straight brandy," Jake answered. "You have a brother?"

Rebecca returned with two drinks in her hand. "Yes. He's in Scotland with his girlfriend's family over the Hogmanay. He won't be back until sometime in early January."

Jake accepted his drink with a smile. "I guess both of you are going to end up inheriting this place."

Rebecca's face contorted to disgust. "It was always supposed to be that way. But I know Daddy all too well. It'll all go to Robby, and I could give a shit anyway."

Jake raised an eyebrow. "Why's that?"

Rebecca explained that while in the country of Zambia, her father had millions of kwacha, but didn't have even one cent of any real negotiable currency, such as sterling, US dollars, Swiss francs, or South African rand. "If our farm was ever sold, the money would be useless. The Zambia exchange control regulations disallow the transfer of funds out of the country."

As Jake stewed on the thought, she added that it didn't really matter to Robby, as he would always live and eventually die on their property.

"Robby will probably marry the poor Scottish girl he's on vacation with right now," she said coldly. "And he'll schlep her out to the middle of Africa to breed for him." She sighed, coming down from her rant. "My only hope is there's a thriving black market buying US dollars or sterling."

Jake leaned back in his chair. "Funny you should say that. When I was going into a bank in Livingstone, a southern European-looking gentleman, maybe Greek, offered five kwacha cash for every US dollar."

Rebecca moved to the edge of her seat. "Did you take it?"

"I couldn't. I had no cash and was accessing an American bank account, so I only got Zambian money, one kwacha for one dollar."

Rebecca laughed. "You got screwed."

Jake shook his head and decided it was time to change the subject. "So what do you do professionally?"

"Besides looking good and having a venomous mouth?"

Jake grinned. "You said it."

Rebecca sat up straight as though she was at an employment interview. She responded proudly, with tongue in cheek. "I'm finally a chartered accountant who was firstly kicked out of the Universiteit van Pretoria. It was mostly due to my bad comprehension of Afrikaans. I basically stunk at it."

"So then?'

Continuing her job interview line, she revealed that she eventually ended up at the University of Cape Town, where she attained her chartered accountants degree. She explained that it was during the days when her father could pay from Zambia with approved foreign exchange. She had the degree for what it was worth, but had no idea what to do with it when it came to being gainfully employed within the boundaries of the country.

"I guess I'll just have to leave Zambia and get a job," she said.

"Shame," Jake said sarcastically.

"Fuck you!"

Jake continued with a broad smile. "If that's a question, then I think maybe I'll have to pass. If it's not an invitation to fornication, but rather, I'm suddenly out of sync with your rapport, then at the very least, I believe we're going to be good friends."

Rebecca arched one lovely brow. "Really?"

Jake offered a solemn nod. "Really. We may find that we can help each other."

She edged forward once more. "How so?"

Jake hesitated only for a moment, questioning himself internally as to whether the time was right to spring a plan on her. Maybe it was the booze. Maybe it was her legs. Whatever the case, he found himself opening up to the lovely young woman.

"Ever think you might like to be in the States?"

She smirked. "It's a dream that my father cannot ever help me to fulfill. Who wouldn't like to be in the States?"

"Well then," Jake said, pointing to himself and then to her, "you help me and I'll help you."

Rebecca was rather slack-jawed now, and the effect was adorable. "How?"

Now Jake realized that he'd gone too far. He couldn't reveal more on this night, lest he risk ruining the entire operation. He'd have to earn her trust first, and she his. "In time, you'll see."

Rebecca started whining. "How? How?"

Jake smiled. "Later, later." Then, before she could protest, he directed the conversation to a subject he'd been longing to discuss since he'd first set eyes on her. "Lovely baby," he said as coolly as possible. "What's the deal there?"

"Oh, that subject is taboo."

Jake cocked his head to one side. "Come on, it's only conversation. The baby looks so sweet. But I noticed that your father never touched her. What's that all about?"

"He never does." She rolled her eyes as she took a long drink of her brandy, choking it down with a disgusted face. "And he doesn't allow me to be overly friendly, either." She sighed. "And how come you knew she was a girl?"

Jake realized his error all at once. *Wake up, Jake!* he warned himself. *This girl's really on her toes. No more mistakes.*

"She's simply too cute to be a boy," he said. "So tell me . . . why does he not want you to be friendly to the baby?"

"I'm a woman, for one," she said emphatically. "So I'm naturally more drawn to babies than a man might be."

"Why's that a problem?"

"I don't know." Rebecca leaned back and crossed one long leg over the other. "Daddy just doesn't want me to take too much interest in this one. This baby's different, almost as white as the driven snow."

"This concerned you?"

"I had to pretty much force Daddy into telling me where she came from."

"And?"

"You're getting a little touchy with the questions."

Jake tried to look aloof again, taking a nip of his drink and turning his head away. To his delight, it apparently appeased her.

"According to Daddy, the baby's the offspring of one of his Scottish section managers. I guess the story goes that after he made some local woman pregnant, he skipped the country and headed back to the safety of his homeland."

"Why didn't the baby stay with the mother, then?"

"Daddy said her mother came to the house and dumped the baby on one of the houseboys, then promptly disappeared into the bush."

"And you believed him?" Jake asked incredulously.

She shrugged. "What else can I believe? I guess this isn't the first time something like this happened. The house staff tells me it happened once before, back around the time I was born. But Mom couldn't handle it, so they sent the baby away."

"So this is like history repeating itself." Jake got up and took her empty glass. He had made the statement knowing that he would be opening a kind of Pandora's Box. He waited for her to say something as he walked quietly toward the refreshment tray.

Rebecca looked oddly at him when he turned back to meet her gaze. "I don't get you."

Jake turned around again and fetched a bottle and a glass. Then, without a word, he got back to refilling their glasses.

"Never mind," she said. "I was just saying that it's strange, considering the same thing has happened before." Rebecca accepted the drink from Jake with a swirling little loop of her eyes. She was clearly well into a drunk now. "It was twenty-four years or so ago," she said dreamily, "and I suspect that it had something to do with my father being a bastard and always jiga-jigging with the Africans. It killed my mother." She picked her head up drunkenly. "Do you know what I mean by jiga-jigging?"

"Oh, yes," Jake said, taking a seat. "I learned that from a girl I met."

"Well, my father has jiga-jigged so much, I wouldn't be surprised if it's his baby and that's why he keeps me away." She pointed a finger at Jake, her lips parting into an impish little smile. "That girl you met . . . did you jiga-jig with her?"

Jake chuckled. "Sure did."

Her legs parted subtly and she leaned forward and flashed him a bedroom smile. "Care to jiga-jig with me?"

Jake practically choked on his brandy. "Is that an invitation this time?"

She pointed to the bedroom off the verandah that Jake was occupying. "Why did you think I made sure Daddy put you in that bedroom? It has a communicating door to guess whose room?"

Jake stood up and took her drink. Without a word spoken, he balanced the two glasses in the palm of his hand and offered her his free hand. She took it and stood up, following him toward the bedroom door.

~ ~ ~

When Jake awoke in the morning, he was alone. It had taken some time to convince Rebecca that he was a good Christian man and that he didn't care to sleep with someone he'd only just met. "I respect you too much to turn this into a one-night thing," was the line that had eventually won her over. He'd ensured that she got into bed safely, of course, and had even kissed her on the forehead goodnight. And in truth, it had taken a great deal of self-control not to take her up on her offer. But Sarah remained foremost in his mind. Lovely Sarah – the love of his life. He couldn't betray her now. Not after all he'd been through to right the wrongs and repair their young family.

Still, he dreaded how deeply he'd gotten in with Rebecca. It was one thing to hold off her advances now. But he was a man, after all, and she was a beautiful woman. He wasn't sure how long he could hold out. And in the end, to achieve his goal, he knew he would have to succumb.

CHAPTER 27

It was Christmas Eve on a hot day with little humidity as Jake and Rebecca embarked on fishing from a small boat on the manmade dam. Silently, they watched their fishing lines bob in the water as the boat sat motionless in the center of the dam some fifty yards from either bank.

"You've been rather aloof lately," Rebecca said, tossing her beautiful hair back over her shoulder.

"Have I?"

"I'm worried, Jake. I thought we were having a good time, you and me."

Jake grinned. "We're having a wonderful time, sweetheart." But then he sighed. "I guess I've just been kind of put off by the nightly ritual of your father's, where we have the baby viewing and the almost instant goodnight."

Rebecca furrowed her brow. "Hmmm."

"It's starting to get to me. It just seems so insane, his behavior."

"Daddy's always been erratic." Rebecca began to reel in her line. "Especially lately. I don't know why that should trouble you, though."

Jake followed suit and started to reel in his line. "I have my reasons."

Rebecca chuffed. "What reasons could you possibly have?"

"It's complicated." He blurted the words before he could even consider the weight.

"It's us, isn't it?" Rebecca asked sadly. She cast her line with something that looked like frustration. The lure darted into the water awkwardly, only skittering a short way from the boat.

"Partly," Jake lied. "But it's mostly other things."

"I get it," she cooed. "You think I'm in love with you. Or *worse*; you're in love with me."

Jake felt rather rejected. "*Worse?*"

Rebecca sighed. "Jake, I'm not in love with you. I like you and I would very much like to fuck you. But I don't love you. I'm in love with seeing the world and getting away from my father and his insanity, as you so aptly put it."

Jake felt a wealth of relief come over him. "Thank God."

"Then you don't love me, either?" she questioned with a hint of relief.

"No."

"Then thank God for a second time." She gave him a suggestive smile. "But you still want to fuck me, don't you?"

Jake wasn't sure how to answer that question, and felt somewhat remorseful. "Oh yes. But thinking about it always fills me with sorrow and regret."

She pursed her lips. "That's not terribly flattering."

"It's not you. You're witty and beautiful and great fun to be with." Then he took her hand in his and continued. "The sorrow and regret follows, simply because I'm married to your half-sister."

Rebecca burst into astonished laughter. "I don't have a sister, half or otherwise."

"Yes you do, like it or not."

Rebecca let go of his hand, looking as if she felt this joke had gone far enough. She eyed him with obvious confusion. "When, how, and where is this so-called half-sister now?"

Jake spoke in a calm and convincing voice. "You ask when? That was about twenty-four years ago. As for the how, your half-sister was brought into this world by your father and an Ethiopian woman. And regarding the where, well, she's with my family in the States."

Rebecca sat upright in her seat and eyed him with suspicion. "So, Mr. Jack Dillon, if that's your name, meeting me was not by accident."

"No it was not," Jake admitted. "It was a must."

Rebecca reeled in her line and set the pole down beside her. "This is bullshit. And too much to absorb." She scowled. "Row me to the bank."

Jake picked up the oars and did as asked.

Rebecca remained silent until they reached the edge of the shore. Then she scoffed, climbed from the boat, and headed straight for her Vanette. There, she turned to him, still scowling. "Prove this to me, or you'll have to prove it to Samuel Cameron."

"I will," Jake said. "Back at the house. I'll also prove that the baby we see every night is my child."

Rebecca's face became somehow more furious. "*What*?"

Jake remained calm. "That baby that your father looks at every night is our baby, Sarah's and mine."

"Sarah?"

"That's her name. Notice that it's biblical, like yours. Your old man is a creature of habit; Scottish names for your house staff and daughters with biblical names." He paused for a moment. "What was the name of the mystery baby?"

"Ruth," Rebecca said dolefully.

Jake cast his hands to either side. "There you go."

Rebecca climbed into the Vanette and slammed the door behind her. Jake got in on the passenger side.

She looked over at him. "So is Jack Dillon at least your real name?"

"Actually, it's Jacob Fallon. 'Jake' to my friends."

"Am I a friend?"

"Don't hate me, Rebecca. You're more than a friend; You're part of my family."

"Big deal."

"Please forgive the deception. There was no other way for me to gain access to my daughter."

She sighed. "You're really not joking, are you?"

"No joke. But if your father finds out, he'll kick me off his property."

She smiled in an admonishing way. "More than that, if he doesn't have you arrested, he might take you for a long walk in the bush. You'd get 'lost' and never come back."

"Then you understand why you can't mention my real name to your father," Jake said adamantly. "I was lucky in that he didn't know my face. But he knows full well my name."

Rebecca sighed again, looking defeated.

"You have to help me," Jake pleaded, taking her hand in his. "If not for me, or for your sister, then for your niece."

Rebecca pulled her hand away and started the Vanette. Without a word, she guided it along the dusty farm road toward the house. As she drove, her jaw tightened.

"If what you say is true," she said after a time, "then not only do I have a sister, but I am, as you state, an aunt. So prove it to me."

~ ~ ~

At the door to Jake's bedroom, Rebecca stood with her hands on her hips in silence. Jake cast a sideways glance in her direction as he riffled through his bag for the proof he had promised her. Shortly, he produced the documents. Rebecca sat on the end of the bed and gazed at his passport for a time, then unfolded the birth certificate Caldwell had written for him.

When she'd finished, she looked up at him in clear astonishment. "This is signed by Willie Caldwell. We know him well."

Jake nodded. "And so you should. He not only delivered our baby, but he also delivered Sarah, your half-sister."

"And *me*," Rebecca added. "My father had him come up to Monze to deliver me. He didn't like the doctor at the local hospital, so Willie had to trot up."

Jake watched her for a moment, looking for signs that she was beginning to crack. None came. In fact, she appeared more resolute than ever that her company was a liar.

"I need a little more concrete proof than you've shown me," she said.

Jake's eyes never wavered from hers. "I understand. And I can give it."

She cocked her head to one side, obviously intrigued.

"In less than a week, it will be New Year's Eve. Your father has invited me to the country club. How would you feel if we pretended to be an item, and how would that sit with your old man?"

Rebecca looked confused. "Oh, I think it would sit well. He's always trying to marry me off to one of the sons of his farmer friends, here or in Rhodesia."

"Well, if we can play the game—" Jake pointed at the birth certificate in Rebecca's hand "—and if the good doctor will be there, then I'll give you the mother-load of proof. All the proof you'll ever need."

Rebecca chuffed. "Willie's *always* there. By the time the piper pumps up the bagpipes, he'll be sitting in his favorite corner, a cigar in hand, looking like a bloated Winston Churchill."

Jake chuckled. "Well, I promise you that if he sees me, he'll shit. So we'll have to get him outside before he sees me. And before he's drunk. If you can do that, I'll be able to prove everything."

Rebecca suddenly appeared to melt. Her eyes went from disdainful to loving in one rash moment. Before Jake knew it, she had her arms around his neck and was kissing him.

"If we're to be an item," she said, "Daddy will expect to see us act as such."

"But, Rebecca—"

"No," she interrupted. "There's no way out of this. If we're going to pull this off, we have to be more than friends."

Jake opened his mouth to protest, but it fell short the moment he looked into her blue eyes. "Can I see the baby?" he asked meekly.

Rebecca smiled. "Only if you do as I ask of you."

~ ~ ~

Rebecca's leg was draped over him as he lay in bed. She slept, her blonde hair covering her face, her head resting on his shoulder. Jake was wide awake, remorseful as he gazed up at the twirling ceiling fan with its incessant clicking. His thoughts were of Sarah and what she would do if she knew he had just bedded her half-sister. He felt confused and annoyed at how easy it had been to end up in bed with Rebecca. But she had coaxed him, after all, with threats against the mission he'd come to complete – and he would do *anything* to regain his daughter.

He brushed back Rebecca's hair. She opened her eyes and smiled at him.

"Mmmm," she cooed. "I thought that was a dream."

Jake opened his mouth to speak, but was cut off by a loud knock on the bedroom door that startled them both.

Rebecca leapt from the bed, naked, and rushed into the en suite bathroom. She peered out from behind the half-closed door. She giggled. "Probably Angus with the coffee."

"Angus, a Scotsman with the coffee," Jake quipped.

Rebecca laughed. "No. It's silly old Angus, one of the house-boys. They've all got Scottish names. Remember I told you: Daddy's a weird old bastard."

Jake shouted at the door. "Come in."

The African came into the room, and in silence, placed a tray beside the bed.

"Good morning," Jake said.

"Good morning, Bwana," the smiling African replied.

"I need another cup of coffee; I always have two in the morning."

The African pointed to the coffee pot. "Look, a full pot."

"I still need a fresh cup."

The African scratched his head, obviously confused as he left the room.

Rebecca strutted out of the bathroom. She was still naked and in glorious form as she crossed to the communicating door. She crossed into the bedroom opposite – her bedroom – and returned wearing a dressing gown of bright red silk. She also held a cup in her hand.

"My coffee was already beside my bed," she said. "So we can drink coffee till the cows come home." She took a sip, then opened her gown just enough to reveal her beautiful breast. "Maybe a little more, jiga-jig?"

Jake chuckled. "Let's try a little coffee in bed first. We'll see where it leads."

She grinned. "You're right. That sounds much nicer."

CHAPTER 28

New Year's Eve had arrived, and with it the annual New Year's Eve party at the Solebury farm home of Patrick and Mary Fallon. As always, it would be a formal and exorbitantly catered affair attended by the usual list of Philadelphia Main Line guests. Bill and Sarah had slipped in the house via the home's back staircase, wanting to get dressed in one of the guest bedrooms without being seen. As he fiddled with his cufflinks, Bill could hear the chatter of early arriving guests as they talked and clinked their glasses.

He turned to Sarah, who looked stunning in her Versace gown. She appeared to be having trouble working the clasp of the diamond necklace he'd given her for Christmas, so he stepped forward to help her. He fumbled with the clasp himself for a moment before finally getting it to close.

She turned to face him. "I'm scared, Bill."

Bill smiled sympathetically. "You've got nothing to be scared about. You look stunning."

"All those influential people." Sarah's eyes grew dewy. "How will they look at me?"

"There will not be an eye in this house that will not want to focus on you." He smiled and stepped back. "How do I look?"

"Are you two coming down at any point tonight?" came a ragged voice that Bill immediately recognized as his mother's.

He turned toward the door, realizing that his mother was yelling from the bottom of the stairs. "We'll be down in a moment."

He rolled his eyes and Sarah grinned, kissing him on the cheek.

"You look handsome as always," she said. "Well . . . I'm ready for the slaughter."

Bill nodded and offered his arm, which Sarah took gracefully. The two made their way to the staircase and descended slowly, Bill always one step ahead of her. When they came into view of the main hall, guests began to turn their heads and stare. A great roar of whispering rose up, everyone clearly sharing their opinions on the new addition to the Fallon family at once.

"She's absolutely stunning," Bill overheard.

"Not as black as I thought she would be," came another whisper.

"Which of the boys is she married to?" It was this question that made his heart sink. He knew at that moment that despite his best efforts, he had failed to hide his affection for Sarah. When he turned to look at her, he could see that she had heard it, too, and that she was equally troubled.

The moment they reached the bottom of the stairs, Bill saw his mother come into view beside them. He turned to see her waving her hands for attention. The moment she had it, she began to speak in loud tones, as if delivering an especially important announcement.

"Our dear friends," she said, "Patrick and I want to thank you for coming, and in a few hours, we'll be watching the ball drop in Times Square and entering not only a new year, but a new decade; a decade that, I may add, will be filled with love and hope for us all." She looked directly at Sarah. "Pat and I welcome

Sarah into our family, as we sincerely hope you will welcome her into your lives."

There was a loud burst of applause from the invited guests. Bill smiled at Sarah, who returned the smile.

"And now I have a surprise for my new daughter-in-law," Mary said, unable to control the wide grin that followed. "We've just learned that within the month, our Jake, Sarah's husband, is finally coming home!"

More applause followed. Bill exchanged a solemn glance with Sarah, feeling as if all eyes in the room were melting him.

"Come on, everyone!" Mary called out, oblivious. "Let's celebrate! Let the party begin!"

Bill felt like crawling into a hole. And in the eyes of his love, he could see the same feeling.

CHAPTER 29

It was nearly midnight outside the country club. Jake stood beside Rebecca's Vanette, waiting for the inevitable confrontation. Just when he felt like he could wait no more, he saw a pair of silhouettes heading in his direction. The one was unmistakable: Rebecca, in her alluring form, swayed from side to side with the familiar-looking rotund frame of a man in tow. Shortly, he could hear their voices rise up from the darkness. Dr. Caldwell, with his clear baritone, was doing most of the talking.

"So what type of symptoms have you been having that we need to talk so privately about?" he asked. He stopped, pulling her to face him. "Don't tell me you're pregnant."

Rebecca laughed. "No, Willie, I'm not pregnant. It's just that someone wants to talk to you, and I thought it would be wiser to do it outside."

"Who wants to talk with me?" He sounded more than a little drunk. "It's closing on midnight, and your old man's getting ready to pipe in the haggis."

Jake stepped out of the darkness. "That would be me."

Caldwell's face reflected instant recognition. Quickly, he turned on his heel to retreat, but Rebecca held him fast. "Oh my sweet Jesus," he said. "It's you again."

Jake grabbed him by his arm, wrenching him from Rebecca's failing grasp. "In the flesh."

Caldwell pointed to his bandaged hand. "What the hell do you want now?"

Jake released his grip on Caldwell's arm. "I'm not going to hurt you. I just want you to tell Rebecca here the truth."

He glanced at Rebecca, who looked quite frightened. She hugged her arms to herself, sending quick glances back over her shoulders.

"But I can't—"

"She's already sworn not to reveal anything to her father," Jake interrupted. "But as a young woman in her own right, she deserves to know the truth about her life and the life of her half-sister and niece."

Caldwell looked at Rebecca for a sign that what Jake had said was true. Rebecca nodded, showing through her eyes her desire to know everything. Caldwell sighed and took her by the hand. He led her away, toward a well-worn bench under a tall Mopani tree. Jake lit a cigarette as he watched from beside the Vanette. He could see that Caldwell was imparting all he knew on Rebecca. Occasionally, Rebecca would put her hand to her mouth as if in disbelief. In short order, they finished conversing, and Rebecca got up from the bench and started to walk back toward Jake. Caldwell arose a few seconds later and raised his hand to Jake.

Jake responded and raised his hand back at the doctor. "Not a word to Cameron."

Caldwell could be seen clearly to nod in the dim light. He then silently returned to the club.

Rebecca appeared extremely angry by the time she reached the Vanette. "It's true! All of it's true."

Jake shrugged.

"What the hell has my father done?"

"Hurt a lot of people for a lot of years," Jake said. "He did it to you and to Sarah by keeping you apart."

Rebecca's eyes brimmed with tears. "He had no right."

Jake clasped her by the shoulders. "Will you help me?"

A tear rolled down her cheek. "Whatever it takes."

Jake embraced her.

"But not now," she said. "It's almost midnight." She pulled away, taking him by the hand and offering a sad little smile. "Let's go, then. You won't want to miss Daddy in his kilt, piping in the haggis."

"You have a weird sense of humor."

Jake followed her. Up ahead, he could hear the warm screech of a pair of bagpipes being made ready. Midnight would soon be upon them.

~ ~ ~

The following afternoon found Jake and Rebecca sitting on the verandah, indulging in afternoon tea. Cameron entered the verandah and joined them, picking up a cup of coffee on the way. He appeared in good spirits, with not a hint of late-night drinking visible in his deportment.

As he sat down with the cup and saucer in his hand, he addressed both of them. "I'm leaving for Salisbury tomorrow."

Rebecca looked at him, clearly unconcerned. "Oh, really," she answered with only a hint of contempt.

"Yes," the old man said. "I've a meeting at the Salisbury Club. I'll be gone for a week." He turned to Jake. "What about you, Jack?"

Jake did not respond, having momentarily forgotten his pseudonym.

Rebecca elbowed him. "Jack, are you deaf? Daddy's talking to you."

"Sorry," Jake replied. "I was lost in thought."

Cameron repeated himself.

"Well, I've got to get back to the States," Jake said. "So I guess I'll be gone when you return. But allow me to thank you again for your hospitality."

Cameron offered a rare smile. "Not at all, laddie. It was a pleasure piping in the haggis with you."

"Pleasure was all mine."

Cameron turned his attention to his daughter. "You'll be all right on your own, won't you, love? Robby won't be back from Scotland until next week, after all. I could call John Blake and see if—"

"I'll be fine, Daddy," Rebecca interrupted.

Jake interjected with a wave of his hand. "If it's all right with you, sir, I could stay on at the farm until your son returns."

Cameron offered a rare smile for the second time. "That would be nice, but I'll wager you're more interested in Rebecca than my hospitality."

"I could use the company and a man about the house," Rebecca said dismissively. "Jack here would be far better suited."

Cameron chuffed.

"Blake's son would probably have a coronary if anything untoward happened here." She looked at Jake. "I guarantee at the first sight or sound of any trouble, I would end up having to look after his pimply white arse."

"My God, girl," Cameron admonished, "you have a mouth on you."

"I had a hell of a good teacher in you, Daddy."

After a bit of an uncomfortable spat, Jake brought the conversation back to civil by reminding them that he would need to return his Mazda, now that it had been outfitted with the new points that Cameron had ordered. Cameron offered his own Range Rover in exchange for Jake's agreeing to stay with his daughter. He would return the Mazda to Livingston, and the matter was settled.

"All set then," Cameron replied, standing as if to take his leave. "I'll see you two at dinner." He waddled away toward the side of the house, waving his hand above his head.

Now alone, Jake and Rebecca smiled at each other.

CHAPTER 30

Jake walked out of the American embassy in Lusaka, firmly holding his daughter's new emergency passport in his hand. He examined the document once again, then turned his attention to Rebecca's Zambian passport, ensuring that the visitor's visa for the United States was in order. He crossed the street and got into a taxi.

"Intercontinental Hotel," he said to the driver.

In less than fifteen minutes, they reached the destination. Jake paid the driver, then decided he would kill some time over a cup of the hotel's miserable and always-burned coffee. He checked in quickly, took a seat in the foyer, ordered a coffee, and waited.

An hour later, he was relieved to see Cameron's Range Rover pull up outside. Jake put down his empty mug on the receptionist desk and dashed out to meet the vehicle.

When he arrived, he was startled to see not Rebecca, who he had expected, but Zena, the baby's wet nurse. She clutched Jake's daughter close to her chest as she climbed out of the Range Rover. Rebecca then came around from the driver's side, smiled at Jake, and kissed him on the cheek.

"What's she doing here?" he whispered to her.

"I'll explain later," she said in hushed tones.

Jake gave instructions, and a tall African porter took Rebecca's bags from the back of the Rover. The group then followed the porter through the foyer and on toward the elevators, where they would ride up to the room. With Zena and the baby bringing up the rear, they followed the porter down the corridor and arrived at their room. Jake tipped the porter, who withdrew without a word.

Rebecca turned to Zena. "Danka stelek *(thanks a lot)*, Zena. Now you go to your brother in Lusaka and stay until tomorrow night. I'll take Ruth to the doctor for all her injections."

"Yes, Dona," Zena replied nervously as she handed the baby to Rebecca. She was a simple farm girl, Jake noticed, and she appeared quite out of place here in the big city.

Rebecca cuddled the baby to her shoulder. "I promised my Baba *(father)* that I would do this."

This seemed to calm Zena a little. She cupped her hands in a small clapping sound, as was customary in greeting or farewell – an age-old ritual used in the presence of a village elder or chief as a greeting or goodbye, one designed to show the elder that the hands were free of an offensive weapon.

"Ngomso *(tomorrow)*," Zena replied, and then she departed.

Rebecca turned to Jake and handed the child to him. "Delivered as promised."

Jake looked lovingly at the baby. He felt so lost in the child's lovely eyes – Sarah's eyes, he noted – that he feared he might never look away. But then the sound of Rebecca cracking down into the wicker chair in the corner snapped him out of his delighted reverie.

"Why did you bring Zena?" he asked.

"She was too suspicious of me taking her alone without Daddy's permission. So I had to tell her that Daddy asked me to take her to the city for shots."

Jake's eyebrows arched in surprise. "Shots?"

"It's all nonsense, of course. Willie Caldwell did all of that already."

"But Zena didn't have to—"

"I told you she was adamant," Rebecca interrupted. "And besides, did you really expect me to drive and hold a baby for two hundred miles?"

Jake nodded distantly, finding that he had lost himself in the vision of his child once more. Such a beautiful little face. The tiniest nose and mouth he had ever seen. The most adorable hands. And here, she seemed to smile.

"Are you listening to me?" Rebecca demanded.

Jake snapped out of it, turning his frustrated attention on Rebecca. "Yes, absolutely. But what do we do about Zena?"

Rebecca's eyes took on a mischievous quality. "I've got it all worked out." She explained that they would leave money for Zena at the front desk. They would tell the head receptionist that there was an emergency and that they had to leave right away. "The money we leave will be adequate for her to take the train back to Monze."

"By then we'll be on the nine o'clock flight to Heathrow," Jake said.

"The very one."

He sat on the edge of the bed, resting his daughter on his legs. "What about your father?"

"I left him a letter."

At that moment, the baby started to cry. Jake felt his heart leap and then sink. He turned to Rebecca, who was rummaging through the bag of baby items Zena had brought. In short order, she pulled out the baby's Simalac formula and an empty bottle that appeared well sterilized.

"Come on, big girl," she said, taking the baby. She glanced at Jake. "And as for you, big boy, call room service. We need hot water. It's time you learned a few things about babies."

Jake picked up the phone. "I'm on it."

"And off me." She sighed as she filled the baby's bottle. "To think that this is the day that jiga-jiga comes to an end for us." She cooed at the baby. "No more sex, especially in the same room with your daughter and my niece."

"Eventually all good things come to an end," Jake said solemnly.

~~~

Zena stood in troubled attention before Cameron, a look of despair etched on her face. Cameron was visibly upset as he dismissed her and picked up the letter on the tray that sat beside his bottle of scotch. He poured himself a stiff shot before sitting down to open the letter. His hands shook as he unfolded it. Then, as he read, he could almost hear Rebecca's cutting tone echo in his ears.

Dear Daddy,

By the time you read this, I will probably be changing planes in London and bound for the United States. Please tell Zena that I am sorry for putting her in your crossfire, but it had to be. The Jack Dillon that you knew actually goes by the name of Jacob Fallon. I have assisted Jake in leaving the country with his child and the child of my unknown half-sister.

Cameron wiped his sweating brow, poured another shot, and continued to read.

How could you have done such a despicable deed to deny me the knowledge that I had a sister with the same blood as you and I? Moreover, how could you act like the Gestapo and take away her child? Now I know why I
~~~

was always the bane of your life and why Mommy had so much disdain for you. You always loved another woman and had a daughter that you housed in an orphanage. No wonder you were always down on me, while my brother Robby was the white-haired angel. It would seem that I was the reminder of your indiscretion.

So, Daddy, it should make you proud that, on behalf of the Camerons, I am doing the right thing by helping deliver my sister's baby into her hands. This awful secret is in the open now and there is no more time for regret. Jake has promised me he will take no action against you. Please remember that you will always be my father, and although I cannot live with you, I will love you to the end and will let you know how and what I'm doing.

I really do love you, you old codger.

Rebecca.

PS: Tell Robby I'll be in touch. Your Range Rover is in the parking lot at the Lusaka Intercontinental. The keys are with reception.

Cameron got up and wiped his eyes and quickly downed his third scotch. As he folded the letter and put it in his pocket, Angus the houseboy arrived on the verandah.

"Bwana Robby is home," the African said.

"Thank you, Angus," Cameron managed. "I'll go and meet the lad. Time to bring the boy into the picture."

"Bwana?"

Cameron patted the African on the back and followed him toward the kitchen. "It's nothing, Angus. Nothing at all. Suddenly, it's no longer a cloudy day."

CHAPTER 31

They settled into an oceanfront room at the Cable Beach Hotel in Nassau. It was a pleasant Bahamian day with little humidity in the air and a cool breeze from the Atlantic Ocean. Rebecca was stretched out on the bed, cradling the baby in her arms as Jake came out of the bathroom, having shaved. He was buttoning his shirt as he studied them together on the bed. Rebecca picked up the baby and smelled the diaper.

Jake banged his watch to get her attention as to the time. "She'll be here any minute."

She made a face at the smell of the diaper.

"You're not listening," Jake said. "It's noon, and she'll be here any minute."

Rebecca spoke quietly to the baby. "Oh my word, Ruth. Or should I say Mary? You are a smelly-poo. Let's change you before this room becomes contaminated and ultimately condemned." She got up with the baby in her arms and went into the bathroom, leaving the door slightly ajar.

There was a knock on the bedroom door. Jake opened it to find his mother, Mary Fallon, standing in the hall.

"Mother!" Jake said excitedly, diving into her arms. "Oh, Mom!"

Mary grabbed Jake, trying to surround his frame with her arms. She held on to him for a long while and started to cry with joy against his chest. Then she wiped her eyes and stepped back to look at him. Her voice was hysterical. "Jacob, Jacob, Jacob," she said with a long sigh. "How we have missed you and been worried sick about you every day."

She took another step back and her face became suddenly furious. Without warning, she whacked him hard on the chest with her open hand. "You little bastard! Have you any idea what we've been through?"

Jake grabbed his mother's wrists as she reeled back to strike him again. "I'm sure it was hell for all of you, but I've also had my share of hell. I just couldn't leave until I avenged Brian's death."

Mary's eyes started to well up again. "The poor Wilsons. What those terrorists did to their son! We thought you would end up the same way."

"Well I didn't," Jake said with a hint of anger. "And I got the bastards."

"And a wife, I may add," Mary said with a sour tone. "Why did you ever have to marry an African?"

"Do I smell disapproval, Mom?"

Mary was about to answer when the baby began to whimper in the bathroom. Jake and Mary turned to stare at the door.

"Come on out, Rebecca," Jake said. "Time to meet the dragon lady."

Rebecca appeared in the doorway with the baby in her arms. Mary looked confused.

"Mom," Jake said proudly, "this is Rebecca. She's Sarah's half-sister. And this little bundle is one Mary Josephine Margaret Fallon."

Mary Fallon staggered backward, where she fell onto the bed and sat down. Her face paled as she stared at Rebecca, who was offering the baby into her arms.

"Lost for words, Mom?" Jake said mockingly.

Mary didn't respond to her son. Instead, she addressed Rebecca. "Is this baby yours and Jacob's?"

"Hell no," Rebecca said. "This is Mary, your son Jake's daughter, my half-sister's daughter, and your granddaughter."

Mary's face suddenly beamed as she took the baby and cradled her in her arms. After a time, she looked up at Jake. "I need a drink."

Jake scoffed. "Mom, it's only noon."

"I don't give a crap what time it is."

Rebecca extended her hand to Mary. "I'm Rebecca Cameron, and I'm pleased to meet you. And I'll join you for that drink because I'm a Rhodesian. We can drink at the drop of a hat, and this is a hat-dropping occasion."

"But you're blonde and she's colored," Mary blurted.

"She?" Jake said furiously.

Mary appeared rather glassy-eyed when she looked at her son. "Sarah. I mean Sarah."

"Let's say a little indiscretion on behalf of my father, the randy old bastard," Rebecca said, returning from the mini-bar with a pair of small bottles of rum. She handed one to Mary, who took it gratefully.

"You don't like Sarah, do you, Mom?" Jake asked.

"Of course I do," Mary said defensively, but she seemed only to have eyes for the murmuring baby in her lap. "I didn't like her to start with, what with the initial shock of a colored girl." She turned to Rebecca and said apologetically, "Excuse me, child, I meant no offense to your family."

Rebecca shrugged. "No offense taken. We've never met. I might hate her. Who knows?"

"I didn't say I disliked her," Mary said in a dignified tone. "I was shocked to begin with, but not anymore. She's quite the lady these days." She looked with adoration at her granddaughter once more. "And the baby?"

"This is our so-called stillborn," Jake said proudly. "It's a long story, and the main reason I stayed on in Africa. If it wasn't for Rebecca—"

"Then you two are not involved," Mary interrupted.

"Not quite my type," Rebecca lied.

"Ugh!" Mary said, making a face at her rum. "I need something more adventurous than this."

Jake sighed and picked up the phone. He placed an order for three Bahama Mamas.

"I hate those," Mary said.

"That's all you're getting at midday," Jake said with authority. "So lump it."

"Is there alcohol in the Mama thing?" Rebecca asked.

"Rum, rum, and more rum," Jake said, exasperated.

"Excellent." She turned to Mary. "Sometimes he's fanagalo baby."

"Fanagalo baby?" Mary inquired.

Rebecca smiled. "It means like a baby."

Mary returned Rebecca's smile. "I like you, girl. I think the dragon lady and you will be good friends."

"A match made in heaven," Jake said with a groan.

A knock on the door halted the banter. Jake answered it, and a waiter brought in a tray bearing three frozen red drinks. The waiter placed them on the desk in the corner of the room as Jake signed the tab. The waiter smiled and withdrew. Jake handed a drink to Rebecca and one to Mary. Mary took a dainty sip, and Rebecca gulped down a third of the glass.

The younger woman then looked at the red mixture as if examining a rare specimen. "Rum's on the short side. A couple stiff shots of brandy wouldn't hurt."

Mary smiled at Rebecca, a smile she held as she turned her attention back to the contented baby on her lap. "So, Jacob . . . I'm sitting here, trying to assimilate the current situation. Why on earth did you want to meet here and not come straight to the villa?"

"It's Bill," Jake said coolly.

"Bill?" Mary asked.

"Yes, Bill." Jake began to stroke the stubble on his chin. "When we were changing planes in London, I spoke to Dad on the phone. He told me about . . . what you've feared."

"Oh!" Mary exclaimed. Her face ran red.

"Oh what?" Rebecca asked, looking confused.

Mary spoke directly to Rebecca as if Jake was not in the room. "I think his brother is in love with his wife. Maybe they're having an affair. Who knows?"

"Oh, how wicked," Rebecca said, her lips curling at the corners. "And so intriguing. I guess this Sarah and I most definitely come from the same gene pool." She laughed.

"Whatever do you mean?" Mary asked, shooting a strange look at Jake.

"I'm glad you find all of this funny, Rebecca," Jake said, ignoring his mother's stare.

Mary gazed toward the ceiling as if looking for guidance or confirmation that she was not being conned. "I'm going to assume, dear Jacob, that what I'm hearing means that you haven't been so faithful this year, either."

Jake turned away.

"Well, that doesn't matter," she added. "All that matters now is what you plan to do from here."

Jake sighed and leaned against the wall, nursing his drink for a moment. "Well, all I know is that I wanted you to see the baby.

Here. Out of sight of Bill and Sarah because I'm not sure yet how I'm going to deal with that situation."

"How do you *feel*, though, Jacob?"

Jake shrugged. "I'm crazy about Sarah. She's my life. And she *saved* my life. If what Dad said about her relationship with Bill is true, I'm scared, Mom. What if she doesn't want me back?"

"If she's got an ounce of that Scottish Cameron blood," Rebecca offered, "she'll want you back. You're the one who persevered and brought her baby back to her, after all."

Jake hung his head low. "That's the point . . . I don't want her back just because we have a baby. That's not the life we planned. If she's happy with Bill, then I have to be happy for her. Happiness has eluded her all her life. If she's found happiness, I can't destroy it now."

"So what's your plan, Jacob?" Mary asked. "I don't buy this self-pity routine for one minute. You always have some ridiculous fucking plan."

"Yeah, Jake," Rebecca said. "What's your mad fucking plan?"

Mary smiled at Rebecca, but Jake could only sigh again, shaking his head.

"Bill and Sarah are in the air right now on their way from Manhattan," Mary said. "They'll be home by three."

"Mother, Rebecca," Jake said furiously, "would both of you just sit down, shut up for a moment, and listen?"

CHAPTER 32

On the golden stretch of sand in front of the Fallons' luxury villa overlooking the blue Atlantic, Jake and Rebecca stood talking to Patrick Fallon. The old man hugged Jake several times. It was as if he never wanted to let go the hold he had on his youngest son.

Finally, Patrick lovingly kissed Jake on the cheek once more, and Jake willingly returned the affection. The old man released his hold and turned toward the villa. "You've got no idea how relieved we are to have you back with us, son," he said softly as he walked away.

Jake shouted after him. "I love you, Dad."

Rebecca touched his arm, and Jake saw that she was smiling. "There's a lot of you in his strong face," she said, still watching the departing older man.

It was four in the afternoon, and the sun was starting to descend in the west as they looked out over the calm sea. Jake sat down by the water's edge and patted the sand beside him, inviting Rebecca to join him and look out over the ocean. Rebecca wore a bikini, while Jake wore jeans and little else.

Jake tried to remain calm, as he knew that by now Bill and Sarah must have joined his father on the veranda some fifty yards behind. No words were spoken between him and Rebecca as they gazed out to sea. As if by telepathy, the two of them turned at the same time to look at the veranda, where Jake saw something that brought his heart to skip. There stood a group of three, and in spite of the distance, he could see that Sarah was among them.

Jake got to his feet and offered Rebecca his hand. She arose and smiled at him, then turned and ran into the calm water. Jake started to walk toward the verandah. As he did so, he watched as one of the figures, the shortest and most slender, kicked off her shoes and dashed toward him. As she neared, he could see that it was Sarah, and his smile grew with every passing step. She ran through the sand feverishly, sand that to Jake's touch, seemed to be losing its heat by the late afternoon.

Jake felt utterly filled with joy, so much so that he started to run toward her. They reached each other, and Sarah leapt into his arms, wrapping her legs around his waist as he held her there in silence. Her tears fell freely on Jake's shoulder, and then he eased her face to his and kissed her. Finally, Jake sat down in the sand, still holding his wife in his arms.

"Sarah," he whispered into her ear. "My Sarah. I love and have missed you so much. I'm so sorry for leaving you alone for so long." He sighed, and then looked her in the eyes for what felt like the first time in many years. "Just look at you. Look at the Sinazongwe girl. You seem to have left Africa in the distant past."

She climbed from his legs and sat in the sand beside him. Both looked out at the sea, their hands laced together.

"Oh, Jacob," Sarah said sadly. "I've been lonely without you in the strange new world. If it was not for Bill—" she turned and pointed to the verandah "—I never would have made it. He was always there to help and comfort me. He's made me what I am today." She paused. "But it has cost me so much." She broke down, trying to get her breath. It was a long while before she could look him directly in the eyes, and as she did, she cried. "I have been unfaithful to you."

Jake put his finger to her lips. "I know. And I know my brother. Do you love him?"

"I do."

"And me?"

"I'll always love you, Jacob."

His lips began to quiver as the pain set in. "Here and now and today?"

Tears rolled down Sarah's cheeks. "Always means always. Here, now, and forever."

Jake turned and held her close for a time. Then he let her go. "I'm not about to share you. So what about Bill?"

"Bill knows that you are the love of my life," Sarah said, looking down. "He's been living with that for months."

Jake felt short of breath, but knew he must ask the question that had been plaguing him for days. "You'll take me back, then? No matter how long I left you alone?"

Sarah offered a deep, shuddering sigh. "You were never away from my heart."

Jake heard footsteps in the sand. He turned to see his brother approaching, the older Fallon's limp appearing almost as a thing of the past. Jake and Sarah stood to greet him. He reached them just as Jake and Sarah were brushing the sand from their clothing. When Jake stood to his full height, he was grabbed into an embrace by his brother. He felt a kiss on his cheek just before Bill pulled away.

"Welcome home, my brother," Bill whispered. "Time for you to take care of your wife."

Jake offered Bill his hand, which he shook. "Thanks for looking after her. And a special thank you for giving her back."

Bill wiped the tears from his eyes with a soft chuckle. "Must be the blowing sand." He pulled himself together. "Sarah never was mine. For a brief moment in time, I could have had my dream, but it was not to be."

Jake looked to his wife, who clasped her hands before her and stared at the ground demurely.

"What God has joined together and all that jazz," Bill added.

An uncomfortable moment of silence followed.

"I'll always love her as I will always love you. So I guess that's just—" Whatever Bill intended to say, he seemed to lose his resolve.

Jake watched his wife, who stood motionless, seeming unsure of whom to comfort. He thought it a strange twist of fate that a simple African girl had conquered both Main Line men – and not with her newly found sophistication, but with her honest simplicity. After a time, she took both of them by the hand and they threw their arms around her in a collective hug. Jake faced the veranda, where he saw his father watching them. Bill faced the ocean.

Bill released himself from the huddle. "Who's that?"

Jake turned to see Rebecca, bikini-clad, standing with her back to them, waist deep in the water with her hands on her hips. Jake slipped his hand around Sarah's waist. "Oh, that's surprise number one. That's Rebecca, Sarah's half-sister."

Sarah put her hand to her mouth. "Sister?"

Jake nodded. "Yes, that's Rebecca. Her father is also your father. He's Samuel Cameron, the man who visited you in the orphanage."

"I have a sister?" Sarah asked, sounding more excited now.

"Yes, you have a sister." Jake grinned. "And quite the pistol she is."

Sarah turned toward the ocean. "I have to go to her."

Jake held her tightly. "Bill will bring Rebecca to the verandah." He turned to Bill. "Go, Bill. Introduce yourself. And watch your ass. She can sting."

Bill nodded, looking almost like a young boy working up the courage to ask a girl to dance. Jake and Sarah stood in the sand for a moment, Jake smiling and Sarah looking confused. The two watched as Rebecca came out of the water and extended a wet hand for Bill to shake. Bill took her hand, and Rebecca pulled him to her, soaking him in her embrace.

Jake watched for a time, hearing their voices carry in on the breeze.

"I'm Rebecca, Rebecca Cameron. I repeat: 'Rebecca,' not 'Becky,' not 'Becks,' not 'Reba,' but 'Rebecca.'"

Bill laughed. "What synergy! I'm Jake's older brother, Bill Fallon. Neither 'Billy,' 'Willie,' nor 'William,' but 'Bill.'"

Rebecca smiled her heartrending smile.

"I'm very pleased to meet you, Rebecca."

Jake chuckled. Sarah glanced up at him, looking anxious.

"Jacob, I'm so excited!" she said. "I just have to go and meet her."

"Not yet," Jake said quietly. "I have surprise number two."

"What surprise could be better than having you by my side and finding out that the girl from Sinazongwe has a sister?"

Jake turned to her, held her close, and smiled. "How about instead of finding a family, we make one?"

She looked up at him, clearly puzzled.

Jake turned Sarah away from the ocean. He looked into her deep brown eyes.

"What do you mean, Jacob?"

Jake grinned. "I mean our baby. Our daughter. There was no stillborn, Sarah. It was Cameron, your father. He took our baby."

Sarah stared at him as though she couldn't comprehend what he was saying.

Jake pointed to the verandah. "Look!"

At that moment, Mary appeared on the verandah, holding the baby in her arms. She held her up toward them, in a futile attempt at offering them a clear view.

Sarah looked at Jake, then back to the verandah. She clearly couldn't believe her eyes. Then she became suddenly hysterical. "My baby?" she shouted to Jake. "My baby's alive?"

Jake nodded proudly.

"God, I never thought I could love you any more." She tumbled into him, weeping. "My baby! My baby! *Our* baby, Jacob!" She took a deep breath and collected herself before pointing up at the verandah. "Can we?"

"Of course!" Jake said, chuckling.

She took his hand in hers and squeezed it. "Today, Jacob Fallon, you have made my life begin."

Then, with all the speed she had, Sarah ran. Jake watched his wife's feet move quickly through the dry, fine sand until she reached the verandah. He trotted behind, watching as his mother smiled warmly at her daughter-in-law and passed the child into Sarah's arms. By the time he reached his family, Sarah was holding her daughter close, kissing and cuddling her with a fire that could only be maternal.

"This is Mary," Jake whispered.

Sarah gasped with pleasure while everyone else on the veranda looked on and smiled. She held little Mary back at arm's length to get a good look at her from head to toe, then clutched the baby to her chest, and fell into Jake's strong embrace. For a brief moment, their life was suspended in time, and the world seemed to stop revolving. Jake's family was finally home.